DEVIL'S BREATH

LANG JOHNSON

"There are some who can live without wild things, and some who cannot."

— Aldo Leopold

ACKNOWLEDGMENTS

Without the support of my amazing husband, Jared, none of this would be possible. You encourage me to write when I feel like giving up, and to rest when I work through the night. Your faith in me never wavers. I am blessed to have you in my corner.

I am eternally grateful to my agent, Léonicka. Your keen insight and ongoing guidance keep me afloat in this complicated but wonderful industry. Thank you for believing in me. Partnering with you was my wisest career move.

My utmost appreciation goes out to my editors, Laura and Stephanie. This novel needed your unique editorial touches. You polished it up and turned it into a story worth telling.

To my mother, Minerva: You taught me to cultivate my dreams and never surrender. Thank you for captivating me with the magical world of stories from a young age. You are and always will be one of my biggest cheerleaders.

To my daughter, Nika: Thank you for showing me how strong a young woman can be. You lift me up when I am down. And you are forever there to make me laugh until my face hurts.

A giant thanks to my beta readers: Chloe and Kenzie. I

appreciate the time and love you poured into my novel. This story needed you.

I also want to express my gratitude to my family, friends, and the Instagram bookish community. Thank you for being a part of my journey. Your continuous support means the world to me.

Last, but definitely not least, I want to thank you, the reader, for choosing this novel. I wrote this book from my heart to yours. The thought of just one of you falling in love with Cassius and Sera brings me true joy.

CHAPTER 1

The moment Cassius saw her, he knew she was going to be his demise. *Sera Dwari.* His brother, Christian, referred to her as the ice queen. The viper. The—

"You have *no* chance in hell," Christian yelled in his ear. He had to yell. The music in the club was so loud that the table they sat at vibrated. "Look, little bro, you begged me to tell you what I know about her. And I did. She's a fucking snob. Stop obsessing over a chick you haven't even spoken to."

"What are you talking about?" Cassius knew exactly what Christian was talking about. Sera walked past their table five minutes ago and nodded...*merely nodded*...at Cassius, and he was captivated. He'd never met her before. They'd never said a word to each other. Up until a few minutes ago, Cassius didn't know she existed. But ever since she crossed his path, he couldn't keep his eyes off her.

In truth, he zoned in on the stunning woman and her

equally stunning friend the moment they entered 1 Oak—the most exclusive hotspot in New York City, or so Cassius was told. What did he know? Sure, he'd been to his fair share of luxurious establishments. But he usually avoided the party scene. He wouldn't even be out that evening if his brother, and his brother's accomplice, Damion, hadn't dragged him there. Cassius wasn't a nightclub kind of guy. He was more of a mountain climbing, dirt bike racing, bungee jumping, skydiving, open-adventure-adrenaline-rush kind of man. A scene where people drank overpriced liquor and tried to entice one another didn't appeal to him.

He couldn't deny the club was exquisite. The small bars in his hometown of Gillette, Wyoming, paled in comparison. Cream leather couches surrounded private tables—one of them occupied by Cassius, Christian, and Damion. Atop their table were expensive libations: four-hundred-dollar bottles of vodka and equally pricey bottles of tequila. Dim lights hung from the ceiling, swirling like diamond-encrusted snakes. Crimson foliage overflowed from giant vases and wrapped around the columns framing the dance floor. On the stage was a famous R&B singer. And Cassius could've sworn he saw a few celebrities walking around. *Definitely, not Gillette.*

Even with all the extravagance surrounding him, Cassius wasn't a fan of New York City. He was only there to help his degenerate brother with a business endeavor. "Help" meant funding Christian. Because the man was forever broke, and Cassius had billions to spare. Literally, billions.

"I told you coming out tonight was a good idea,"

Christian said. *"But,* if you're looking for some action, there are plenty of other whores that'll love to ride you until the sun comes up. Sera isn't one of them. She's out of your league. That's saying a lot since you're handsome and rich."

"Yeah, she's a bitch," Damion chimed in. He nodded toward the woman standing next to Sera. "Her best friend is stuck-up too."

"I don't want to hear that disrespectful shit. Cut it out, or I'm leaving." Cassius sipped his vodka and club soda, swallowing his aggravation. Christian and Damion were the poster boys of misogyny. Two thirty-two-year-old assholes who acted like privileged frat boys. Cassius fought with Christian numerous times about his behavior, but there was no getting through to his brother. If Cassius didn't need to be around Christian, he would've left New York days ago.

"Hey, man, calm down. We're messing with you." Damion's blue eyes glazed over. A mixture of too much alcohol and cocaine.

"I forgot, you're a fucking feminist." Christian sneered. "Quit being such a prude. You're thirty, loosen up." He patted Cassius's shoulder. His diamond-encrusted watch shimmered like sunbeams.

The man loved to flaunt wealth he didn't have. Whatever money he made was spent on extravagant items. Yet, he barely had enough funds left over to fill up his Mercedes. *How are we from the same family?* Their parents raised them better than that. But there was a reason why Christian had been disowned.

Cassius rubbed his forehead as if he could wipe away

his growing headache. "I'm asking you to tone it down, that's all."

"Can't you drop the Wyoming-bred, old-fashioned manners for once?" Christian swiped the condensation on his glass with a napkin. "Chivalry is dead here. City girls love to take co—"

Cassius raised his hand, palm forward, silencing his brother. He opened his mouth, an argument forming on his tongue. It was shut down by some commotion on the edge of the dance floor. *What the hell?*

A man twice Sera's size grabbed her hips. With a quickness Cassius had never seen before, Sera—donning six-inch stilettos and a tight dress—landed a low sweep kick to the back of his legs. The impact brought the man crashing to his knees. Slamming her palm into his chest, he collapsed on the ground. She held him down by placing her spiked heel against the hollow of his throat. Then...she smiled. It made the hairs on Cassius's arms stand up.

Sera's eyes were calm as a lake on a windless day. *That smile, though.* It was a feral nightmare. Like a wolf grating at her manacles, on the verge of breaking her confines. It was a glimmer of unhinged desire. A flicker of blood behind ravenous teeth. Her foot pressed down on the man's neck. Cassius thought she'd sink her heel deeper and sever his jugular. The music kept playing, and people continued to dance. Most were oblivious to what was happening around them. But Cassius watched Sera with unbridled intensity.

After a couple of agonizing seconds, she released him. Sera's smile dropped, and her face turned to marble. Like an exquisitely callous sculpture. Leaving the man on the ground, she walked away. Her friend—who had watched the entire scene with remarkable indifference—waved the bouncers over to take care of the mess Sera left behind.

"That was...that was..." Cassius didn't know how to finish his sentence. He had already been fascinated with Sera, now he was borderline infatuated.

"Oh shit! Sera's *really* caught your attention." Christian slapped Cassius's back. "Mãe and Pa say I'm the crazy one. But *you're* the one who's fucked up in the head. It's not like it hasn't been proven by doctors."

Cassius glared at his brother. For a blissful instant, he forgot Christian was there. "Don't—"

"Stop being so goddamn sensitive." He slapped Cassius's back again. "Forget Sera. Let's talk about more important shit, like how Damion and I are going to be filthy rich once our business opens up." He flashed the diamond-studded chain around his neck. "Everyone wants to buy gemstones."

"The babes are going to swarm us," Damion added. "Chicks are suckers for rubies and emeralds. They love those stupid crystals too. They think rose quartz is going to bring them love, and amethysts will protect them." He snickered. "It's bullshit if you ask me. But if they believe it, then whatever. As long as the money rolls in." He nudged Cassius's knee with his own. "Thanks for hooking us up with the funds, man. I appreciate it."

Christian's lips set into a thin line. "Yeah, thanks, brother." It looked like it pained him to show any sort of gratitude. "Anyway, when our first shipment comes in..."

His brother continued to talk, but Cassius blocked him

out. Nursing his drink, he concentrated on Sera. She was speaking to the DJ by the stage.

All of a sudden, she looked over at him.

Their eyes met, and her pouty lips twisted into a smirk.

Then, she strolled toward him.

"Did you say Sera was out of my league?" Cassius spoke to Christian, but his attention remained on Sera. "We'll see about that."

Christian followed Cassius's gaze. "I guess we will."

Cassius tracked Sera as she crossed the floor, observing her. He couldn't help it. She took up all the space in the room. Cassius wasn't the only one mesmerized by her presence. Everyone she passed—men and women alike—stopped to gawk at her and her best friend.

A dark-skinned woman who could've been on the cover of both *Vogue* and *Rolling Stone* magazine accompanied Sera. Her asymmetrical lace dress, strappy thigh-high heels, and chunky Chanel necklace screamed haute couture. Metallic gray lined her brown eyes, which matched the silver dye in her tresses. Her hair was buzzed on the sides, the top layered and styled into a faux-hawk. She had a sleek body, and her legs went on for days. A fashion designer's dream. Yet, there was something lethal about her as if she were ready to strike at any moment. She moved with extraordinary grace, like a snake with a fixed focus.

Sera was the complete opposite of her friend. Tiny and all curves. She was no more than five feet once she removed her designer stilettos. *Louboutins.* Cassius spotted the red bottoms when her heel decorated a man's throat. He was no stranger to fancy things. He was born into money. Though he preferred not to parade his wealth, the woman bathed in hers. From the thousand-dollar shoes to the diamonds adorning her body like a second skin.

Cassius convinced himself that Sera was a goddess in another life. Her jet-black hair, pulled back into a high ponytail, shone like obsidian. Her gray eyes glowed like a cat's at night. And her bone structure could've only been crafted by the hands of a skilled artist.

Cassius had been with his share of women. Their beauty was gentle and welcoming, akin to soft rays warming his skin. Their presence was soothing, like song-birds preening their colorful feathers under the sun. They embodied soft kisses, tender caresses, and sweet whispers in his ear.

Sera's beauty was different. It was cruel—biting, like a freshly sharpened blade. And she was...*lust*. Pure, raw lust. It shimmered around her like heat haze. She embodied carnal pleasure. Secret rendezvous that left you with teeth marks and sticky skin. She was the kind of woman that doused desire on your flesh, making you yearn for more. If the other women were songbirds basking in light, then Sera was a jaguar prowling the dark jungle.

People parted for her when she approached Cassius's table. Sera walked as if she owned the place. She knew how to work the room. Sera shook hands, smiled, and laughed with those she seemed to know. But there was something off about her. Cassius had always been good at reading people. It was one of his gifts. Right now, the emotions in her eyes were...*blank*. They were flat as a sheet of glass and cold as ice. He understood why Christian and Damion called her the ice queen. She was frozen to the core.

"Cassius, right?" Sera asked when she reached him. Her voice managed to sound soft and husky over the squall around them. "Christian frequents this club. He mentioned his brother was visiting from Wyoming." She and her friend sat in the two empty seats across from the men. Sera had pulled her chair out far enough to where Cassius still had full view of her body.

Christian mentioned me to Sera? Why? "And you are?" Cassius asked as if he didn't already know—as if he hadn't been fixated on her for the past hour.

Sera flashed a smile—closed-lipped, no joy. "Sera. This"—she briefly glanced at her friend—"is Raine."

"Pleasure," Raine said, glorious boredom lining her pretty face.

"Nice to meet you both," Cassius replied. He said nothing else.

That's it.

That. Was. It.

Where was the smooth talker? The one who made women want to jump in his bed, even when he wasn't trying. Where was the CEO of a billion-dollar corporation? The one who could close a deal in two minutes. *Nice to meet you?* How generic.

Christian chuckled, clearly amused by Cassius's awkwardness. "You'll have to excuse my brother. He's a little overwhelmed. This isn't his scene. He prefers low-key bars with his rancher buddies." Christian poured two shots of tequila and handed them to Sera and Raine.

Sera held it in her hand, her flat eyes slanting at Christian. "Drink it first."

Much to Cassius's surprise, Christian obeyed. He took a swig out of the bottle. "I'd never slip either of you a roofie," he snapped. But there was no bite in his tone.

Raine downed her shot. "Thanks." The woman somehow managed to make it sound like an insult.

Sera took one small sip of her drink and placed it on the table. She tapped her fingers on her lap. Her red polish was a stark contrast against her white dress. "So, Cassius, what do you do for fun in Wyoming?"

Christian spoke before Cassius could. "Gillette is a town of thirty thousand people. There's nothing to do there. It's the energy capital of the nation, thanks to our parents. Oh, and *of course*, thanks to my brother. He runs the family business now—the *handsome* face of Batista Holdings." Christian poured himself another drink and tossed it back. "Cassius loves Wyoming. He's the outdoorsy type, so that dinky place is a dream for him. His idea of fun is climbing mountains with no rope. He thinks he's immortal. It's easy to believe when everyone worships you." There was a hint of disdain in Christian's voice. "Isn't that right, golden boy?" More than a hint.

Cassius didn't think he was immortal. There was more to it. *Much* more. His brother knew it. As for the family business, Christian would forever be bitter. But it wasn't Cassius's fault that Christian threw his life away. It wasn't his fault their parents cut Christian off. He had dug his own grave. And Cassius was in New York bailing him out one last time.

Sera seemed to ignore Christian's ire and focused her

attention on Cassius. "You're in the energy business?" She crossed her legs. "How's that working out?"

Cassius willed himself to keep his attention on her face. "It's great. We own oil, coal, and methane." Was she interested or making polite conversation? "We—"

"Pa's retired," Christian slurred. The man was on his...*tenth or eleventh* drink. It was nothing new. Christian partied like a washed-up rock star. The more he drank, the more obnoxious he got. "Cassius runs it all. He controls more than one-third of the nation's coal. Cool, right?" He nudged Cassius's arm a little too hard. Christian was usually decent at reining in his jealousy, but now it dripped off him like sweat on a hundred-degree day.

Sera seemed unfazed by Christian's temper tantrum. Quirking a brow, she said, "I just wanted to introduce myself. If there's anything you gentlemen need, let my manager, Nikki, know. She's behind the bar."

She does own the club. Why didn't Christian tell him? Oh yeah...*because he's Christian*...synonymous with asshole. The man got a kick out of watching Cassius squirm.

Sera uncrossed her legs. Cassius's traitorous eyes snapped down to her lap. And lower. Her knees were slightly apart. He caught a glimpse of the bare slit between her thighs. *Fuck.* The woman wasn't wearing any underwear.

"It doesn't go with the dress," Sera said. "The lines would show through." There was humor in her voice, but when he looked into her eyes, he saw hollow voids that held no amusement.

A flush heated his cheeks. "I'm sorry. I didn't mean to..."

"Have a fun time in the city, Mr. Batista." Sera stood up and tossed her ponytail over her shoulder. "Maybe we'll cross paths again."

"Okay." *Okay?* What was wrong with him? This was his chance to say something slick, but apparently, he forgot how to talk.

"Hey, Raine," Damion finally spoke. "Want to hang out later?"

Raine pushed her seat back and hopped up with effortless elegance. The look of contempt she gave him was impressive. It was as if a pauper had asked a queen to marry him. "No." One dispassionate word before she walked off with Sera.

Damion whistled. "I told you they were bitches."

Christian picked up the shot Sera left on the table and drank it. "That's the damned truth."

Damion snorted. "*Anyway*, what the hell was up with you, Cassius? Is that how you pick up chicks in Gillette?"

Christian burst into a fit of laughter. "That was bullshit, little brother. It was embarrassing to watch."

"All right, I get it." Cassius rolled his shoulders back. "Trust me when I say that it was way more painful for me than it was for you guys."

The two men roared. "Don't sweat it, Wyoming," Damion said. "Sera has that effect on men. Shit, she has that effect on chicks too."

Cassius picked up Sera's shot glass. The one Christian emptied. A red lipstick mark graced the rim. "I'll never see her again anyway. I'm going home in less than a month."

"You'll see her," Christian said, his slur worse than it was a few minutes before.

Cassius disregarded his drunk brother's comment and watched Sera for the millionth time. He recalled the bare slit between her thighs. What did she feel like? How soft was her skin? Cassius wasn't into one-night stands. He wasn't into relationships either. He was always in a limbo phase with women—committed enough to leave his toothbrush at their house but not committed enough to move in together. It boiled down to the fact that he didn't know what he wanted when it came to relationships. But he knew damn well what he wanted at the moment—Sera in his bed. Just for a day. *Maybe two.* That was not considered a one-night stand, right?

Cassius leaned back on the plush leather seat. "She owns this club. Go figure…"

"We're still talking about Sera?" Christian pushed up the sleeves of his button-down shirt. "If you had any chance of sticking your dick in her, you blew it."

"Cut it out, Christian. Your brother has sensitive ears." Damion covered up his laugh with a yawn. "What Christian meant to say is that no one fucks Sera—she fucks them."

"What the hell does that mean?" Cassius asked.

Damion didn't have a chance to respond. A cocktail waitress came up to them with a bottle of champagne. Not just any bottle. A 1998 Boerl & Kroff Brut Magnum, which cost three thousand dollars. Cassius drank it many times. Placing it on the table, she said, "Compliments of the owner."

Christian chuckled. "I guess you did make an impression on the frigid bitch. We've been here a ton, and she's never given us anything for free."

Cassius gazed at Sera. She and Raine were seated a few feet away with a man in a pin-striped suit. A fedora sat on his head, and an unlit cigar dangled from his mouth. He looked like a gangster from the Prohibition Era. On the table was a bottle of Grey Goose. When he picked up the glass, Cassius spotted his tattooed hand.

Sera leaned over and whispered something in his ear. The man laughed in return. Was she interested in him? He looked too old for her, but age wasn't a concern to most people. *Why did she give me the champagne?* It certainly wasn't because he captivated her with his conversation skills.

"What are you guys doing when you leave here?" the cocktail waitress asked, jolting Cassius from his thoughts.

Christian popped the bottle open and sipped from it. "Damn, that's good." He glanced at the waitress. "We're going to my brother's suite, Mandy. Want to come? Maybe you can bring some of your girls with you?"

Mandy looked at Cassius. "We'd *love* to hang out with you."

Cassius didn't want to hang out with her, nor did he want a group of strangers in his room. The plan was, he would come to the club and go back to his suite. *Alone.* Christian and Damion would go home to their separate apartments.

"I'm not in the mood," Cassius said.

Christian elbowed him. "Come on. We won't stay long. Promise."

"Please?" Damion asked with pleading eyes.

Christian always managed to put him in tight situations. Cassius grabbed the bottle out of Christian's hand and took a large gulp. "Fine, you can hang for an hour."

Damion pumped his fist in the air and yelled, "Yeah!"

Christian blinked innocently. "Of course."

Mandy leaned over the table, her auburn hair sweeping over her shoulders. Her cleavage was in full view. "I get off in thirty minutes. But it won't take me that long to get you off." She licked her lips. "Where are we going, handsome?"

Cassius had no intention of sleeping with her. But for his brother's sake, he said, "The Mandarin Oriental."

"Great, see you soon." Mandy stood straight up. "I almost forgot, don't worry about the tab. Sera said everything is on the house."

What? Cassius glanced at Sera's table again.

She was already gone.

CHAPTER 2

It was midnight by the time Sera walked into the New York Skyline Suite of the Mandarin Oriental. Raine was already there. *Good!* Sera scanned the entire room as she always did when she was on the job. Hell, she did it even if she wasn't working. It had become a habit of hers.

She fixed her eyes on *him*. Their lovely guest.

The man donned a white robe and was sprawled atop the king-size bed next to Raine. "It's great to see you, Carlo. I hope you weren't waiting long."

Carlo Esposito was the head honcho of the New York drug trafficking industry. His latest project was creating a brand-new drug called Devil's Breath and was planning to release it to the public in a few months. Sera was certain it would be a gold mine. The drug's euphoric effects were greater than cocaine and heroin combined, and it was ten times more addictive. Most importantly, it was Sera's recipe. Carlo didn't steal it from her. She'd given him the information. But plans changed, and the price he'd have to pay was more than he'd bargained for.

"You're a little late." Carlo loosened the belt on his robe. "I'm sure you'll find a way to make it up to me."

Sera tried not to gag at the sight of his hairy chest. She knew Carlo personally, and he trusted her and Raine since they aided him with a few of his targets. He paid well, but he was a chauvinistic pig who constantly tried to get in their pants. That reason alone tempted her to rid the world of Carlo at no charge. Except Sera didn't do anything for free. *This contract is different, though.* She and Raine weren't getting paid directly. But the money they'd make in the end would be worth it.

Removing her stilettos, Sera placed them by the door along with her oversize purse. "Sorry, I had to stop by the house before I came here." *Lies.* Sera had to wait until Raine fixed the surveillance cameras in the hotel, setting them to run on a loop.

To kill time, Sera drove around the city after leaving 1 Oak. It gave her a solid hour to think about her next target: Cassius. She finally got to meet him. She waited months for their encounter to take place. Cassius, on the other hand, would regret crossing her path for the rest of his life. *Good thing he won't live long.* Murdering Cassius didn't sit well with Sera. But a job was a job.

"No worries, doll." Carlo cut into Sera's reverie. Grunting, he sat up and rested his head against the head-board. "You two have finally come to your senses, huh?"

"We've always been down for a good time. We were waiting for *you* to come to your senses," Raine teased. Her long, dark legs were crossed, and her manicured fingers caressed his thigh. Her silver faux-hawk was slightly disheveled. Sera knew she'd been running her hands through it. A sign of her agitation.

The hard set in Raine's jaw revealed how much she despised Carlo. The woman turned on the charm when she needed to, but it took everything out of her. She was too much wolf. Sheep's clothing didn't fit her. Most men disgusted Raine. In her mind, they wanted one thing. And the majority of them weren't even good at that one thing.

"Raine's right. We've been eager for this day to come," Sera said. Little did he know how true that statement was. "Gorgeous room, Carlo. I assume it's up to your standards." As the name boasted, the suite had a panoramic view. *Too bad we aren't city gazing tonight.* Sera walked straight to the windows and closed the curtains.

Her eyes continued to roam the suite, pretending to admire its beauty. In truth, she was still scanning for threats. She went through the checklist in her head.

Cameras scrambled.

Sodium hydroxide in the safe.

My and Raine's rooms booked.

Sera had booked three rooms. The first was reserved for Carlo. It was Sera's treat. It was his birthday month, after all. She used one of her many fake credit cards for the special occasion. Another room was for her and Leo— Sera's sometimes lover. The last was for Raine and Diana —Raine's sometimes lover. Both were fast asleep, dosed with a small amount of sleeping powder slipped into their drinks. It had to happen. They needed other alibis.

Prudence and precaution were how they'd survived this long in the business.

"Coming to join us, Sera, or are you going to stand by the window all night?" Carlo slurred.

Wonderful! He was nice and drunk. Sera made sure the staff at her exclusive nightclub pumped him full of alcohol. Jobs were easier when the mark was incoherent.

Flashing him a seductive smile, Sera said, "Let me freshen up. I'll be right back."

"Hurry," he called after her.

"Yes, *please* hurry," Raine said, her voice strained as a tightrope.

"I will. I promise." Sera entered the bathroom located in the right corner of the suite, a few paces from the bed. Closing the door, she glanced at the hot tub. It was large enough to fit five bodies. *Perfect.*

Standing over the sink, Sera gripped the counter with her hands, bent forward…

And threw up. Once. Quietly.

Sera always vomited before a job. She wasn't quite sure why. Guilt or fear never crossed her mind. The vomiting was an annoying inconvenience, like getting the hiccups. A therapist would probably tell Sera it was her subconscious begging for attention. Since she bottled up her trauma, it manifested in her body. *Blah. Blah. Blah.* She'd been to therapy twice and never returned. The woman didn't tell her anything she wasn't aware of. Sera just didn't care.

People don't change. As wealthy as she and Raine were, they'd always be inner-city girls who lived among the roaches and rats. They lived eighteen out of their twenty-nine years of life in the slums. They'd forever be chasing money, selling their souls, and shielding their hearts. *All in the name of survival.* The jewelry that draped Sera's body cost more than what her father made during his years in the Marines. And it certainly cost *way* more than what he made at the glass factory. It had been ages since he worked. She made enough for both of them.

Sera gargled mouthwash that the hotel provided. Digging in her bra, she pulled out the homemade capsule she had developed. It was a one-inch cellulose tube packed with a potent drug. The tube had a piece of film on one end, so the contents couldn't be released unless Sera blew on it. That made the likelihood of poisoning herself minimal.

Sera was proud of her creation. She modeled it after a dart blowgun. One that fit in her mouth. She was just as pleased with what was inside of it. *Devil's Breath.* An uncut dose of white powder. There were no other ingredients added. Ingredients that were needed to create a perfect high and lessen the chance of an overdose. No, this was pure. The tenth of a gram in the capsule was enough to kill a small horse. Carlo was about to get a taste of his own medicine. Literally.

"What's taking so long in there?" Carlo's voice rang through the walls. "Are you playing hard to get? Do I need to come get you?"

"I'll be out in a second." Sera tried to make her snarl sound like a laugh.

She stepped out of her dress and stared at her reflection—stared at the curves every man drooled over and every woman coveted. Even with her scars and burns, she was gorgeous. Her tawny-brown skin, long black hair, and storm-gray eyes—compliments of her Japanese-Filipino heritage—did wonders for her sex appeal. At times she hated it because no one saw past it. Most of the time, she used it to her advantage. *People are so predictable.*

Slipping the capsule under her tongue, Sera stepped into the room. As planned, Carlo was handcuffed to the bed with Raine on top of him. This was going to be too easy. Raine shot Sera an "are you okay" look. Her friend knew about her vomiting compulsion.

Sera nodded and plastered a smile on her face. "Don't be greedy. Learn to share, Raine. It's my turn."

"He's all yours." Raine jumped off Carlo with lightning speed. It was obvious to Sera that she couldn't bear to touch him anymore.

Sera didn't want to touch him either. If she could've put the drugs in his drink, then she would've. But there was no way she was going to kill Carlo in her own nightclub. Besides, it took too long to kick in when swallowed —a span of two minutes. Within that time frame, Carlo could've caused a ruckus. Sera didn't need that kind of mess. If inhaled, Devil's Breath killed within seconds. Effortless and uncomplicated.

Pushing down her disgust, Sera crawled on top of Carlo and straddled his lap. She dug her nails into her thighs as he ground his hard length against her. It took everything in Sera not to punch him.

Batting her lashes, she leaned forward. Her lips grazed

his. "I've been waiting a long time to do this." She wasn't lying. Sera wanted him dead years ago.

"Let me slide inside of you." Carlo panted like a dog in heat.

"Patience," she said, her teeth nibbling his bottom lip.

Sera had no issues killing people. Poison, guns, knives— she wasn't particular about her weapons. Nothing about murder bothered her. Not the stench of blood. Not the scent of rotting corpses. Not severed vessels oozing out of necks like grooved pipes. Sera didn't mind any of it. Maybe it was because she'd seen her father kill a man when she was seven years old. Sera helped him stuff the body in the bathtub. That was where the corpse stayed for weeks until the neighbors complained of a nasty smell coming from somewhere in their vicinity. Her dad finally dumped the body. Sera didn't know where, but she recalled feeling a deep sense of loss.

When the man resided in their bathtub, Sera had spoken to him as if he were alive. She'd sit on the ledge of the tub and talk for hours. She remembered wishing the man were her father because he listened so well. That wasn't the last person she saw her father kill. By the time she was nine, her sense of loss was gone. It was replaced by utter indifference.

"I'm so hot for you ladies. It's hard to be patient." Carlo's handcuffed wrist banged against the headboard. "Put me out of my misery."

"As you wish." Sera flicked the pill out from under her tongue, placing it between her teeth.

Her mouth hovered over the tip of his nose.

She held her breath...

21

And blew.

Flecks of powder fluttered onto his face like snowflakes. Once it hit Carlo's nostrils, his legs flayed and foam oozed out of his mouth. Sera tried to conjure up some form of sympathy, but the only thing she summoned was sheer displeasure for the man. A beat later, Carlo coughed, wheezed, and died. Just like that—in less than a minute. It was completely anticlimactic and slightly disappointing.

Still straddling him, Sera sat up and spat the cellulose tube on the floor. She scrubbed her face with the sheets to remove any powder residue that might've gotten on her skin. Then, she released the hold on her breath. Raine plopped beside her on the edge of the bed. Both stared at Carlo as if he were a fetal pig about to be dissected in a high school science class.

"And your father said your master's in chemistry would never come in handy." Raine nudged Sera with her elbow. "Now look at you, saving the world with your drugs."

Sera glanced at Raine and rolled her eyes. "You have a terrible sense of humor."

"Oh, and yours is better?" Raine chuckled. "Carlo asked you to put him out of his misery, and your reply was, 'as you wish.'" Her tone husky as she imitated Sera's voice. "It's like a bad line from a 1980s Sylvester Stallone action flick."

Sera picked up a pillow and hit Raine with it. Raine lost her balance and tumbled to the ground, bringing Sera along with her. "Why are we friends again?" Sera asked.

She flopped onto her back, the plush carpet embracing her skin.

Raine turned to her side, propping herself up on her elbow. "Because no one knows us like we know us."

That was the truth. When they were together, the icy facade they showed to the world faded away. They could be themselves—goofy and authentic. "And because no one trusts us like we trust us."

"Agreed." Raine chewed her lower lip. "Are you nervous about Cassius? You've been studying—"

"Nope." Sera hopped up. "I'm not having this conversation with you."

Raine stood slowly, her eyes searching Sera. "He was sexy in pictures. But in person"—she fanned her face—"hot damn. Those dimples, that smile, *those lips*. I can only imagine what he can do with those lush lips."

Sera scowled. "I don't think about him in that way."

She *absolutely* wasn't visualizing his dark curls and unnaturally black eyes. She *totally* wasn't picturing his amber-brown skin, gifted to him by his Afro-Brazilian heritage. And she *definitely* wasn't imagining his sharp jawline, muscled frame, or corded neck that sat on top of broad shoulders. Nope, not at all. Sera didn't fall for her marks. *I'm a professional.*

"*Anyway*"—Sera shook her head—"we have work to do. Since you want to bring up my degree, why don't you put your computer science degree to use before we get caught?"

"Hmmm...all right." Raine's eyes were still fixed on Sera. "We're going to talk about it eventually. This thing you're doing...it's not healthy."

23

"Can we start working, please?" She didn't want to have this discussion with Raine. *Ever.* She didn't want to have the discussion with herself.

"Okay, okay." Raine lifted her hands up in mock surrender. "I'm just telling you because I...*lylas.*" *Love you like a sister.* A silly term they made up when they were children. It stuck with them because it was true. Their bond was unbreakable, their connection forever.

Raine was an anomaly in Sera's eyes. She was both honey and venom. Her venom was lethal. All poison, no remorse. *The honey, though.* It trickled down to the people she cared about—Sera was one of them. Raine's affection was fragrant, floral, and sweet. It was an offering and a gift.

The good qualities Raine had didn't apply to Sera. She was also venom, but with no honey. Her kindness was saccharine—artificial, gritty, and toxic. But she adored her friend to no end. "Lylas, too, Raine." She let out a sigh. "Now, let's get this over with before Diana and Leo wake up and question where we are."

Raine was on it. She rummaged through Carlo's slacks, which were strewn on the floor. Pulling his cell phone out of the pocket, she put the screen up to his face. "Damn it, he doesn't have facial recognition set up. I'll have to do it the old-fashioned way."

Sera knew Raine wasn't truly bothered. The woman was a tech whiz. Raine was coding before anyone in their school knew what coding was. In college, Raine made the dean's list every time. She hacked anything and everything. It was as simple to her as breathing. Sifting through her purse, Raine retrieved a flash drive, a tiny keyboard, and two USB cords. She sat at the table across from the bed and began to work her magic.

Sera went to the living room. Passing the extravagant chesterfield sofas and mahogany coffee table, she opened the closet door next to a seventy-inch flat-screen television. Inside was a large safe with a keypad lock. Raine, in all her clever glory, had attached a removable latch with a biometric fingerprint sensor over the keypad. They had entered the room the day before Carlo checked in and set it up. Sera and Raine were the only ones who could unlock the safe. Once unlocked, Sera would remove the latch.

Carlo could've complained to the front desk that his safe was not working. But Carlo never worried about someone taking his possessions. He thought he was untouchable. It was his biggest flaw. The man didn't realize anyone could be a mark, especially those on top.

Sera pressed her finger on the sensor. When the safe clicked open, she pulled out two five-pound plastic jugs filled with clear liquid. Sodium hydroxide. A powerful chemical that dissolved bodies within hours. It was mainly used for roadkill. Sera had only used it on humans.

She carried the jugs to the bathroom and set them down beside the hot tub. Reentering the bedroom, Sera grabbed her purse and pulled out a plastic poncho, a pair of gloves, goggles, a surgical mask, and a shower cap. "Are you done, or should I wait?" she asked Raine.

"Just a second…almost…almost…" Raine's brows furrowed, her lips twisted in concentration. "Done." Raine unhooked the gadgets from the phone. "I am an evil genius. Muhahahaha," she said, rubbing her hands together.

Sera laughed. "I *never* want to hear you make fun of my one-liners ever again. That was *horrific*."

Raine grinned as she walked over to her purse. "Let's spend next weekend working on our lines because we have no life."

It was a joke. But it was also accurate. Sera spent most of her time with her father and Raine. Raine spent most of her time with her grandmother and Sera. They associated with others only for business or sex.

Raine stuffed the flash drive and cords in her bag. "Let's do this." She pulled out her own surgical mask, poncho, gloves, goggles, and shower cap.

Without speaking, they got dressed. They didn't need to talk. They knew each other's moves as much as they knew their own. Heading to the bed, Sera uncuffed Carlo's hands. Wrapping her arms under his shoulders, Sera hoisted him up while Raine held on to his legs. Together, they carried him to the bathroom and dumped his lifeless body into the tub.

"Ready to turn him into soap?" Sera asked. Sodium hydroxide liquified bodies, but it was also the main ingredient in soap. Lye was the known term for it.

Raine smirked. "You're sick."

"That's why you love me." Sera picked up the lye and dumped it in the tub.

"That, chica, is a fact." Raine popped open the cap of the other jug and doused Carlo with the liquid.

As Carlo melted, they ripped the sheets from the mattress and replaced them with the ones they stole from a cleaning cart. Afterward, they wiped the room down with an oxygen-producing detergent in order to get rid of incriminating evidence.

They performed their tasks quietly and carefully. Their moves were perfectly in sync. The women were flawless when they worked. Graceful. Elegant. It was a dance between them. A ballet. And they were prima ballerinas.

CHAPTER 3

Cassius woke up the next morning with a pounding headache. How much did he drink last night? *Too much.* He rubbed his temples, swiping the cobwebs of sleep out of his mind. The memories came rushing back. Christian, Damion, and three women came to his suite. One of them was Mandy. There was lots of alcohol and...*sex*. Not on Cassius's end. Mandy sure as hell tried, but he wasn't in the mood to have a stranger in his bed. Christian and Damion were another story.

Cassius walked in on them, stark naked in the bathroom, with two women who were also clothing-deprived. Dirty condoms sat on the sink along with lines of cocaine. That's when Cassius kicked them out. There wasn't enough alcohol in the world to blur that disgusting scene. *A few more weeks and he's out of my life.* One last favor and the family would be rid of Christian.

Cassius's phone buzzed on the side table. Picking it up, he glanced at the screen. There were three missed calls from Ava, the family attorney. *Shit.* Cassius immediately dialed her back.

Ava answered on the first ring. "Good morning, Sleeping Beauty. It's ten a.m. You never sleep this late. Fun night?"

"Not really. I was with Christian, remember?" Cassius hopped out of bed and grabbed a bottled water from the fridge in the living room.

Ava huffed. "Let me guess. Alcohol, drugs, and women?"

Cassius gulped the water down before replying. "Yes to all three."

"Any women in particular?"

"Why? Jealous?" Cassius teased. Ava was certainly not jealous. She'd been the Batista's attorney for decades. She had known Cassius since he was in diapers. Not to mention that Ava was in a committed relationship with a woman.

"Are you avoiding my question?" Ava teased back.

Flopping down on the couch, Cassius said, "No women. Okay, maybe one." A vision flashed in his mind— Sera, with her legs slightly spread, showing what was underneath her dress. "I met her last night at a club she owns. She seems...*interesting.* But I'll probably never see her again."

There was a clicking noise on the other end. Cassius knew Ava was lighting a cigarette. The woman smoked like a chimney. "Hmmm...by interesting you mean exciting," Ava said matter-of-factly. "Make sure you don't let that brain of yours take over."

Peeling the label off the water bottle, Cassius said, "I think the saying is, don't let your cock take over."

"That applies to other men, not to you," Ava grumbled. "You can't commit because the women you've been with aren't thrilling enough for you. The thrilling ones are dangerous. They might hold your attention but not in a healthy way. Remember, Cassius, it's not real. It's your mind—"

"Ava," Cassius interjected. He knew he was wired differently. The dozens of brain scans confirmed it. He didn't need a reminder. "I know you didn't call to talk about my love life, which is nonexistent. What do you want? Or were you blowing up my phone because you missed my voice."

With a snort, Ava said, "Hardly." A moment of silence. Then… "The guy's name is Henry Fisher. He has all the details you requested, plus more. I gave him your hotel information. He'll meet you there Monday afternoon. I'll text you his contact number in case you have to change plans." A long exhale of cigarette smoke. "You're safe for now, but be careful, okay?"

Cassius scrubbed a hand over his face. "What do you mean?"

"Henry will explain everything. It's best to talk to him." When Cassius didn't respond, Ava said, "Go eat breakfast and forget about it. What's done is done."

Cassius scratched his chin in contemplation. "Thanks for everything, Ava."

"I'll be in touch." She barked out a loud cough.

"You need to quit smoking. It's going—"

"Can't hear you. The signal is fuzzy. Bye." Ava hung up.

Cassius shook his head. She heard him loud and clear. *Stubborn as hell.* He didn't have time to dwell on their conversation; the rumbling of his stomach took over his concern. He showered and changed into jeans and a navy-blue polo shirt. He patted down his jet-black curls, forgoing a brush. Slapping on his watch and sliding his phone in his pocket, Cassius headed to the hotel's restaurant.

The one thing Cassius liked about New York was that no one scrutinized his every move. In Gillette, he was the son of an energy tycoon. The man who took over his father's business. Like Christian relayed to Sera, he was the face of Batista Holdings. Cassius was aware of the reputation he had to maintain. He was the golden boy, after all. *If people only knew what I did.* His and his parents' characters would be ruined. Thankfully, the incident had been hidden from Christian. Who knew what his brother would've done with that information. *How could I have been so selfish and careless?* It was a question he asked himself repeatedly.

Approaching the host station, Cassius brushed his guilt aside. "Morning," he said to a tall blond man in a suit.

"Good morning to you, sir. I hope your day is off to a good start." The man clasped his hands in front of his chest. "Do you have a preference on where you'd like to sit? The window, perhaps?"

Glancing around the room, he looked for an empty table. His eyes swept over the bar. And he froze. Leaning against it, with her left elbow propped on the countertop, was Sera. In her right hand was a champagne glass filled with orange liquid. *Probably a mimosa.* Her gray eyes looked at nothing, but Cassius was certain she was aware of her surroundings. Every person—male and female—stared when they passed her. How could they not? The woman was a marble statue—frozen in her flawlessness. She oozed with desire and sex and arrogance. So. Much. Arrogance.

It didn't help that she resembled someone who had stepped out of a high-priced boutique. Her red lips and nails matched her red-bottomed stilettos. Her tight black Gucci top and skin-hugging jeans flattered her curves. To complete the look, her wrists and neck were adorned with gold and emeralds.

"I think I'll seat myself," Cassius told the host.

He made his way to the bar, hoping his mouth formed proper phrases this time. "Sera, right?" Cassius asked when he reached her. He leaned the side of his body on the bar. "I want to thank you for comping us last night." Sera sipped her drink while he studied her profile. She didn't face him—didn't acknowledge his presence. *Walk away before you embarrass yourself.* It was apparent she didn't want to be disturbed. "Sorry to bother you. I guess I'll go now."

Sera's eyes slid over to him. "You're welcome." Her tone was flat. Indifferent. "Christian has blown plenty of paychecks at my club. I'm a generous woman. I don't mind showing his brother a good time."

Her gaze slipped down his body and back up to his face again. The intensity of it burned through his clothes. Cassius was half hard just being near her. Like a teenage virgin who got aroused when the wind blew.

What's wrong with me? He was normally bold and

assertive. He needed to get his act together. "Can I take you to dinner?"

"Why? You don't even know me." A bored question.

"I can get to know you over dinner. I kept thinking about you last night. I can't believe I ran into you today." Cassius had never been good at being aloof. He hated the dating game, where people who were interested acted uninterested. It wasn't his style.

Sera took a long sip of her drink. "Do you want to get to know me, or do you want to fuck me?" She turned her entire body to face him. "Last night, were you thinking about what an intelligent conversationalist I'd be, or were you picturing me naked and wriggling underneath you?"

Cassius flushed. He wasn't expecting her to say *that*. "The second one," he muttered. "I was picturing you...I was picturing you naked." Honesty was the best policy. Sera knew the truth. She was merely baiting him. "But I only want to take you out to eat. I won't make any moves. Promise." He meant it. Sera caught his attention at 1 Oak, especially after what she did to the man who tried to grab her. The woman captivated him. He genuinely wanted to find out more about her. "What do you say?"

Sera twirled the stem of her glass. The seconds ticked by slowly. Finally, she said, "Tea, not dinner. Meet me at Lenox Coffee Roasters in Central Harlem tomorrow at three. I'm sure you can find your way. Don't be late."

A full-fledged smile settled on Cassius's lips. "Why tea instead of dinner?"

Sera finished her drink and set the empty glass on the counter. "It's less of a commitment. Dinner is similar to a proposal. Tea is more like speed dating."

His smile widened. "So, this is a date?"

"I'm willing to fulfill a small part of your fantasy," Sera said, studying her nails.

"You think I fantasize about taking you out?" Cassius quirked a brow.

Sera cocked her head to the side. "Everyone fantasizes about taking me out."

Cassius laughed. "Beautiful and modest, I see."

"It's one of my many talents." Sera stroked the emerald that hung on a gold chain around her neck. "Did you have fun with Mandy last night?"

What? "What?" He couldn't mask his shock. "She came to my room, but I didn't do anything with her." It sounded like a lie even though it wasn't.

"Okay," was her only response. Before Cassius could explain, Sera slid a hundred-dollar bill on the counter. "I have to go. See you tomorrow." She glanced at the bartender and said, "Keep the change."

"Wait." A thought triggered his mind. "What are you doing here? Do you usually go to hotels alone and drink mimosas? Most people prefer coffee at cafés with friends."

Sera brushed back a strand of her silky hair. "Who said I'm drinking a mimosa? That was orange juice." Cassius took note of how she avoided his other questions. "Alcohol and caffeine aren't part of my diet. That's why I suggested tea." He was fairly sure her suggestion wasn't a suggestion at all. It was a command. "I don't put toxins in my body."

Cassius recalled how Christian handed Sera a shot of tequila at 1 Oak, barely sipping it before putting it down. "Do you have any other dietary restrictions?"

"I'm thinking of giving up meat." Sera's eyes swooped to the crotch of his jeans. "It's unsatisfying."

"Is that right?" Cassius crossed his arms over his chest. "You should give it one last chance. Everyone knows Wyoming meat is the best."

"Are you saying you can change my mind?" Sera purred.

Cassius shrugged. "It depends if I'm interested in you after we meet up."

Sera's husky laugh heated his skin. "I'll make sure to impress you then."

Cassius was about to respond when a man with short brown hair and a full beard approached. "Are you ready?" he asked Sera, ignoring Cassius completely.

"Of course, Leo." She grabbed the man's hand, entwining their fingers together. Winking at Cassius, she said, "Remember, don't be late tomorrow."

Cassius watched as Sera left the restaurant with this Leo. As his eyes followed their exit, one thought ran through his mind. *What am I getting myself into?*

Sera and Leo parted ways once they reached the valet, his car already there. *Thank God.* She could only take so much of him. It's not like Leo cared. He wasn't even attached to Sera. They had an understanding—a relationship based on sex. They weren't even friends. Hell, if she didn't need him as an alibi, she wouldn't have spent the night with him.

That was true with all of Sera's partners. Why complicate things? Raine was her friend. Her father was her friend. That's all Sera needed. She never came, anyway, unless she did it herself. Sex was something she did to pass the time. It wasn't particularly enjoyable, but it wasn't terrible either. Kind of like eating a salad with no dressing. Sera had been close to coming with a few partners, but she always stopped herself. A therapist would tell her she had control issues. Sera wasn't concerned enough to delve into it.

She handed the attendant her ticket, and a few minutes later, her Tesla arrived. Sera hopped into the driver's seat, dug her burner phone out of her purse, and dialed.

"Hello," a raspy voice answered.

"Are you *still* asleep?" Her irritation flared. She did all the work while this imbecile partied and slept till noon.

The man cleared his throat. "I had a long night."

"Yeah, so did I," she said through gritted teeth.

"Don't be upset, babe." His lackadaisical tone grated Sera's nerves. "You're about to get the biggest paycheck of your life, so is your dad."

That was the only reason she agreed to the monstrous plan. Sera would pillage the world if it made her dad happy. "Well, it's done. We have the information." Sera didn't need to explain that they killed Carlo, hacked his phone, and gathered the data of where the drug lab was located. The drug lab she and Raine were expected to raid. It was all part of the plan. Clarification wasn't needed.

"Good job, babe," the man said. "And Cassius?"

Sera grabbed her sunglasses from the cupholder and

put them on. "I ran into him at the restaurant." Sera didn't exactly run into him. She knew he was staying at the Mandarin. That's why she booked rooms there for Carlo, herself, and Raine. She also knew he'd be at the restaurant for breakfast. He arrived later than expected, but Sera was a patient woman. "We're going out for tea tomorrow."

"Cassius is a charming man. Make sure you don't end up falling for Mr. Perfect. Otherwise, you'll end up marrying him instead of murdering him." The man's tone was light, but bitterness seeped through.

Swerving around cars to beat the traffic, she said, "I have to go. I'll touch base with you later." She wasn't in the mood to listen to someone sulk. "Oh, and if you call me babe one more time, I'll cut your fucking fingers off."

She hung up the phone before he could respond. The entire thing sickened her. Sera had taken many jobs, but the people she assassinated were killers themselves. Now she had to eliminate Cassius, an innocent man. She often wondered what the real motive was behind this job— money or jealousy. Sera had an inkling it was the latter. Because who puts a hit on their own brother?

CHAPTER 4

Sera never worked with people like Christian. He was an amateur who partied too hard and spent money he didn't have. She honestly preferred working with Carlo. At least he was professional when it came to business. But this time Sera made an exception. *The things you do for love.* She had one true love in her life: her father. He wanted this, so she'd make it happen.

Sera entered her penthouse and removed her shoes, placing them by the door. Sauntering to the living room, she jumped in surprise. Sitting on the sofa was Lorenzo Dwari. "*Tay,* I wasn't expecting you."

"Hello, *iha,*" he said.

Iha. The Filipino term of endearment her father used when he wanted something. Acid ate at Sera's stomach. Lorenzo's jet-black hair was disheveled, and his gray eyes had rings underneath. "What's wrong?"

His heavily tattooed arms draped over the top of the couch. "Why don't you get your tay a glass of scotch, then we'll talk."

"Of course." Sera walked to the opposite side of the room, where the bar took up half of the wall. She didn't lie to Cassius about not drinking. The bar was for her father. Lorenzo enjoyed his alcohol. Sera wanted to make sure he was comfortable when he visited her. Putting a bar in her living room was his idea, after all.

"Pour me the Highland Park, the forty-year one. Make it neat," he called to her.

"Yes, Tay." Sera filled a glass with the four-thousand-dollar bottle of scotch. Only the best for her father. The man sacrificed his whole life for Sera. He raised her when her drug-addicted mother ran back to Japan. They might've been poor, but Lorenzo found ways for the two of them to survive. He'd go hungry so she could eat. He'd wear tattered shoes so she could sport a decent pair. He'd sleep on the couch so she could have the only bed.

Now he didn't have to grind anymore. Sera made sure of that.

She handed Lorenzo his drink and sat on the accent chair across from him. "What's going on?"

"You know what I was thinking about this morning? All our fun escapades," he said, snubbing her question. "Remember when I used to take you to Coney Island? You'd eat so much cotton candy that it made you sick for days. I should've cut you off, but I couldn't say no to my *prinsesa*." He beamed with pride. "And remember ice skating at Rockefeller Center? We'd go every New Year's Eve. Those are my favorite memories of us. I hated working overtime at the factory. And pawning some of my stuff hurt. It was worth it, though. You're the most important person in my life. I'd break my back all over again just to take you on those adventures."

He neglected to mention that he wasn't always kind and selfless. *But what human is? He did the best he could.* "I'll never forget what you've done for me," Sera said. "You're an amazing father."

"And you're an amazing daughter." Lorenzo took a few sips of his drink before putting it down on the coffee table. "Anyway, we're both tired from our long night, so I'll cut to the chase. I need you to do something for me. I got into a jam."

"I'm always here to help you. How much money do you need?" Sera already paid for his apartment in the Lower East Side, bought his groceries, and had a cleaning service fix his place up once a week. Not to mention she gave him five thousand dollars a month to spend on whatever he desired. It never seemed to be enough.

"It's not that." He shifted in his seat. Sera noticed the letters of her name—tattooed on his left knuckles—were scraped up. "I went out drinking after I left your club last night. You know how I get when I'm blitzed."

Yes, Sera knew all too well. The scars on her body never let her forget. Especially the iron-shaped burn on her lower back. Lorenzo always apologized after he hurt her. He'd buy her something fancy: a dollhouse, a new dress, whatever she wanted. He spent all his money to make up for his mistakes. How could Sera not forgive him? It wasn't his fault he had a bad temper. That's what happens when you've been dealt the wrong hand all your life.

Leaving her chair, Sera sat beside her father. She took his hand and held it in hers. "Tell me what I can do."

Lorenzo smiled. A sad, lonely smile. The kind that wrenched her heart out of her chest. "What would you do for me, iha?" It was a question he had asked her many times before.

There was only one response. "Anything, Tay."

"Just anything?"

"Everything," Sera said.

"Good." Lorenzo released her hand and picked up his drink. "I went straight to Quiapo after I jetted out of 1 Oak."

Shit. Sera knew where this was going. Quiapo was a bar in Woodside where most of the patrons were Filipinos or Japanese. It was also where the Yakuza hung out.

Sera steadied her breath. "Go on." She couldn't show fright. Lorenzo would ridicule her for it. *Fear is weakness,* he'd say.

"I went with Butch. We were partying it up." He downed his scotch. "When we left, we ran into three tough guys a few streets down. They were at Quiapo earlier that evening. We recognized them, but they didn't recognize us. These suckers were so juiced they couldn't see straight. They wanted to throw down."

Bullshit. Butch was a wild card. The man started fights if someone looked at him the wrong way. And he was a killer. Not a trained one like Sera. A reckless one, like a rabid dog in a frenzy. Butch was who Lorenzo called if he wanted someone dead and didn't want to do it himself. *That was a long time ago, though.* Now Sera was old enough to do Lorenzo's dirty work.

As a child, Lorenzo used Butch to incite fear in Sera. Normal parents would say things like, "You better be good, or the boogeyman will get you." But Lorenzo wasn't a normal parent. He'd say things like, "If I ever leave you alone with Butch, you know your time is up."

"So...you want me to take care of these guys?" Sera sat on her hands to keep them from shaking. He was the only person who could break through her layers of ice. It had taken years to build her image: cold, impassive, and untouchable. Lorenzo managed to shatter her in seconds.

"Yeah, I do." Lorenzo traced the rim of his glass with his finger. "We busted them up pretty bad. Butch is lying low at my house right now. But I doubt those Yaks can identify us."

Yaks. That was the keyword. "They're Yakuza?" She already knew the answer.

Lorenzo adjusted the butterfly collar on his vintage Armani shirt. "A bunch of scumbags. Butch has seen them around the way. He knows their reputation—some over-sensitive bitches."

"What are their positions?" *Please don't let them be important.*

"Kyodai."

Fuck! "What Yakuza family are they from?"

"Ichiwa-kai."

Double fuck. Lorenzo had to—*just had to*—mess with high-ranking members from the most ruthless Yakuza family. There was no going back from this. "I'll take care of it." Butch would handle it if she didn't. The job would be a mess. The man was a certified psychopath.

"That's my baby." Lorenzo ruffled Sera's hair. "There

are three of them. I'll text you everything you need to know on the burner phone later. An inside source told me that on Saturday nights, they have dinner at Kusina. They arrive around seven and stay till the place closes."

Saturday night. Tomorrow. "Got it."

"I knew I could count on you." Lorenzo smiled like a cat over a bowl of cream. "Let's discuss more important shit. How's our business venture going?"

Our venture was really *his*. Except Sera did all the work. She always did all the work. "It's fine. Carlo is dead."

Her father rubbed the star tattoo on his neck. He got it during one of his many jail stints. "What else?"

"I'm meeting Cassius tomorrow."

"What do you think of him? Is he an easy mark?" This time he rubbed the tattoo on his forearm—a globe with an eagle sitting on top of it. He had it done when he was in the Marines. "I bet he's an arrogant fuck. He probably wipes his ass with bills just to prove he can."

He said the same thing to Sera at 1 Oak. Lorenzo rarely went to her club. He preferred dive bars with his hoodlum buddies. The patrons at those establishments worshiped him because he was the richest one there. He'd toss money around like a celebrity to remind them how well-off he was.

When he found out Cassius was going to be at 1 Oak, he decided to show up. He spent the evening scrutinizing the man while polishing off a bottle of Grey Goose. He despised Cassius with a passion. Lorenzo would never admit it, but Sera knew her father was jealous. Successful people intimidated him. They made him feel insecure and inadequate.

Sera crossed her legs. "Based on my investigation, the man is shrewd in his business dealings. I don't think those kinds of people get duped easily."

Lorenzo's stormy gaze met hers. "Iha, you're the perfect woman for this job. Men melt in your hands. That pretty boy doesn't have a chance." He abruptly seized her wrist, squeezing it tight. His giant hand felt like a vise. Sera's fingers tingled from lack of blood supply, and her pulse galloped in fear. Lorenzo stopped hitting her years ago. But his forcefulness was a reminder of the things he'd done to her. What he was *still* capable of doing if it pleased him. "We have a lot riding on this. Disappointing me isn't an option. *Entiende?*"

"Yes, I understand," Sera croaked out, licking her dry lips.

Draining Cassius's bank accounts and killing him would be the hardest job she'd ever taken on. But she couldn't tell her father that.

If she wasn't terrified of failing—terrified of Lorenzo —she'd actually have room to be annoyed. The entire operation landed on her and Raine. Cassius was just one part of it. They had to take care of much, much more. Sure, Christian, Damion, and Lorenzo would manage the logistics. But Raine was the one who flew to Colombia and negotiated the contracts for the farms. Because of her, they had seventy acres of Devil's Breath trees.

Sera was the one who handpicked the chemists in Colombia. Her recipe—the one Carlo was going to utilize before she killed him—was being used to create the most powerful drug on the market. The drug that was going to make them all extremely rich.

Who funded most of it so far? *Me.* Christian and Damion sure as hell didn't have the money. Neither did Lorenzo. Who helped her the most? *Raine.* The woman didn't want to be involved, but she did it for Sera. She was loyal to the bone.

"Now that that's settled, do you have a sample?" Lorenzo released Sera's wrist and patted her head. "I know I've seen it a million times, but I adore being reminded of what your brilliant brain can create." How he managed to dole out a threat and a compliment in the same breath was beyond her.

Despite his harsh behavior, Sera couldn't help but smile. She was pathetic when it came to her father. Like a puppy eager to please her master no matter how many times she'd been kicked. Sera removed her bracelet and popped two emeralds out of it. "Here you go." She handed the gemstones to her father.

He held the stones against the sunlight. "Beautiful." He sighed. "You're incredible. I did something right when I raised you."

Sera cringed internally. She produced illegal drugs, laundered money, and killed. *How is that amazing? I end lives.* But it's what Lorenzo wanted. It's what he trained her for. He passed along his martial arts knowledge and the combat skills he learned in the Marines to teach her how to be lethal.

Begrudgingly, she admitted that the emeralds were impressive. Lorenzo was right: she had a brilliant brain. If only she used it for good instead of evil. In all honesty,

Sera wanted nothing to do with the Devil's Breath business. But how was she supposed to say no to her father?

"The chemists in Colombia know the exact formula, right?" Lorenzo asked, pocketing the stones.

"Yes, I trained them myself," Sera responded.

Uncut Devil's Breath killed quickly, as it did with Carlo. Sera found a way to mix it with an antidote called physostigmine to treat Devil's Breath overdoses. Another ingredient was meclizine—a drug used to alleviate withdrawal symptoms. Those who snorted the end product claimed sheer euphoria.

"Good girl." Lorenzo nodded his approval. "I still can't believe you managed to turn powder into an imitation emerald."

"It wasn't easy." Sera lay down and rested her head on the arm of the couch. "I had to find a way to freeze it without disrupting the chemical compounds. Removing the food coloring was a task on its own. Melting the polymeric—"

Lorenzo's hand slammed the table, causing her muscles to lock. His whole mood shifted. *Again.* The man was constantly on edge. "Why *the fuck* are you talking to me about things I don't understand? Are you trying to prove you're smarter than me? I could've gone to a fancy college, too, if I wasn't stuck raising an ungrateful brat."

A familiar sensation crept into her: bitterness and remorse. The bitterness she swallowed. She had no right to resent the man who raised her. The guilt she allowed to settle in her throat. She shouldn't have made her father feel intellectually inept. It was her fault he was upset. "I'm sorry, Tay. I got carried away. I appreciate all you've done for me and what you gave up because of me. I couldn't ask for a better dad."

Lorenzo's jaw twitched. Twice.

His face softened as he squeezed Sera's ankle. "I shouldn't have gotten pissed off. You did an excellent job. Be proud of yourself. Everything is falling into place. Soon, we'll have Cassius's money *and* profits from the Devil's Breath." He had a faraway look in his eyes. "When we lived in the slums, I was happy to have a fridge full of food. Now look where we're at."

Yes, now look. Sera was a millionaire, but it wasn't enough for Lorenzo. Her father didn't need to get involved in the drug trade. They didn't have to kill Cassius. Sera made enough money for both of them. "We could leave Cassius alone," she said with reluctance. "I can fund the entire operation. Christian can deal with his brother on his own."

Lorenzo scowled. "You can't afford it. We have to compensate the Colombian police. The farms have to be maintained. We have to pay for the ingredients, our workers, security, trucks..." Lorenzo counted the expenses on his fingers. "The starting fees are going to be *at least* fifteen million. You're rich, but not Cassius rich." A glint of steel shone in his eyes. "Don't forget, the fifteen million isn't shit compared to what we're *really* taking him for."

"I don't want anything bad to happen to you. This is the riskiest thing we've done. Why don't we just start small?"

Lorenzo patted his daughter's knee. "Iha, when have you and I ever done anything small?"

· · ·

After Lorenzo left, Sera sat on the couch for an hour, biting her manicured nails until they were chipped and jagged. She wouldn't sleep tonight. Not because she had to kill people to help her father...*again*. It was because she'd worry about him until the three Yaks were dead. As usual, Sera would send him numerous texts to ensure he was safe. Lorenzo would get irritated and ignore her.

When will this end? Sera knew the answer: *never.* Her father was her weakness. Sera honed her coldness—her control—like a blade. Except when it came to Lorenzo. With him, she was soft. All water, no ice.

Picking up her burner phone, Sera dialed Raine. She hung up before she could hit the call button. Rubbing her thumb against her chin, she rethought her plan. Sera was about to ask Raine to be her alibi, but the woman worked better in the shadows. Raine was a criminal, tried and true. She wore blood like a cocktail dress, and her lips were perpetually stained in poison. Sera needed her assistance for something else.

Honestly, Sera didn't want to tell Raine about Lorenzo's encounter with the Yakuza. The woman despised her father. Sera didn't need her to hate him even more. But Raine was the only person she trusted. With reluctance, Sera called her. Raine agreed to the plan because that's what Raine did. She'd do anything for Sera. *And I'd do anything for her.*

Everything was in place except for the alibi. Leo was usually her unknowing alibi. Hopefully, he'd be free. If not, she had a list of people who'd love to spend time with her. How ironic one can be so popular yet feel alone at the same time.

Picking up her main phone, Sera scrolled through her contact list. Her eyes lingered on one particular name. Cassius Batista. *Shit.* She had to cancel their date. What would she say? *Sorry, I have to take a rain check. I'm massacring three Yakuza gangsters tomorrow night.* Another thought crossed her mind. Cassius hadn't given her his number. She got it from Christian. How was she going to explain that?

Your brother hates you and hired me to kill you. Would you like to reschedule our date? Sera had seen sibling rivalry before, but nothing compared to Christian's animosity toward his brother. Christian told her bits and pieces of his childhood when he was drunk. He was the outcast of the family—ignored and disinherited. He came to New York and worked odd jobs until he became a low-level criminal. In Sera's opinion, Christian had no redeeming qualities. He was a selfish, egotistical man-child.

Then there was Cassius. The thirty-year-old tycoon who didn't just live off his parents' money. He had overhauled and optimized Batista Holdings, allowing for all employees to earn a living wage. The man's integrity helped him gain dedicated business partners. And the calculated risks he took doubled the company's profits.

He was the complete opposite of his brother. He trumped Christian in every way possible. Even in the looks department. They were both over six feet tall with jet-black curls, amber-brown skin, and obsidian eyes. But Cassius was the more handsome of the two. Christian was not revolting by any means. It was like comparing a tiger to a lion. They were both stunning, but the lion was the king of the jungle.

Sera had studied everything there was to know about Cassius. It was her job to research her marks. She didn't pry Christian for information. She listened when he voluntarily talked about Cassius, but it was apparent he hated discussing his brother. Sera was a professional, though. She had her own ways of learning about people. And learn about him she did. It got to the point where Raine intervened because her research became an obsession. She couldn't help it. She'd never met anyone like Cassius. The man was perfect. His looks were stunning, his success remarkable. But what drew her attention was his generosity.

Kindness might've been normal to others. To Sera, it was a foreign concept. The people she associated with were criminals. Acquaintances one day and foes the next. These weren't people who committed crimes because they were destitute. They did it because they loved the thrill of it.

They were driven by greed.

Including Lorenzo.

Including myself.

Sera could've gone legit years ago but chose not to.

Because of Lorenzo.

Because of myself.

Cassius wasn't a criminal nor a terrible human being. The man donated billions of dollars each year to charities around the world. He gave hefty donations to organizations in Brazil, where his parents originated from. He created a private foundation, which held five billion dollars in assets. The foundation's goal was to reduce poverty and expand educational opportunities in South

America. In Wyoming, he founded three nonprofits: one that helped those affected by substance abuse, another for domestic violence survivors, and a no-kill animal shelter. Not only did he establish the organizations, but he also volunteered his time. And he was in the process of setting up more nonprofits. If that wasn't enough, he organized holiday feasts for the homeless every year.

The man is a saint. Compared to him, Sera was a demon. She'd never known anyone who could make her feel bad about herself. *Cassius sure does.*

There *was* one thing she couldn't figure out about him. Cassius made monthly contributions to three families residing in the Solukhumbu District of Nepal. These funds came out of his personal account. His other contributions were withdrawn from accounts designated for charitable giving. *Why is this different?* Sera was aware Cassius climbed Mount Everest in his teens, but that was his only link to Nepal. It didn't make sense.

What does it matter? Cassius's dealings weren't Sera's business. Her only concern was catching his eye, which she did. *Thanks to Christian's advice.* He told her to be mysterious. Be the challenge he couldn't refuse. "Challenges" were Cassius's weakness.

Their quick interactions at the club, a glimpse under her dress, the free drinks, and the altercation with a man were all part of the plan. Even Christian's behavior was an act. Most of it, at least. His jealousy was definitely real. Showing up at the hotel restaurant that morning was part of her process too. Sera knew how to play people like a game of chess—how to get them to notice her. That was how she made it this far in life. Still, at times she wished she were normal. She shoved the dangerous thought away every time it entered her mind. Why dwell on the impossible?

She'd never be like the women Cassius dated. Sera studied them too. *I am a truly sad case.* Those women were the epitome of class and elegance. They were the type who wore pearls and pleated skirts while having Sunday brunch at the country club. They represented old money sophistication. Sera could bet her last dollar they'd never tasted a ketchup sandwich before. A meal Sera was all too familiar with.

Rolling her neck, Sera tossed aside the self-deprecating thoughts. She'd wasted enough time feeling sorry for herself. Ten minutes had passed since she spoke to Raine. She needed to finish setting up her plan. Glancing at Cassius's name on her phone again, she hit the call button.

It took four rings before he answered. "Hello," he said in a jagged voice.

"It's Sera." Her tone was flat. The ice queen mask was strapped on, skintight. "Christian gave me your number." She figured it was best to be honest. "You sound out of breath. Were you in the middle of getting to know your right hand better?"

Cassius laughed. "I just got back from a run. I'm about to take a shower."

"Perfect, let's video chat." It was a joke, but she wouldn't have minded if he agreed.

"Maybe another time." There was smile in his words. "I got your number from Christian too. I realized I had no way of contacting you if plans changed. That's why you're calling, right? To change plans? Or are you canceling? You know my heart can't handle that," he teased.

Little did he know she couldn't flat-out cancel on him. She'd have to see him at some point if the plan was going to work. *But not tomorrow.* It was too risky.

"Wait…are you canceling?" he asked quietly.

Yes, I am. I'm totally *canceling tomorrow's date.* "I need to change the location and time." *Damn it!* Why wasn't she able to control what came out of her mouth? "Kusina at seven. It's a restaurant in Woodside."

"I thought you didn't want to do dinner? Something about it being too much of a commitment. Our relationship seems to be progressing fast." Sera heard the shower turn on. "Should I propose? I bet you're a round cut ring kind of woman."

Sera stifled a laugh. It wouldn't go well with her performance. "You're free to gift me diamonds. I won't stop you." He was right, though. She was a round cut kind of girl. "Are you available tomorrow night?"

"I'd meet you at five in the morning if you asked me to."

"Men are always willing to go through obstacles for sex." It was something she used to her advantage. Giving it or withholding it. "If you think I'm going to spread my legs because you're paying for a plate of food, then you're mistaken."

"Who said I was paying?" Cassius asked with a joking cadence. "Look, Sera. I'm not trying to have sex with you. It's just dinner. I promise."

Sera was taken aback. It was the second time he had said those words. No one had ever said *that* to her before.

They didn't necessarily tell her up front that they wanted to have sex with her, but their motive was clear enough. "Fine." She feigned disinterest. "See you at seven. And Cassius—"

"I know." He chuckled. "I won't be late."

Sera hung up the phone and blew out a breath. She glanced at her chipped nails. The ones she'd bitten down like a rabbit chewing on carrots. As tired as she was, she had to go to the salon. Chipped nails just wouldn't do. Because it wasn't perfect. And another lesson Lorenzo taught her: it wasn't worth it if it wasn't perfect.

CHAPTER 5

Cassius arrived at Kusina five minutes before seven. It was a quaint establishment with little lamps that sat atop dark wood tables, and the black leather seats were plush and shiny. A bar stood to the right of the room, and to the left was a jukebox that played a soft jazz tune. Pictures of rice fields, cerulean oceans, and erupting volcanoes decorated the walls, and one of them dedicated photos of Asian celebrities who had visited the restaurant.

The patrons were primarily Asian men dressed in black tailored suits. Some had their jackets off, exposing full-sleeve tattoos. Cassius spotted a few customers with missing fingers. He immediately thought of the Yakuza. He watched a documentary once where the members cut off their own digits to atone for their offenses. He shook the silly thought from his mind. These men weren't gangsters.

He scanned the room until his eyes found Sera. She was standing next to a table, engrossed in a conversation with a silver-haired gentleman. Cassius watched her before he approached. Her beauty was addicting. He could stare at her for hours. Tonight, her hair was slicked into a high bun. She wore a strappy burgundy dress with gold stilettos that matched her hoop earrings. And her nails...*hmmm*...they were a different color. The last two times he had seen her, they were red, but now they were matte gray.

He analyzed her as if he were a scientist who discovered a new species. Cassius had always been good at reading people. When he looked at Sera, he saw a downright predator. It was written in her smile. In the way she rested her hand on the man's forearm. In the way she examined him when he talked. The woman was exquisite, but there was something deceiving about her magnificence. Like a carnivorous flower devouring anything that graced its path. Realizing this, Cassius still went over to her.

Sera's eyes flicked to him, slick as oil. "You're on time." For a brief moment, her dead eyes came to life. *Or am I imagining it?* "This is my friend, Manny. He owns the restaurant."

Manny extended his hand, giving Cassius a firm handshake. "Nice to meet you," he said in a thick New York accent. "Sera tells me you're from Wyoming."

"Yes, Gillette. I'm here for a few weeks visiting my brother," Cassius responded. *Manny: tailored suit with a slight sheen. Flashy. A gold pinkie ring. Pricey. Italian leather shoes. Classy.*

The man was new money, Cassius decided after sizing him up. Manny wanted people to know how successful he was. Old money rarely did that. They were used to their wealth and had nothing to prove. Cassius wasn't judging. It was simply an observation. He admired people who built their own empires.

"I hope you're enjoying the city." Manny nodded at one of the waiters. A pale man with blond hair, donning a white blazer and black slacks, approached. "Timothy, bring this table our best bottle of wine. Compliments of the house." He winked at Cassius. "A friend of Sera's is a friend of mine. Now, if you'll excuse me, I'm going to greet some acquaintances of mine. I hope you two enjoy dinner."

Manny walked over to two men who were seated a few strides from Cassius and Sera. Both had spiky black hair and matching dragon tattoos on their arms. They glanced at Sera and gave her a slight nod. She smiled in return.

"You seem to have lots of connections," Cassius said, taking a seat.

Sera slid in the chair across from his, her face utterly blank. He could've been staring at someone in a casket. "It's all about connections. You should know...being a businessman and all."

"Who are those two men?"

Sera's smile was slow-dripped molasses. "Why? Jealous?"

Cassius grinned. "Maybe."

Sera tapped her bottom lip with her finger. He tried not to stare. "The one on the left is Angelo Del Rosario. The other one is Stevie Del Rosario. They're brothers. They belong to the Yamaguchi-gumi. They come here every night for dinner. Yakuza loves this place." Sera spoke in such a casual manner. It was as though she were telling him they were surrounded by priests instead of notorious killers.

Cassius's initial observation was correct. Kusina was crawling with gangsters. "What exactly is it that you do for a living? I know you own 1 Oak; I have a feeling you're involved in other endeavors."

The waiter came back with a bottle of wine. He poured the red liquid into their glasses before stepping away. "Do you think I'm a Yakuza princess?" She didn't wait for him to respond. "I'm a businesswoman," she said, opening her menu.

Cassius opened his menu as well. "What kind of business?"

Sera looked at him from underneath her thick lashes. "I own 1 Oak, a strip club, two cash checking stores, and a funeral home."

Cassius raised a brow. "A funeral home, huh? Interesting choice."

Sera put her menu down. Her dull eyes clipped his face. "Everyone dies. Why not profit from it? Besides, there's something fascinating about death. Isn't it interesting how we spend our life rotting away until one day our bodies cease to function? Unless the person is murdered." She picked her menu up again. "I'm going to order the tofu adobo. How about you?"

Cassius took a sip of the delicious wine. "That's an interesting take on things." The woman was either joking or a sociopath. Cassius suspected the latter. Yet he had no desire to walk away from her. "You talk about murder like it's nothing."

Sera clasped her hands atop the table. "We kill animals all the time. If people slaughtered one another at the same rate we slaughter animals, we'd be extinct in seventeen days." The statement rolled off her tongue with lazy indifference. "Humans are natural killers. Why is taking a human life different from taking an animal's?"

Cassius blinked. "You can't be serious?"

Sera cocked her head and flashed her perfect white teeth. The action had the charm of a panther before it ripped your throat out. "Would you walk out the door if I was?"

Everything Sera said and did made him want to delve deeper into her mind. She triggered the dopamine in his brain. It was the same feeling he had when he was about to jump off a plane, parachute at the ready. "No, I'd stay."

"Why?" There was a challenge in her question.

"Because I'm pretty damn hungry," he said, calling the waiter over.

A reaction flickered across Sera's face, quick as a scuttling spider. It almost seemed like admiration. "All right, let's eat."

After the waiter took their order, Cassius said, "I forgot to compliment you on your nails. It's my favorite color. Two of my cars are custom painted matte gray."

"I'm happy to please." Maybe it was her feline smile, but he had a feeling Sera somehow knew that fact already.

"That makes two of us," he said with a wink. "See, we already have one thing in common."

He was about to continue the topic when three heavy-set men walked into the restaurant and sat at the bar. Bruises covered their faces, and their glassy eyes exposed how drunk they were. It was apparent they were regulars there. Manny and the bartender greeted them personally. Their drinks were brought over before they ordered.

Sera stared at them with the intensity of a boxer assessing her opponent.

"Don't tell me you know them too," Cassius said.

"No," she replied, her focus back on him.

There it is. Her tell: the quiver of her right hand. It revealed her lie. The tremor was minor, nothing anyone would notice. Anyone but Cassius. He was gifted in that way. His mother used to tell him that if Batista Holdings tanked, he could become a special agent for the FBI. He was talented at picking up on nonverbal cues. That's how he figured Manny was nouveau riche. But Cassius wasn't about to press Sera. Whatever her relationship was with those three men was none of his business.

The waiter delivered their food—tofu adobo for Sera and a ribeye steak for Cassius. "Why did you choose this restaurant?" he asked, taking a bite of his steak. It was the best cut of meat he'd come across. That was saying a lot for someone born and bred in Wyoming.

"What do you mean?"

"I thought you were giving up meat? You said it was unsatisfying." He pointed at the menu on their table. "Most of the entrees have pork, steak, or chicken in them."

Sera twirled a piece of rice noodle around her fork. "I stated that incorrectly. I gave up meat years ago."

"Why not choose a place with more options for you?"

Her leg brushed against his. "I like to tempt myself."

Lust curled in his stomach. "Are we talking about food or something else?"

"I'm here with you, aren't I?" Her foot traced the inseam of his pants, halting at his crotch. The sole of her shoe pressed firmly against it.

He hardened immediately. Carnal desire surged within him, the strength of it half-blinding. The urge to rub himself against her foot was overwhelming. The ache between his thighs required a form of relief. *Just dinner. Just dinner. Just dinner.*

It took every ounce of self-control to grab Sera's ankle and move it away from him. Gritting his teeth, he said, "I am three seconds from bending you over this table." He forced himself to take a bite of food, hoping it would calm the impulse to tear her dress off. "But I want more."

"More?" Sera arched a brow. "I had no idea you were so kinky. We have another thing in common. What's your favorite kink? Mine is when people watch." She traced the line of her cleavage with her fingers. "Do you like to watch, Cassius?"

He inhaled a sharp breath. *This woman is killing me.* He took a few minutes to collect himself. Once his severe craving for her subsided, he spoke. "I do have a kink." He gave her a slow, edged grin. "Let me get inside that pretty head of yours."

"I'd rather you bend me over." Sera's chin tilted up. Her eyes narrowed. "But I'll indulge you. What would you like to know?"

"Everything." Sera was like a book that kept you up at night. You couldn't rest until you knew the entire story. "Who are you? The *real* you?"

A bolt of lightning struck through her eyes before settling into gray clouds. The sexy vixen had retreated. The insatiable lust between them had been put on pause.

"What you see is what you get," she said dryly.

Cassius picked up his wineglass and whirled the stem between his fingers. "I don't think that's true."

"So you're an entrepreneur and a therapist?" She leaned toward him. "Tell me who you think I am."

"All right." Cassius took a sip of wine before placing the glass back on the table. "When I was seven, my parents allowed me to purchase a hundred fireflies. I wanted them as pets. They're—"

"What does this have to do with me?"

Cassius raised his hand, palm facing her. "Hear me out."

She gave him a curt nod.

"Fireflies are magical and whimsical. They're creatures of fantasy novels. I had a giant terrarium built for them. I know," he said when Sera raised a brow at him. "The things money can buy. Believe me, I understand my privilege." He pushed up the sleeves of his button-down shirt. "I didn't realize I bought two types of fireflies—the run-of-the-mill ones and femme fatales. I found out the hard way that femme fatales are savage creatures. What they do is mimic the mating signal of regular fireflies to attract them. Once the fireflies are lured in, the femme fatales eat them. I had the fireflies for less than a week before they killed the regular ones."

Sera burst into laughter. It almost seemed genuine. Except those damn eyes remained callous. "Why ask me out if I'm a femme fatale?"

Cassius shrugged. "As Aldo Leopold said, 'there are some who can live without wild things and some who cannot.'"

"And you cannot?"

"No, I cannot," he replied with quiet steel. "There's a lot to be said about those who haven't had all the rough ridden off them."

"Another Leopold quote?"

Cassius took a sip of his wine. "A Wyoming saying." He leveled his gaze at her. "Besides, no relationship is without conflict."

"We're in a relationship now?" She wiped the corners of her mouth with a napkin.

Cassius took a bite out of his meal. "You're the one who wanted dinner instead of tea. I assumed we took things to the next level."

"Maybe I just needed *someone* to do on a Saturday night." A small smile. "Wild things, huh? Most people prefer to take the safe route."

To tell her or not to tell her...tell her. It wasn't a secret anyway. "My brain doesn't function like the majority of the population." He wasn't necessarily embarrassed by the fact, but explaining it made him feel like a science experiment. "I always knew something was off about me. When I was young, my parents took me to get brain scans and other tests. The exams revealed that I have an extremely low level of dopamine and serotonin."

He tapped his fingers on the table. "Without getting too technical, my brain's fear center doesn't work properly. The response to threat misfires. People who participate in extreme sports have the same condition. They call us high sensation seekers. There was one test where three hundred images were flashed in front of me. It's similar to channel surfing. The images were meant to frighten or excite a normal person. It had no effect on me."

Sera peered at him, head slanted. "You're attracted to things that spike your adrenaline. Others get a rush from riding roller coasters, but you need more of a thrill. Highlining, perhaps?"

"Yes," Cassius said. "I've actually done that, along with volcano surfing, free diving, wingsuit flying, and more."

Sera ran a thumb over her chin. "Do I give you a rush?"

"I think so." Cassius roamed her face. Although he wondered how her lush lips would feel wrapped around his length, her lifeless eyes intrigued him more. He wanted to uncover the emotions hidden behind them. "You're different...fascinating..."

"How romantic." Sera stirred the water in her cup with a straw. "You make me sound like an organism you just discovered."

"That's not what I meant. It's—"

Sera waved a dismissive hand. "How do you know it's real?"

Cassius popped a piece of steak in his mouth. "If what's real?"

"How do you know if you actually wanted this date? What if I'm simply triggering your dopamine and serotonin levels because *I'm different...fascinating...a femme fatale firefly.*" Sera shoved her plate aside and clasped her hands on top of the table. "What if I'm not this person you imagine me to be? Maybe I enjoy knitting and watching reruns on TV. Would you still be enamored by me?"

"It's real because it's who I am. I was born with this brain. It's all I've ever known." He popped another slice of steak in his mouth and chewed slowly. "You're right...I don't know you. Yet."

"Yet?"

"*Yet*," he repeated with conviction.

"This really is your kink. Look, I don't mind bondage, but I find *bonding* a bit dull." Her tone was light, but Cassius heard the dark undertow in it.

Folding his arm behind his head, Cassius leaned back in his chair. "Sex is better when you have a connection with the other person. Don't you think?" Sera didn't respond. He figured she wouldn't. "Back to my earlier question: Who are you, Sera?"

"I thought you had me figured out with your femme fatale theory."

"There's more to it." He sat up, crossing his forearms on the table. "I think this"—he looked her up and down—"is all an act."

"Is it?" Mimicking Cassius, Sera crossed her forearms on the table. "Do you love running Batista Holdings, or would you rather do something else?"

Cassius knit his brows together. "Yeah, I love it. I could've walked away from the company if I wanted to. My family would've supported my decision."

"Are you sure you love it?" Sera watched him like a hawk ogling a rat's nest. "I bet when you were a kid, your parents took you to the mining sites. They introduced you to the people who worked for them. They discussed the business with you, the profits it brought in, the luxuries it provided, the opportunities your family gained from it."

"True." The sharpness in her tone unsettled him. He wasn't sure if he preferred *this* or her normal impassiveness. "What are you getting at?"

Sera blinked, and suddenly there was a storm in her eyes. It was the first sign of emotion he'd seen from her. "You were groomed since childhood to run Batista Holdings. You think you had a choice, but you didn't. The life you were meant to live was embedded in you by your parents. You love it because you know nothing else."

She blinked again, and the storm was gone. A listless sky took its place as if revealing any hint of passion exhausted her. "I was groomed as well." She pointed at herself. "This is the result. How can it be an act if it's rooted in me?"

Cassius almost believed her, but the tremor in her hand told him something different. Maybe she didn't know she was lying to him because she was also lying to herself. The question was...*who fed her this bullshit?* "Sera, it doesn't matter how you've been raised. We have choices. We're freethinkers. I get your point: certain traits have been instilled in us. It doesn't mean they're stuck with us forever. We learn and grow. We're forever evolving."

"Says the man who can buy all of New York three times over. People born into wealth have choices. They have the privilege to be freethinkers. That's one percent of the population. What about those who didn't enter this world draped in money?" Cassius could almost see a coating of ice slither over her skin, like frost on a windshield. "Do you want dessert?" she asked.

Just like that, the conversation was over.

"Sure. You can pick it out for me." Cassius wanted to continue the topic. But he had a feeling Sera revealed too much of herself and wasn't willing to expose more.

She waved her hand, and the waiter came over. "Can you bring over the dessert sample platter for my friend? Nothing more for me."

"Of course." The waiter nodded three times.

After he left, Sera flashed Cassius a practiced smile. Her walls were back up. They never collapsed, but for a few fleeting minutes, they had faltered. "So, what do you think?" She was asking about the restaurant.

Cassius had another answer. "I think I should stay away from you."

"Oh?" Sera caressed the lobe of her ear. "Why?"

"You're complicated." That was an understatement.

"You enjoy complicated, remember? 'There are some who can live without wild things, and some who cannot.'" Her eyes were dark patches of water. A deceptively calm rip current. "Just don't fall in love with me, Cassius. I'll only break your heart."

CHAPTER 6

The waiter nodded three times. That was the signal.

Sera had known Timothy since elementary school. They'd done a couple of jobs together throughout the years. Nothing fancy, a few robberies and carjackings. They were stickup kids. Although they weren't exactly friends, Sera knew Timothy wasn't a snitch. Growing up in the Bronx was tough. Sera, Timothy, and Raine looked out for one another. They needed one another to survive Hunts Point. That was a long time ago. Sera and Raine graduated to the big leagues. Timothy chose a simpler life. He was a starving artist who funded himself by waiting tables and pushing drugs.

Sera glanced at the bar where the three henchmen had sat. Their stools were empty. That's what the three nods meant. The men were now in the bathroom getting high off free cocaine. Timothy dealt to them whenever they came to Kusina. This time he offered them complimentary drugs. Sera paid Timothy a substantial amount to help with the logistics of her assassination plan.

It's game time. Ten minutes. That's the time frame she gave herself. She was on a date, after all. First, she needed to calm her mind. Cassius managed to worm his way into it. His presumptions about her were eerily accurate, and his comments made too much sense. Sera didn't like it one bit.

With a steady breath, Sera pulled her phone out of her purse. "Shit, I missed a bunch of calls from Raine." That was a lie. There wasn't a single missed call on her phone. "It must be important. Do you mind if I call her back?"

"Of course not," Cassius replied. "Take your time."

"I'll try to be quick." Sera stopped at the table where the two Del Rosario brothers dined. She greeted them before heading outside to take her fake phone call.

It wasn't *exactly* fake. She did call Raine. "Hey, what's up?" Sera asked when Raine answered. "Did you get him to talk to you?" They weren't on burner phones, so they spoke in code. Sera really asked Raine if she had been able to grab Cassius's financial information.

It was part of their plan. While Sera dined with Cassius, Raine broke into his suite to hack banking information off his laptop. That way Cassius was distracted, Raine was able to work, and Sera had an alibi for when she killed the three Yakuza gangsters.

"Nope," Raine grumbled. "He won't commit." *She can't get the data.* "I've never experienced a relationship like this before." *She's never seen encryptions like the ones on Cassius's computer.* "I've been talking to him for over an hour now, and I'm not getting anywhere." *She's been there for a long time and can't get past it.*

"Okay, don't stress. No need to dwell on 'him' all night. You'll figure it out soon enough." Sera wasn't worried; Raine was the best hacker around.

"I'll keep trying for a while. Go do your thing."

Instead of hanging up, Sera put Raine on mute. Another part of the plan. There needed to be proof of what she was doing when she wasn't in the restaurant. Call logs were proof. Although the chance she'd be implicated for the murders was low, being careful was a must.

Sera walked down an alley lined with dumpsters. She vomited behind the garbage bins. *Now* she was ready to make the kills. She reached the door to the back of the restaurant where Timothy was waiting for her. In his hand was a tote. "Thank you," Sera said, grabbing the tote.

"Sure," Timothy responded as Sera stepped inside. "It's eight o'clock. Ten minutes, right? I can't do more than that. The boss man will get suspicious. Especially if customers have to use the bathroom and find out that it's locked." He nodded to the door a few feet in front of them. "Manny will start asking who's responsible for the out-of-order sign."

Sera scanned the space. It was a narrow hallway with the women's bathroom to the left and the men's to the right. Around the corner was a staircase that led to the main floor of the restaurant. "Ten minutes, I promise." She patted his cheek. "You're the best, Timothy."

He smiled. It was so sweet that Sera's heart twisted. She recalled the times when they were still young and innocent. When they played hopscotch near the basketball courts and ate tubs of ice cream at Bronx Park. *Now look at us.* Swallowing the lump that formed in her throat, Sera asked, "Is everything in the bag?"

"Yup," Timothy replied. "Good luck, Sera."

She waited until he left before she opened the tote. Placing her phone inside one of the pockets, Sera pulled out a Glock with a silencer attached to it. The Yaks would have guns too—9mm Berettas with suppressors.

As he promised, Lorenzo sent her their information via the burner phone. Sera did additional research on them as well. That's how she knew who they were when they entered the restaurant. Ernesto Aballa had a long scar going down his left cheek. Roman Dy had slicked-back hair. And Danilo Velasco had a bald head. The men were in their forties, but their hard-living lifestyle made them look older.

After examining the gun to make sure there were no issues with it, she placed it by her side. Next, Sera grabbed the shower cap and tucked her hair inside it. The gloves came after. Then, the surgical mask. The last thing she pulled out of the tote was a small bag filled with uncut Devil's Breath powder—a tenth of a gram to be exact. Sera dumped the entire contents into her gloved hand and balled her fist. With her other hand, she picked up the Glock.

Here I go. Sera pushed the tote behind a radiator and walked into the bathroom, locking the door behind her. Ernesto was at the sink to the left, brushing cocaine off his nose. Roman was at the urinal a few steps in front of her. There was a closed stall to the right of the urinal. Sera assumed Danilo was in there.

"Hey, doll," Ernesto spoke first, his voice a deep slur. His pupils were the size of pennies. It took him a moment to register the shower cap, the gloves, the surgical mask. The gun.

"Shit!" He reached for the 9mm tucked into his waistband.

It was too late. Sera leaped toward him, opened her fist, and slammed her powder-coated palm into his face. Like Carlo, Ernesto was dead within seconds. No agonizing screams, only slight convulsions followed by instant death.

"What the hell?" Roman's eyes widened when he saw his friend's body slam to the ground. Frantically zipping up his pants, he grabbed the gun strapped to his hip. "Danny, come out *now*."

Danilo started to open the stall. "What's going—"

Sera aimed her Glock at the aluminum door and shot through it. She didn't see Danilo fall, but she heard the *thump* of his body as he hit the floor. Through it all, her focus never once left Roman.

"Who sent you?" Roman had his gun pointed at her.

Sera had hers pointed back at him. "I heard you're a hit man. The best one in town. I'm better." She prowled closer to him.

"We'll see about that." He sneered. "I'll bite, though. How about...whoever pulls the trigger first gets to live. So, *puta*, who's going to shoot first?"

Sera was.

And she did.

Then...

Nothing.

Her gun jammed. *What the fuck?* She thought she checked it thoroughly. It wouldn't have been Timothy's fault. This was her own personal gun. She'd given Timothy the tote right before her date with Cassius. It was an amateur move she'd beat herself up for later.

Roman smiled like a wolf with a rabbit between its teeth. "I guess I'm the better *asashin.*"

Before he could make his next move, Sera threw her gun to the side and pounced. There was no way she was dying today. She certainly wasn't about to be killed by a drugged-out Yak. Sera grabbed Roman's wrist with both hands and placed her thumbs over the hammer of his gun. She couldn't prevent him from pulling the trigger, but the action stalled him. Lifting a spiked heel, Sera kicked Roman in the stomach and knocked the wind out of him.

He released the gun and doubled over. Sera caught the 9mm before it hit the floor. She slammed the butt of it into his head. Roman fell forward. The crack of his face on the tiles echoed over the bathroom walls. Turning his body over, Sera slammed the gun into his forehead. Roman was still, but the rise and fall of his chest proved he was alive. "This is for Lorenzo, you dirty Yak." Sera pummeled him until he took his last breath.

Blood covered her gloves. A few drops speckled her dress. She wasn't concerned. She wore burgundy for a reason. Glancing at the watch on her wrist, Sera realized she'd been in the bathroom for four minutes. *Perfect. Three Yaks dead, and six minutes to spare.* Now, she could get back to her date.

Sera eyed Roman one last time before looking at the stall to get a glimpse of Danilo's body. The stall door—

which had barely been cracked—was now wide open. And Danilo wasn't in there.

A cold barrel pressed against the back of Sera's head. "Drop the gun and face me, *puta*." *Danilo.*

The hit had turned into a disaster. First her gun jammed and now this. It was too sloppy—so unlike her. *I'm distracted.* Sera hated to admit it, but her distraction was sitting upstairs awaiting her return.

"Okay, okay." Sera carefully placed the 9mm on the floor.

"Turn around," Danilo growled, kicking the gun away from her.

Sera did as she was told, discreetly glancing at her hand. There were some remnants of powder stuck to her glove. She prayed it was enough.

"Don't shoot me, please." She raised her hands in surrender and forced a quiver in her voice. Sera wasn't truly scared. She never was. At times, she welcomed death. Her life had always been a struggle. Living in the projects had been tough, but *this* was worse.

"*Sino ka?*" Danilo asked. The gun dug into her forehead —cold metal that impatiently waited to claim her.

Who are you? He wanted to know, so she'd tell him. "I'm the person who's going to end your life." She smashed her palm into Danilo's nose.

It wasn't enough Devil's Breath to kill him, but it was enough to leave him dazed. He stumbled back and the gun fell out of his grasp. He mumbled phrases Sera couldn't understand. But he wasn't as far gone as she wanted him to be. Danilo was able to regain his footing and close the distance between them.

His giant hands wrapped around her throat. He squeezed her neck effortlessly as if it were a slice of lemon. Sera's lungs tightened, and her vision turned hazy. Black dots formed in front of her eyes. With the last ounce of strength she had, Sera rammed her hand against his nose once more.

Pushing up.

And up.

And up.

Blood poured out of his nostrils, streaming through her fingers like a waterfall.

Danilo released his grip and stepped back. His vacant eyes searched her face as though he were trying to decipher what caused the bleeding. The confusion was a side effect of Devil's Breath. *Good.* Muttering a string of incoherent sentences, Danilo lunged for her again. Sera caught the gleam on his belt. A stiletto knife with a silver handle was sheathed on his hip.

Sera made a grab for it. Yanking the knife out of his belt, she flipped the handle, exposing the blade. Danilo stared at her blankly as she sliced his throat from ear to ear. Soft as a lover's caress. Deep as a farmer gutting a pig. Danilo gurgled as he collapsed, drowning in his own blood. *Done.* Lorenzo was safe now.

Sera glanced at her watch. *Three minutes to spare.* She took the sheath off Danilo and slid the knife in it. In her free hand, Sera retrieved her Glock and left the bathroom. *Two minutes.*

Stepping into the hallway, Sera stashed her Glock in the tote. Next, she removed the tainted gloves, shower cap, and surgical mask. She wrapped them in plastic and placed them next to her gun. She then used wipes to scrub the blood off her skin and clothes. Before she touched the sheathed knife, Sera pulled out liquid adhesive and dipped her fingertips in it. She couldn't risk the authorities lifting her prints. Grabbing an empty Ziploc bag, she placed the sheathed knife in it and tucked it in her underwear. *One minute.*

Sera left through the same door she entered. She grabbed her phone out of the tote before stuffing it behind a garbage bin. Timothy would take care of it later.

When she reached the front of the restaurant, she unmuted her phone. "How's it going, Raine?"

"Still here." Raine yawned. "Are you good?"

"My period was messy. There was so much blood this month." *The hit was a chaotic massacre.*

Raine chuckled. "That's unlike you. Wyoming must have your hormones all ramped up." *You're slipping because you have Cassius on your mind.*

"Not true," Sera said, entering Kusina. *Zero minutes.*

"If you say so." Raine sounded doubtful. "Listen, I'm getting out of here. I need to think things over." *She still can't crack Cassius's encryptions and needs to research the situation.*

Sera went to the table with the phone at her ear. "Let me know if you need anything from me."

"All right, chica." Raine lowered her voice. "Hey, don't forget to tell me how big Wyoming's dick is. You owe me."

Sera kept her face blank as she sat down. "If it's worth discussing."

Raine burst into a fit of laughter. "He's sitting right in front of you, isn't he? You should tell him—"

"We'll talk later. Bye, Raine." Sera hung up before her friend said anything else. "Sorry." Sera put her phone in her purse. "Work stuff. She's my partner at the funeral home."

Cassius smiled. The dimples in his cheeks made Sera want to lick his face. She was fully aware of how desperate that sounded.

"It's fine. I've kept myself busy." He pointed to the dessert samples in front of him. He'd taken a few bites out of each one. "I'm glad you didn't run out on me. I was beginning to think you left."

"Why would I do that? We're just starting to get to know each other." Sera slid the Ziploc-wrapped sheath out from under her dress and dropped it in the purse by her feet. "Let's go back to my place and get to know each other even better."

"You don't want dessert first?" Cassius's eyes twinkled with amusement.

"Are you waiting for me to say something cheesy like"—her voice softened to a purr—"the only dessert I want is you."

Cassius drained the last of his wine. "It's always best to be honest. You were the one making the moves on me."

Sera's lips quirked. "Yes, but you're the one who admitted to fantasizing about me. Maybe later you can tell me what you pictured us doing in your bed. I'm really good at making wishes come true."

The flush on his cheeks warmed Sera's chest. Most men would've used that opportunity to come up with a vulgar response. Cassius wasn't like most men. That in itself was dangerous. Sera could deal with men who lusted over her. She had no clue how to handle men who *actually* wanted to get to know her—no innuendos.

"Let's go," she said, filling in the uncomfortable silence between them. Cassius pulled out his wallet, but Sera shook her head. She took out her credit card and dropped it on the table. "It's my treat. You can pay next time. Can you wait for the waiter to bring the bill? I have to talk to my friends really quick." She jutted her chin toward the Del Rosario brothers.

"Okay. Thanks for dinner." Cassius put his wallet back in his pocket. "So, are you saying that there's going to be another date?"

Sera stood up and slung her bag over her shoulder. "Sure, why not." She shot him a wink before strolling over to the Yamaguchi-gumi henchmen.

The two men greeted her by devouring her breasts with their eyes. She loathed them. They made their desires too evident for her liking. She knew how to play the part, though—how to morph herself into every man's wet dream. Fixing her lips into a seductive pout, Sera slithered next to Angelo. She made small talk and complimented them. *A lot.* Boosting their already inflated egos. Sera didn't want to be anywhere near the Del Rosario brothers. She was there for one reason.

Sera leaned over and kissed Angelo's cheek. One hand squeezed his thigh, while her other hand slipped inside her purse. Like the connoisseur criminal that she was, Sera pulled the knife—fresh with Danilo's blood—out of her bag. With featherlight fingers, she slid it into Angelo's pocket.

81

CHAPTER 7

They shared a taxi back to Sera's penthouse. Neither brought a car to the restaurant. Apparently, they were both in agreement that trying to find parking on a Saturday night in New York wasn't a good idea.

To Cassius's surprise, the cab ride wasn't as awkward as he expected. Sera was fairly chatty, and the conversation flowed well. The woman seemed to have warmed up to him as much as a cat warms up to a human.

They had just finished talking about their favorite bands when Sera abruptly said, "Three questions."

"What?" Cassius creased his brows in confusion.

"You want to know me, right?" She slanted her eyes at him. "I'll answer three personal questions."

Cassius hid his shock. The woman was giving him a chance to delve into her life. He was certain this wasn't an opportunity she gave most people. Cassius mulled it over. There were many intimate things he wanted to know about her, but he decided to keep it simple. In his experience, people revealed more when they didn't feel intimidated.

"Have you lived in New York your whole life?"

Sera nodded. "I was born and raised in the Bronx. I went to Columbia University."

Cassius's strategy worked. He asked one question. Sera revealed two extra facts about herself. "What was your major?"

"I have a master's in chemistry." She swiped away a piece of hair that escaped from her bun. "I was going to move to Virginia after college. I got offered a job as an environmental chemist, but my dad needed me here. There's not enough money in environmental chemistry anyway." There was a mechanical edge to her tone. Like she was reciting words someone else wrote.

Interesting...

Cassius picked up on something else too.

She said dad. Not mom and dad. "Tell me about your father."

"He's the best." Sera clasped her hands on her lap. "He dedicated his life to me. My mother left when I was six. She was a drug addict." She glanced at Cassius. Her expression was blank. She spoke with such dispassion as if she were listing facts out of a history book. "My dad was in the Marines Special Forces when my mother abandoned me. He was on a mission at the time. Child Protective Services couldn't get ahold of him, so I was placed in foster care. When he found out what happened, he came immediately. He got kicked out because he had to take care of me. Tay lost his entire career. I've never met anyone as selfless as him."

Cassius schooled his face into an unreadable mask. People didn't get kicked out of the military because they had to raise children. If worse came to worst, they'd get a hardship discharge. The man wouldn't *lose* his entire career.

"You've asked three questions. It's your turn," Sera said sharply. She was either upset or embarrassed that she'd revealed too much of herself. *Probably both.*

Cassius rested the back of his head against the window. "Ask away."

"What do you love most about living in Gillette?"

His lips curved into a soft smile as he thought about Wyoming. "I love watching the sunset over the mountains. I love the ruggedness of the forests. I love the rough terrains and the unspoiled wilderness. I love the freedom of nature."

"Your brother was right. You really are the outdoorsy type." Sera's neutral tone matched her blank expression.

Cassius couldn't decipher if her statement was a compliment or an insult. "Yeah, I guess I am. If you ask me to choose between an extravagant resort or a tent under the stars, I will pick the latter." He crossed an ankle over his knee. "My buddies and I get together a few times a month to go mud bogging. At night we sit around the bonfire and drink beer. I prefer the woods over a nightclub. Even one as stunning as 1 Oak." He winked. "You must think I'm pretty lame, huh?"

"Hmmm…" Sera stroked her chin. "You're unpretentious with a small-town soul. What terrible qualities to have." Humor flitted over her face. "Why don't you tell me what goes on at these mud bogging and bonfire parties?

Not that I'm terribly interested or anything," she said with a teasing cadence.

Cassius laughed. "I'd be happy to."

He didn't have the same rules as Sera. He spoke freely of life in Gillette. He didn't count how many questions she asked. He answered them all. And he volunteered information. Cassius described the beauty of the mountains in full detail. He discussed his business, hobbies, family, and friends. For an emotionally distant person, Sera appeared interested in his life. Her eyes continued to hold their flatness, but he could tell she was listening.

Cassius then tried to squeeze more information out of her, but Sera was done sharing. It didn't bother him. He was just as good at pulling data out of unsaid words. When Cassius brought up the topic of friendship, Sera avoided the question. He was sure Raine was her only friend. When he asked about relationships, she stared at him as if the question made no sense. Cassius watched her flirt with the Del Rosario brothers. Sera knew how to work men. But she didn't appear to enjoy it. Like a child at church—her body was there, but her mind wasn't present. She held the same energy at 1 Oak when men approached her. And at the Mandarin, when she walked out of the restaurant with Leo. Cassius wondered why Sera even bothered if she didn't find pleasure in their company.

He also couldn't stop thinking about their disturbing conversation at dinner. The too casual way she talked about death. Her belief that most people had no choice in how their lives turned out. Was it something she learned from her father? Did she recognize that her thought process was twisted and unhealthy?

Cassius glanced at her profile, prepared to ask her about it. A different question popped out of his mouth. "What happened to your neck?" He hadn't noticed the bruises during dinner. The restaurant was dim, though. Still, he was an observant man. There wasn't much that sidestepped his radar.

"You are completely incapable of abiding by the three-question rule." Sera looked at him, a suggestive curl on her lips. "If you must know, I like rough sex." A slight tremble of her hand.

"It wasn't there earli—"

"We're here," Sera said, not letting Cassius finish.

He didn't try. Sera shut down the discussion. Pushing the topic would go nowhere. He stepped out of the cab and admired the Italian Renaissance-style palazzo. "Beautiful building."

"I like it." Sera nodded at the doorman as they entered the building. "It's twelve stories and only seventeen units." They took a personal elevator that led right to her door. "I have lots of privacy."

The inside looked exactly how Cassius imagined it. Clean and spacious, much like his own home. It had an open concept layout, with panoramic windows over-looking Central Park. The interior design was simple. Gray and white furniture stood atop beechwood floors, complementing the bright-white walls. The kitchen—with its spotless, stainless-steel appliances and shimmering granite counters—looked like it had never been used. The living room to the left was equipped with a giant gray couch, matching accent chairs, and a coffee table made from distressed wood. A long bar stood against the far wall. And a glass staircase was positioned a few feet away from it. Cassius guessed it led to the bedrooms.

"You want a drink?" Sera guided Cassius to the living room. She tossed her purse on the coffee table. "There's vodka, gin, whiskey...you name it, I have it."

Cassius followed her to the bar and sat on one of the stools. "Whiskey on the rocks is fine." She poured the brown liquid into a lowball glass and handed it to him. "Why do you have a bar if you don't drink?"

"It's for when my dad visits." Sera walked to an accent chair across from where Cassius was seated. Kicking off her shoes, she leaned against the back of it.

Cassius's mind was blown away. The woman had a fully stocked bar for her father who didn't even live there. Cassius wasn't sure their relationship was healthy at this point. "Why did you decide to get your master's in chemistry?" he asked, steering away from the sensitive topic.

Sera untied her bun. Her thick black hair fell to her waist. Cassius had the urge to run his hands through it. He had the urge to do more than that. "I wanted to learn how to make crystal meth. Life doesn't always work out the way you want it to. Now I'm a boring business-woman."

"You may not be a drug kingpin, but I doubt you're boring." The light in the room hit Sera's neck. Cassius was reminded of her mysterious bruises. He told himself he wouldn't bring it up again, but... "Are you going to tell me what really happened to your neck?"

Sera touched her throat. "I already told you, it's from a lover who likes it rough."

"Do you have many lovers?" he asked, genuinely interested.

"Why? Would you like to be one of them?" Something in her eyes took shape. It looked a lot like resentment.

Sera let her guard down a few times that night. She was quick to drown the emotions beneath pools of gray. The trace of bitterness was harder to hide. It stiffened her jaw and creased her brows. *Hmmm.* It was her idea to come to her penthouse. Yet...she didn't want to sleep with him.

"I only want it if you do," Cassius said.

Sera rolled her eyes. "I forgot. You think sex is better if there's a connection."

Cassius downed his drink and put the empty glass on the coaster. "Have you never had a relationship?" He asked her the same thing in the cab. She changed the subject. He was hoping she'd answer this time.

"I never understood the point." Sera straightened her dress. "People's feelings change all the time. That's why there are more divorces than happy marriages. Have you ever considered that humans aren't designed to be mono-gamous?"

"You believe that?" He leaned forward and placed his forearms on his thighs.

"Yes," Sera said with conviction. "Have *you* ever been in a relationship?"

"There were women I cared about." Cassius clasped his hands together. "We did things people in relationships do. But I could never bring myself to label it as such. If I'm going to commit to someone, I want to make sure it's real. When I tried to take the next steps with these women, something would stop me. I couldn't see them in my future." He blew out a breath. "To answer your question, no, *technically* I've never been in a relationship. But I know how it feels to create a bond with someone. I can tell you it's more fulfilling than casual sex."

"Well, I think casual sex is less complicated." Sera's tongue flicked over her bottom lip. Cassius's eyes went straight to it. She did it on purpose. He cursed himself for falling into her trap. "Less complicated *always* feels better." She slipped her dress off and tossed it on the ground.

Cassius's pulse stumbled. The woman had a body he didn't know existed until then. She put an hourglass to shame. The scars on her skin made her more stunning. He bet they carried stories too painful to be told. He wanted to be the one who tried to unlock the tales. "You're gorgeous, Sera."

Her eyes dipped to his crotch. "Come here and show me what you can do, Wyoming."

Cassius's "creating a bond" speech flew out of his head. *This* is what he'd thought about since he met her. The animalistic side of him yearned to rip through her lace bra and underwear. He wanted to taste her. Touch her. Bury himself inside of her. His hardness strained against his zipper. Forget taking Sera to her room. Cassius didn't have the patience to go up a flight of stairs. He'd fuck her against her panoramic window.

He started to stand, fully prepared to slide inside of her. Then, he recalled the resentment in her eyes. *The bitterness.* His mind wrestled with the aching sensation between his legs. His confusion left him planted on the barstool.

"Well?" Sera stroked her collarbone. "Are you going to fuck me?"

Yes. He didn't have the self-control not to.

No. He couldn't have sex with someone who wasn't truly interested.

Yes.

No.

Yes.

Damn it!

Cassius stood up and walked over to Sera. When he was no more than an inch away, he tucked a piece of hair behind her ear. "I'm not doing this with you tonight." The words cut like razors as he spit them out of his throat. He grabbed her dress off the floor and handed it to her.

"Are you *serious?*" Her veil of indifference lifted. Underneath it was pure disbelief. The woman was obviously not used to rejection.

"You don't want to sleep with me. I don't think you want to sleep with anyone. Sex is part of a preset checklist for you. An activity you perform on autopilot." He slid his hands into his pockets. "Maybe you do it for power. Maybe you do it to prove your theory is correct —all humans are scum. You tell yourself that the only thing they desire from you is sex, so why bother letting them get close." Cassius shook his head. "I'd *love* to spend the night with you. But not like this. I want *you* to want *me.*"

Sera didn't flinch. The veil was back on. "At dinner,

you said you're leaving in three weeks. I think you should try to convince me to *really* want you before then."

Cassius grinned. "I'll convince you in two weeks."

"We'll see." Sera stepped around him. "I'm going to bed. Bolt the bottom lock on your way out."

She didn't wait for him to leave. Sera walked up the stairs.

Cassius was left gazing at what he could've just had.

Cassius entered his suite and changed into gray sweatpants. Flopping down on the bed, he turned on the television. Cassius needed to get his mind off Sera, or else he'd spend the entire night with his cock in his hand. It would probably happen anyway, but he'd at least try to distract himself with something else.

The woman consumed his mind the whole ride back to the hotel. She was complicated and confusing—a mystery he was eager to solve. The way her mind worked challenged and enthused him. If he told Ava about his date, she'd warn him to stay away from Sera. She'd blame Cassius's semi-obsession on his brain. He wasn't going to be in New York much longer, though. He couldn't see their flirtation evolving into something serious. *What's the harm in spending more time with her?*

Cassius absentmindedly flipped through the channels. He tried to watch a documentary about the illegal drug Adrenochrome. But he couldn't get past the part where children were trafficked and killed in order to obtain this drug. He attempted to find another show. Nothing caught his attention. There was never anything interesting on television. *Why do I bother?* He was about to turn it off when a news report caught his eye.

Manny, the owner of Kusina, was being interviewed by a reporter. Three bodies had been found in the men's bathroom of his restaurant. Pictures of the victims flashed across the screen. Cassius recognized them immediately. They were the same men that sat at the bar earlier that evening. According to the reporter, their names were Ernesto Aballa, Roman Dy, and Danilo Velasco. They were members of the Ichiwa-kai, one of the Yakuza crime families. Two suspects had been named: Angelo Del Rosario and Stevie Del Rosario, members of the Yama-guchi-gumi, a rival Yakuza crime family. Apparently, the authorities found a knife in Angelo's pocket. It was coated with blood from one of the victims. According to the report, it was no secret there was tension between the two families.

The last thing Cassius heard before he turned off the TV was that the murders occurred around eight o'clock. It sparked something in his memory. That was around the same time Sera stepped outside to talk to Raine. He knew because he checked his watch when she was walking out of the restaurant. The Del Rosario brothers never left their seats while Sera was gone. *And what about the bruises on her neck?* Cassius was certain they weren't there the entire time. *She also went out of her way to speak to Angelo and Stevie.* She even brought her purse with her. *Why?* Sera left it at the table when she called Raine.

Did she...? It *was* possible. Most restaurants had a back door. *What the hell am I thinking?* The hit was too complicated. *Sera wore a dress and heels for God's sake.* Not to mention that she was on a date. Still, he felt compelled to call her.

She picked up on the second ring. "Did you change your mind? You want to come back over here and fuck me?"

"I do," he admitted. "But I won't."

"I guess I'll have to take care of myself tonight," she purred. "I'll be thinking about you." Cassius hardened as he envisioned Sera caressing herself to thoughts of him. "Want to video chat so you can watch me?"

He was so close to saying yes, but... "I'll pass."

She let out a husky laugh. "What do you want, Cassius?"

What *did* he want? He almost forgot the reason he called. "You know the men at Kusina?" he asked, taking the focus off his aching cock.

"You need to be more specific. There were lots of men at Kusina."

"The three men who sat at the bar." Cassius propped a pillow under his head. "Their faces were battered up."

Sera yawned. "I remember. What about them?"

"They were on the news."

"Are they dead?"

The impassiveness in her tone unnerved him. "How did you know?" *Why is that her first guess?*

"Why else would you be calling me and asking about them?"

Cassius wished he were face-to-face with her. He wanted to see if her hand exposed a lie.

"Do you think I killed them?" A bored question.

94

"I didn't say that. I was wondering…" *What am I wondering?* Sera wasn't a killer. His theory suddenly seemed farfetched. "Forget it. I don't know what I was thinking. I'm sorry I called so late."

"Cassius, they were probably Yakuza. Most of the men who dine at Kusina are Yaks. I bet lots of people wanted them dead. Get some rest." Sera hung up the phone before he could say anything else.

Great. He just accused a five-foot-tall businesswoman of killing three gangsters twice her size. Cassius turned the lights off. Exhaustion was causing his brain to create conspiracy theories.

As he drifted off to sleep, another thought crossed his mind. Cassius's eyes burst open. During their entire conversation, Sera never denied that she was the murderer.

CHAPTER 8

Sera stared at the ceiling of her room. *What happened tonight?* She wasn't prepared for Cassius, which was saying a lot because she was always prepared. Sera figured out how to shape her emotions into a knife long ago, slicing those who got too close. In a span of a few hours, Cassius managed to dull her weapon. The man was like sandpaper, rounding the edges of her blade until it was no longer sharp.

Cassius asked too many poignant questions. And she answered most of them. *Why did I do that? I even divulged information about my mom and Tay. Why do I suck at my own game right now?*

She had never encountered someone like Cassius before. Unlike other men, he didn't constantly stare at her with lust-filled eyes. His gaze delved beneath her skin as if he saw things she wasn't aware of herself. Christian warned Sera that his brother was skilled at sizing up people. She should've taken his caution seriously. Her arrogance got the best of her.

Sera rubbed her eyes, her frustration mounting. How was she going to get through this job without losing her senses? If Raine had been able to hack Cassius's finances that evening, a portion of the money would be in Lorenzo's hands by now. And Cassius's blood would be on hers. *Simple and effortless.* That's how Sera liked it.

But Christian *also* warned her that his brother was painfully...*oh so painfully*...careful when it came to his finances. That's why he needed Sera to get close to Cassius—so she could find a way to gather data from him. *As if three weeks is enough time to make him trust me.* Cassius wouldn't even sleep with her. She never had a problem convincing someone to do that.

She did have one advantage. Thanks to Christian, Sera was aware of Cassius's brain scans prior to their discussion at dinner. That's how she was able to snag a date with him. She knew what to do to catch his attention. The fact that she didn't have to change her personality was a bonus. Sera had taken jobs where she pretended to be ditzy, submissive, or a nymphomaniac. It was refreshing to be herself. At least the version of herself she was most comfortable with.

I know my brother. You're everything he wants in a woman. He's never met anyone like you. Get him to notice you, and he'll be eating out of your hands. Those were Christian's words. The man made it sound easy. Cassius was anything but easy.

He just accused me of being a murderer. And he was right.

Sera's burner phone rang, sweeping the mess out of her head. "Tay," she said when she picked up.

"I saw the news. I'm proud of you, iha."

Shit. She forgot to call him. Sera usually touched base with Lorenzo after a hit, especially one he ordered. He didn't seem upset. That was a relief. "Thanks, Tay."

"We have our meeting tomorrow," Lorenzo said. "Let's have dinner after. We'll go wherever you want. I want father-daughter time with my iha."

"I'd like that." At least something good came out of the disastrous evening. She loved when Lorenzo treated her like she was the most special person on the planet. Raine would've pointed out that their quality time was on Sera's dime. That wouldn't be true for long. Lorenzo was making big moves. He was part of the Devil's Breath business now.

"How did your date go?"

Damn it. She braced herself for this conversation. Lorenzo hated when Sera failed. "I think it went well. He's...ummm...not as straightforward as I thought he'd be."

"You *think* it went well? This is the biggest payday of our lives." Lorenzo's voice raised an octave. "Did you at least have sex with him?"

"He didn't want to," she mumbled.

"Are you *kidding*? All you have to do is get him to like you enough to give up scraps—*tiny* scraps—of data that can help us hack his account. Then, you kill him. You've done this before. What's the problem?" Lorenzo snarled. "Is it because you're pushing thirty? Are you too old for this shit? You're not as pretty as you used to be. I should hire some younger broad to replace you. If you can't get a man in your bed, then what good are you? How do you expect to hook him if he doesn't want you? Hopefully, Raine can hack this pretty boy without your help. You're useless."

Sera's chest caved in. The scars Lorenzo left on her skin were nothing compared to the wounds he carved in her soul. Sera bit her lip until it bled. Her nails dug into her forearm, leaving deep indents. The actions distracted her from weeping. She'd rather her body hurt instead of her heart. Sera trained herself to stop crying over Lorenzo years ago. If she allowed the tears to flow, they'd drown her. "I'm sorry, Tay. Please don't worry. I swear I can do this."

Silence stretched long and thick between them. It was followed by Lorenzo's heavy sigh. "This deal is putting me on edge. It's my shot at building an empire. I never got to live up to my true potential because of all the sacrifices I've made for you. I don't regret it, but now it's my time to shine. Don't you think I deserve this?"

"Of course." Sera scrubbed a hand over her face. "But I don't mind helping you financially. You've given me everything."

"Iha, it's time I set something up for myself. This'll be good for both of us. When I have my own income, I'll take you to all the places you've wanted to go. You won't have to spend a single dollar. Hell, this can be your last job." Lorenzo spoke to her in a tranquil tone. Like a father soothing his toddler. It was strange how quickly he went from berating her to comforting her. Sera should've been used to it by now. But it still shook her every time.

What made it worse was that Lorenzo's words lacked truth. Her father would always demand something of her. His greed was bottomless. "I'll get the job done. I promise."

"Make me proud. I know how much you hate upsetting me," he said quietly. *Dangerously.* He hung up before she had a chance to respond.

I know how much you hate upsetting me. It was a subtle threat. The burn marks on her body itched as the sentence repeated in her head. Sera spent the next ten minutes warding off a panic attack. Her anxiety was finally beginning to subside when her phone rang again.

"How'd it go?" Rained asked when Sera answered.

"Horrible." She groaned. "Can we talk about this another time? I just got my ass chewed out by my dad."

Raine was silent. Sera knew the woman was struggling to bite her tongue. They never argued, except about one thing: Lorenzo. She claimed that he emotionally blackmailed and mentally abused Sera.

Raine would never be able to understand that part of her life. She left her father's house at the age of fourteen to live with her maternal grandmother. Although her dad was toxic, Raine's mother's side of the family nourished her. *And her mom died in childbirth.* Sera didn't want to downplay the tragedy, but it was better than knowing your mother left you—that she didn't want you. Sera and Lorenzo only had each other.

"Fine, we don't have to talk about *him,*" Raine said through clenched teeth. "Can I at least ask about your date with Cassius? How do you feel about him?"

Sera fiddled with the tassels of her decorative pillow. "I don't feel anything. I don't know him."

"Who do you think you're fooling? Listen, chica, you didn't study Cassius like an assassin gathering intel. You studied him like a serial killer plotting to kidnap her next victim." Raine chuckled. "I don't blame you. The man is remarkable. An Ivy League alum who spends his money and time making the world a better place. When he's not doing that, he's climbing the Himalayas and free diving with sharks. He's like the love interests in those cheesy romance novels you read."

"I don't read those anymore." Sera reached over to her nightstand and shoved a book inside her drawer as if Raine could see it through the phone.

"You totally do."

"*Anyway*, what happened with you tonight?" Sera asked, diverting the topic.

"Nothing," Raine grumbled. "I couldn't figure out a damn thing. I installed a keylogger before I left, so I can trace his keystrokes. I don't think it'll matter. He has a code that constantly overwrites data. Fucking old money. No wonder they never go broke. They're ten steps ahead of everyone else. I got in far enough to see that he has four different accounts. I need more time."

"Don't worry, I'm going to work hard to get information from him. This is a joint project, remember?" Sera wiped her sweaty palms on her shirt. The main issue was that they were on a time crunch. Cassius was leaving soon, and her father was putting pressure on her. "I think we both need some rest. Let's regroup tomorrow."

"Agreed." Raine released a breath. "Sera, I know I tease you about Cassius and your romance books, but I like seeing that side of you. It's soft and vulnerable. You deserve to be a normal human being, not some machine. Not...*Lorenzo's* machine."

CHAPTER 9

Cassius glanced at his watch. It was Sunday, which meant he had a meeting with Christian that evening. *Let this be over soon.* Cassius was sick of his brother. They hadn't spent more than a few hours together since they were teenagers. Cassius remembered why. Christian was the most self-centered person he'd ever known. Being around him was exhausting. But Cassius was prepared to do whatever it took for Christian to leave their family alone.

Christian made him a promise. He'd disappear from their parents' lives forever if Cassius invested in his business. Cassius despised the pain Christian caused their mother. Their father refused to speak to Christian, but their mother held a soft spot in her heart for her oldest son. Christian used it to his advantage, coaxing money out of her whenever possible. That was about to end. Cassius wouldn't allow him to manipulate her any longer.

What happened to you, Christian? Things weren't always terrible between them. When they were children, Cassius adored his brother. They did everything together. Christian—being two years older than Cassius—took his big-brother role seriously. He was the one who bandaged Cassius's knees when he fell off his horse. He was the one who showed Cassius how to ice fish. He was the one who taught him how to hunt elk. Now the rift between them was too wide to cross. Christian acted like everything between him and Cassius was fine, but resentment drenched his skin like rancid cologne.

Cassius glanced at his watch again. He wasn't just counting down the hours until the meeting, he was counting down the hours till he boarded the plane for Wyoming. He had a few weeks left, but he was more than ready to go home. The only thing that kept his attention in New York was Sera. She was a mere distraction. Nothing would come of it. The woman enthralled him, but it wasn't likely they'd fall in love and live happily ever after in Gillette. He laughed at the thought of someone like Sera residing there. A lion in a cage would fare better than Sera in a small town.

It was probably best to leave her alone. His instincts told him to run. There was something not right about her. The woman was like a cat toying with a mouse—relishing in anticipation of its upcoming meal. Cassius was the mouse in the scenario. *Definitely, leave her alone.*

The resolve lasted less than an hour. Cassius's traitorous fingers shot Sera a text.

Lunch tomorrow afternoon?

It took two minutes before she replied. *Tea. Lunch is too much of a commitment.*

We're back to that?

Another two minutes. *We can go to your room instead and skip the formalities.*

Are you in love with me yet? Cassius typed.

Sera sent an emoji character rolling its eyes. *The bar keeps rising. I thought I just had to believe you're not a scumbag. That I'm not going to fuck you on autopilot.*

Cassius grabbed his wallet from the coffee table and shoved it in his pocket. *What can I say? I'm hard to please. Are you avoiding my question about being in love with me?*

Ten minutes passed before Sera wrote back. *I'll see you for tea.*

The warehouse was located on a secluded street in Uniondale, Long Island, which was an hour's drive from Manhattan. Once Cassius parked his car, he walked the perimeter, searching for anything that struck him as odd. The brick structure was impressively large. The back had four loading docks, and the entire area was surrounded by barbed wire.

When Cassius was satisfied that everything looked normal, he went inside. There was no furniture or inventory yet, only a steel folding table with six chairs around it. And ten thousand feet of cement floor. Christian and Damion were already there. Both sat on the right side of the table. Seated on the left was a man Cassius hadn't met. *The third partner.* Christian mentioned him a few times. Lorenzo was his name. His brother told him the man's share was funded by a family member.

Cassius *wasn't* the fourth partner. He didn't want his

name associated with the business. All he cared about was making sure it was legitimate. He'd provide Christian with the start-up funds and stay a few weeks to ensure his brother didn't use the money irresponsibly. Otherwise, they'd be back to square one: Christian calling their mother and begging for an allowance. Their mother would grant it to him behind their father's back.

"Nice space," Cassius said, sitting down in the empty chair beside Lorenzo. "It looks like you plan to keep a lot of inventory."

"Yup. We're going to import a shit-ton of gems." Christian cleared his throat. "Like I told you before, that spiritual hippie shit is really popular nowadays. Of course, we're selling expensive gems too. Those never go out of style."

"The security system is going to be super high-tech once it's installed," Damion chipped in.

Cassius leaned back in his chair, his eyes gutting through Christian. He seemed jumpy. *Why so anxious, brother?* "You already have buyers?"

"I *personally* garnered the contracts of the metaphysical and jewelry stores that want our products." Lorenzo was the one who spoke.

Cassius gazed at him. The man looked familiar. Black hair, gray eyes, tawny-brown skin. *I've seen him before.* The information pieced together in his mind.

He was at 1 Oak.

Sera kept him company at his table.

It wasn't clicking together fast enough in Cassius's head.

He resembles someone...

The tattoo on his knuckles...

It spells...

S...E...R—

The door to the warehouse opened. Sera stepped inside, followed by Raine. Gone were the sexy clothes. Both wore black jeans, black shirts, and black boots. Raine's faux-hawk was perfectly styled. And there wasn't a hair out of place in Sera's tight bun.

"I hope we're not late." Sera's demeanor indicated she didn't really care if they were. Her steel eyes flickered over Cassius. "I see you've met my dad."

"Actually, I was just getting ready to introduce myself." Sera's father flashed Cassius a snake charmer's smile. "I'm Lorenzo. It's a pleasure to meet you."

"Likewise," he forced himself to say. Cassius didn't like him already. The man reminded him of a used-car salesman. *Why didn't Sera tell me her dad is working with Christian?* She waited until the meeting to spring the news. Cassius's blood heated. He didn't like being played for a fool.

Damion moved over so Sera could sit across from Cassius. Raine grabbed the chair next to her. "Let's get started," Sera said once everyone was settled. Her eyes were emptier than usual. She seemed almost unhappy.

Cassius clasped his hands on top of the table. "I heard the other investor pitched in two million dollars. Is that you, Sera?"

She yawned. "Damion pitched in a few grand."

"That wasn't my question." Anger sharpened his statement.

Sera merely shrugged.

Cassius's temper flared. "Since I'm the one dumping the most money into this venture, I should be privy to all the details." His voice was a low growl.

Sera gazed at him, unblinking. "Yes, I'm investing two million for my father. What else do you want to know? Would you like to look over my financial statements? My bank information?" She splayed her fingers on top of the table and leaned closer to him. "Would you like to see what kind of underwear I'm wearing?"

"Is it black lace?" Cassius's lips curled. It wasn't a smile. He used it at board meetings to display dominance. "You can email me your bank statements. I'm sure it won't take long to look over." It was a jab at her finances—how little she had compared to him. It was a low blow, but Cassius could be ruthless when he wanted to be. "There's no need to show me your underwear. I'm not interested."

Sera shot him a feline smile. "Thanks for offering to look over my accounts, but I have an advisor who reviews them. I'm not sure I want to take advice from someone whose wealth was handed to them."

"Enough, Sera." Lorenzo cut through their conversation.

"I apologize, Tay." Her smile didn't drop, but her shoulders slumped a bit. It was an unnatural gesture. Too submissive for someone like Sera.

Cassius recalled the way she spoke about her father during their date. Cassius knew she put him up on a pedestal. It was obvious the man was her weakness.

He didn't have the mental space to dwell on the issue. Fixing his attention on Raine, Cassius asked, "Are you an investor too?"

"No, I'm here just in case." Raine's voice was silk-smooth with a cutting edge.

Christian scowled at her. "She's not—"

"In case of *what?*" Cassius snapped. He was tired of the back and forth. When he conducted business, it was professional and to the point. He wasn't going to sit around for hours playing mind games.

Raine arched a perfect brow. "One of you may need a cup of coffee, or you might need someone to jot down notes."

"Fine." Cassius tapped his fingers on the table. "Christian, why don't you give Raine a pen and some paper. She can take meeting minutes." If she wanted to patronize him, he'd do the same in return. He had the upper hand. They needed him for this venture. "I don't have all day. Either we get started or I'm leaving."

Raine glowered at Cassius but said nothing further.

The rest of the meeting went without a hitch. They had everything Cassius asked for: permits and permissions, tax identification numbers, a business license, and more. They even had market, competitive, and cost analysis reports. Cassius was stunned. What shocked him the most was how little Sera talked during the meeting. Two words from her father and the woman shrank into herself. Raine, on the other hand, kept shooting death glares at Lorenzo.

Cassius concluded the conference by gathering the paperwork presented to him. "I should be done looking these over in a couple of days. If I don't find any discrepancies, I'll wire five million to your company account. Once I see the bill of lading for the ship, I'll wire another million." What they didn't know was that Cassius wasn't giving them a dime until he spoke to Ava's friend. "Then, I want to review the inventory, the inventory reports, and I want to inspect the delivery trucks. If I'm satisfied, I'll send the rest of the money."

"We need fifteen million up front. How are we going to buy all the equipment and pay our people if you're giving us a little at a time?" Christian whined.

Cassius shot him a flat stare. "That's not my problem. Start small. Remember, you have no room to make demands. I'm doing you a favor, so act accordingly." He packed up his belongings and left without giving any of them a proper goodbye.

Before he reached the hotel, a text came through from Sera.

I'm sorry.

He tossed his phone on the passenger's seat of his rental car. Cassius planned on canceling their date, but he couldn't bring himself to send the text.

CHAPTER 10

Sera shoved her hands in the pocket of her red jumpsuit to keep from biting her nails. *Skydiving.* Cassius changed their tea date to a skydiving date in Long Island. Sera had no choice but to say yes. The man was obviously displeased that she hadn't told him about her father's role in the precious stones venture... *which isn't really a precious stones venture.* Sera couldn't afford to lose Cassius. So here she was, sitting in a jump plane, her back fastened to his chest.

"Are you all right?" he asked, his cinnamon-scented breath brushing her ear. For a second, she forgot where they were.

The turbulence brought her back. "Yeah, fine." Sera wasn't fine at all. Cassius had no knowledge that she had a massive fear of heights. Plane rides weren't an issue but standing on the roof of buildings gave her vertigo. Falling out of a plane *had* to be worse. "We're jumping at thirteen thousand feet, right? I read it somewhere," she asked with a stable voice. Being the master of nonchalance came in handy at times like this.

"No, sweetheart, that's at skydiving centers." Cassius wrapped his arm around her waist. With his mouth hovering against the curve of her jaw, he said, "This is my private plane. We're jumping at eighteen thousand feet. That gives us almost two minutes of free fall instead of one."

Sera swallowed the vomit creeping up her throat. The heat exuding from Cassius's body was the only thing that soothed her. Sera would've been ready to rip his clothes off if she wasn't so damn frightened. *Imagine that.* She'd been burned and beaten. She'd killed in the most grue-some of ways. But jumping off a plane *terrified* her. "When do you deploy the parachute?"

"Whenever I feel like it," he said, amused. "I'm kid-ding...kind of. Usually, around twenty-five hundred feet. We'll see."

We'll see? What in the—?

"Let's go." Cassius ended her thought.

He hopped out of the seat, bringing Sera along with him.

She must've been in shock because her brain didn't register the passage of time. One minute they were on the plane. At some point, the ground fell away. Around her was a vast expanse of blue. She ingested the scream that was on the tip of her tongue.

Make this end.

Make this end.

Make this end.

"Sera." Cassius's voice was barely audible, gusts of

wind carrying it into the nether. Somehow, it still managed to distract her from fainting. "Look around. It's amazing out here. Focus on the present. Nothing else."

Okay. I can do this. Sera concentrated on her breath. *In, out, in, out, in, out...*

Then, something strange happened. As she floated on her belly, the surge of panic subsided. The silk sky enveloped her, the cool air caressing her cheeks. She was flying. *Flying!* It felt like freedom. Liberation. Sera tossed the shackles the world imposed on her into the abyss. There wasn't anything else to do but believe in the wind, trust the canopy of clouds.

The view below morphed from azure into patches of color—emeralds and sapphires and ambers. Like paint splashed on a canvas. They were nearing the ground. "Are you going to deploy the parachute?"

"Why didn't you tell me about your father?" Cassius asked, his mouth to her ear.

The field beneath them grew closer, the colors growing more vivid.

The shapes on the ground started to take form, and Cassius showed no sign of deploying the parachute. Sera's panic resurfaced. "Cassius, *please.*"

"Answer the question," he said, calm as a wolf at rest.

"I don't know." A brick sat in her stomach, dragging her down.

"Yes, you do."

"Cassius, *please,*" Sera repeated. She wasn't opposed to groveling at this point. They were dropping fast.

"Tell me." His detachment was unnerving.

"Okay," Sera yelled, aware she'd lost complete control

of the situation. "Christian told me to keep quiet. He said the less you know the better, especially since you're interested in me." Sera didn't want to think about the implications of what she was going to say next. *What choice do I have?* "They're doing something illegal with the gems. I don't know all the details, but it's drug-related. I don't want my dad involved. That's why I came yesterday." The half-truths spilled out of her. "I had to see what was happening at the meeting. Christian was pissed, but I don't answer to him."

Her confession was followed by silence.

"Cassius!" Sera screamed. The trees surrounding the pasture lifted toward her, or so her petrified mind thought.

"It's crazy the things people say when they're on the brink of death." Sera assumed she was the expert on maneuvering dangerous situations. Cassius had her beat. His tone never wavered, and his body stayed relaxed against hers. "For example, you would've never revealed Christian's plot if we weren't eighteen hundred feet above the ground."

"What?" Sera's muscles locked up. "I thought the parachute was supposed to be deployed at twenty-five hundred feet." This man was insane. *High sensation seeker indeed.*

"I said *usually* around twenty-five hundred feet." Cassius laughed. *He fucking laughed.* "Sera, why don't you tell me something about yourself. Something real."

"What I told you at dinner was real, you psycho." The scenario was so bad that she—a cold-blooded murderer—

called a billionaire golden boy a psycho. "My master's degree in chemistry—"

"That's not what I mean." When Sera didn't respond, Cassius said, "Fifteen hundred feet...fourteen hundred... thirteen hundred..."

"I read romance novels," she blurted out. "There's an entire wall in my walk-in closet dedicated to them."

"Twelve hundred."

"I vomit when I'm..." *When I'm what?* She squeezed her eyes shut and opened them again. "When I'm about to hurt someone."

"Eleven hundred."

"I wish I could leave my life behind and start new." They were words she'd spoken aloud only once. *To Raine.*

The straps on her body tightened as she jolted upright. The world slowed. An orange parachute hovered above them, bright as sunlight. A few beats later, they landed with dovelike grace in a seated position. Cassius unhooked the belts connecting them.

"You're crazy." Sera snarled. She didn't give him time to stand up. Facing him, she balled her fist and cocked back.

Cassius caught her wrist before the jab landed. His eyes met hers. They burned like freshly lit coal. "You're so composed and guarded. I wanted you to know what it felt like to be free. To speak your truth."

The desire to pummel him was intense. But she had a more intense desire. Sera pushed him to the ground and crashed her lips against his. Cassius didn't resist. He slid his arm around her waist, kissing her back with the same fierceness.

"Take me to your suite." Sera bit his bottom lip, eliciting a groan from him.

Cassius's fingers stroked her back, his hard length pressed against her. Evidence of his desire. "Yeah. Okay. Let's…" He paused. "Shit, what time is it?" Cassius sat up, bringing Sera with him.

He tried to push her off, but she wrapped her arms around his neck and fastened her legs around his waist. "What the hell is wrong now?" Cassius was the most complicated man she'd ever met. It made her job much more difficult.

Cassius looked at his watch. "I have a conference call with my company lawyer this afternoon. It's important. I need to go." He kissed her jaw. "I'm sorry, I *really* am. I'll text you later to discuss our next date."

Sera cocked a brow. "Oh, and what will this date entail? Cutting ourselves and swimming naked with sharks?"

"Don't give me any ideas." Cassius flashed her a bone-white smile. "We'll do whatever you want. Except have sex. I had a weak moment, but I'm holding out until you're hopelessly in love with me."

Sera burst out laughing. "Maybe I'll lie so I can get you in bed."

"I'll know the truth," he replied, bringing her closer to him. "Sera"—he played with a lock of her hair—"I have a question about what you told me up there." He jutted his chin toward the sky.

Heat fanned Sera's face. "I'll get more information on Christian's plans. My dad doesn't like when I meddle, but I'll figure out a way to gather details from him. I wasn't lying when I said I don't want him involved. If I can convince him to leave—"

"That's not what I was talking about." A dimpled grin. "My brother's antics don't surprise me. We'll discuss that later. There's something else I'd like to ask you."

Nooooo. Sera preferred not to expand on her weaknesses. That's what they were. Her father would've shamed her for it. *Rightly so.* "What is it, Cassius?" she asked with a sigh.

"What kind of romance novels do you read?"

That's what he wanted to know? Not the fears that made her sick? Not the fact that she wanted to get away from her life? Cassius wanted to discuss the least embarrassing topic—probably on purpose, to spare her. It was still embarrassing, nonetheless. "Mostly romantic suspense."

"What's your favorite book?"

Sera's brows creased. Where was he going with this? "It's called *Fatal Trap*."

"What's it about?"

Sera had really built a fortress around herself. How pathetic that such a tame conversation made her anxiety spike. It was as if she were disclosing her first kill. That would've made her less anxious. It didn't uncover her insecurities and foolish hopes. Romance novels were for women who dreamed about love. She wasn't one of those women. She couldn't be. Trying not to die from humiliation, Sera said, "It's about a woman who kills men for fun. Until she meets one she doesn't want to murder."

Cassius's hand moved to the nape of her neck,

stroking it with such gentleness. She wanted him to stop. It turned her mind into mush.

"Do they live happily ever after?"

"Romance novels are supposed to have happy endings. This particular author has written a ton of books, and she doesn't always abide by the rules." Sera stared at a patch of grass behind Cassius. "I'm not sure how the book ends. I only read up to the last chapter."

"I thought it was your favorite book?"

She chewed the inside of her cheek. It was a bad habit. One she resorted to when her comfort level was low. Right now, it was at the bottom of the sea. "I don't want to be disappointed."

"How do you think it ends?"

"I thought you had to go," she snapped.

"I do." He kissed her, soft and short. Too short for her liking. "Can you answer the question?"

Sera gave him a one-shoulder shrug. "There's no happy ending for women like her. The love interest probably figures out she's a monster." Sera dragged herself off Cassius and stood up. She couldn't take it anymore. It was too personal a moment. Being intimate with him made a mess of her. She had to put distance between them. Physically and emotionally. "Thanks for taking me skydiving. Other than the attempted murder, it was fun."

"I would never hurt you." Cassius got up slowly. He brushed her cheek with the back of his knuckles. "You should trust me."

Sera tried to find the cold spot in her heart. The one she summoned to transform herself into the ice queen she was known to be. But Cassius's warmth melted it into a puddle. "I don't know you enough to trust you."

"Sometimes you have to take a chance on people," Cassius said, sliding his hands in his pockets.

Sera's eyes narrowed. "Do you trust me?"

"In certain ways. I put myself in vulnerable situations all the time—risky business deals and dangerous hobbies. In order to do that, I have to trust the universe. I trust you want to be here with me. That you liked kissing me. That the fears you revealed are valid." A muscle feathered in his jaw. "Your barriers keep you from getting hurt, but it also stops you from living a full life. Trust isn't a flaw, Sera."

Cassius didn't give her a chance to answer. For that, she was grateful. She wouldn't have known what to say. "I have to go." He kissed her forehead. "I'll talk to you tonight."

Sera walked to her car, her brain unhinged. The locks installed inside of her heart corroded the more time she spent with Cassius. *Why can't I grasp control of the situation?* Hopping in the driver's seat, Sera grabbed the burner phone out of the glove box. She dialed her father's burner number.

"Hey, what's up?" Butch asked in that gruff tone of his. If a bulldog could talk, it would sound like Butch.

"Where's my dad?" Sera never made small talk with Butch. He was her boogeyman. The beast in the closet.

"Lo-lo," Butch yelled. "Your spawn wants to talk to you."

"How did it go?" Lorenzo asked, getting on the line.

"He fell for it." Sera's stomach revolted. The food she ate for breakfast hardened to cement in her belly.

"Good girl." Lorenzo chuckled. "You'll have him kissing your feet in no time."

Sera clenched and unclenched her fingers, disgusted with herself. Cassius trusted her. This is how she paid him back. "I have to go. I'm sitting outside the grocery store," she lied.

"Hey, you did an excellent job today. Why don't you stop by this week for dinner? I'll make your favorite dish: *Pinakbet*." Lorenzo chuckled again. "And how about I treat you to the Givenchy necklace you've been eyeing?"

"You're so thoughtful. Thank you," Sera said, trying to muster up her enthusiasm.

"Love you, iha." The pride in her father's voice reverberated through the speaker.

"Love you too." Sera's mouth was dry as a desert. For once, she didn't revel in her father's affection. She barely registered hanging up on him.

Sera stared at the field in front of her. *This was always the plan*, she reminded herself. Sera never thought she'd have to implement it midair, but the task was done. Cassius's demise was a two-pronged strategy. Plan A and Plan B all at once. The schedule was aggressive, but time wasn't on their side.

While Raine continued her attempt at hacking Cassius's account, which was proving to be more difficult than they thought, Sera resumed her efforts at getting him to divulge pertinent information. She told Cassius about the drug operation to make it appear as if she were looking out for him. He might not give Christian the funds for their Devil's Breath operation, but that wasn't the goal anyway. The entire meeting at the warehouse was an act. *Everything* was an act—getting Cassius to come to New York, having him meet Sera, and making him fall for her. Christian, Lorenzo, and Damion didn't care about the fifteen million. They wanted the four hundred million sitting in Cassius's accounts. And they wanted him dead. If they kept him alive, he'd go after them. No doubt, he'd win. Men as powerful as Cassius always did. They'd all end up facing life in prison.

Get him to trust you. He'll slip up eventually. They all do. Lorenzo's words. Sera had done this many times before, just not on this level. The men always left crumbs, small morsels they didn't realize they had spilled. Sera found ways to piece it together.

Why did Cassius have to make things complex? Why did he have to think that she was a genuine human being? *Because he chooses to see the good in people.*

Resting her head on the steering wheel, Sera inhaled gulps of air. She did something she hadn't done in a while. She cried.

When there were no more tears to shed, Sera wiped her face and fixed her mascara. Then, she called Ruby—an acquaintance with benefits. When the woman picked up, Sera said, "I'll be at your place in an hour. Be naked before I get there."

That's how Sera handled heartache—she didn't. She tossed it aside. She liquefied it beyond recognition, like the body of her victims.

CHAPTER 11

Cassius replayed the conversation he had with Sera during the drive back to the hotel. He wasn't lying when he said Christian's antics didn't surprise him. It was still a disappointment, though. *What are you up to, brother?* As good as he was at reading people, he'd always had a problem with Christian. It was his blind spot. Maybe he chose to ignore signs when it came to his brother.

Where are the drugs going to be hidden? What kind of drugs? Does it matter? If Cassius didn't give Christian the money, he'd forever be a burden to their family. Christian held that over Cassius's head as a form of emotional blackmail. Cassius would do anything to ensure his parents' happiness. But could he really allow his brother to run a drug ring?

His thoughts lingered on Christian for a couple more minutes before they turned to Sera. The skydiving tactic was a bit extreme, but Cassius was a bit extreme. It was a risky move that worked in his favor. When they sat on the grass together, Sera was open and unguarded. In his arms, Sera's eyes spoke words her mouth wouldn't. Their usual dullness was replaced with passion and fire. *Along with agony and loneliness.* Cassius had been right the entire time: the indifference was an act. She'd worn the costume for so long, it attached to her skin. Like a Band-Aid that stung if pulled off. It was easier to leave it on.

The woman was a beautiful disaster. And Cassius wanted her. Not just in bed either. He yearned to explore her mind. It wasn't rational. He'd known her for less than a week, yet his desire was overwhelming. The first time he went skydiving, he fell in love with it. The adrenaline spike. The hard rush. The blissful freedom. The euphoric risk. The sobering realization that life didn't last forever. That's how he felt when he was around Sera. Like he was flying among clouds. It was a sensation that *shouldn't* be explained because it *couldn't* be explained.

All thoughts of Sera and Christian left Cassius's mind the moment he entered the Mandarin. Sitting in the lobby and waving him over was a slender, dark-haired man. He fit Ava's description of the private detective.

"Henry?" Cassius asked when he was less than a stride away.

"That's me." Henry stood up and shook Cassius's hand. "Nice to meet you."

"Sorry I'm late. I got caught up with something." He looked toward the elevator. "Let's go to my floor."

When they reached his suite, Cassius led Henry to the living room. They took a seat across from each other. "So, you're a friend of Ava's?" Cassius asked, crossing his left ankle over his right knee.

Henry shrugged off his blazer. "Twenty-five years now."

"A friend of Ava's is a friend of mine." He gestured toward the minibar. "Want a drink?"

"No, no. I quit drinking ages ago. Thanks, though." Henry sat forward and steepled his fingers together. "I don't want to take up too much of your time, so I'll get to the point. Your brother's precious stones company is a front for a drug enterprise."

Sera was telling the truth. "What kind of drug?" Cassius held his breath. *Please don't let it be Adrenochrome.* Christian wouldn't get involved in human trafficking. *He's not that twisted. Is he?*

"There's a new drug he plans to market called Devil's Breath," Henry said. "It's going to be for the elite. They're the only ones who'll be able to afford eight hundred dollars a gram."

Cassius released his breath. *Good.* His fear was unfounded. But the issue wasn't resolved. His brother was *still* a drug dealer.

"Eight hundred dollars," Cassius repeated. He'd never done illegal drugs. Extreme sports were his drug of choice. He couldn't fathom anyone paying hundreds of dollars to ruin their mind and body. "Where is this Devil's Breath coming from?"

"Colombia. The substance has been altered to re-semble gemstones. The stones are liquefied and turned back to powder before they're sold." Henry scratched the stubble on his chin. "To be honest, I'm a little impressed. It takes a bright chemist to pull that off."

Chemist. Cassius froze. *Is Sera involved in the operation?*

Did she lie to him? They were in the sky when she disclosed the drug deal. He couldn't read her—couldn't see if her right hand quivered. "Do you know about the others involved?"

"Not much. Damion is a petty criminal. He's never done anything this big." Henry flicked a piece of lint off his shirt. "Lorenzo was in and out of jail for a few misdemeanors and two felonies: theft and an assault charge. His daughter, Sera, has a clean slate. I can't find anything on her."

Cassius turned the data over in his mind. He had decisions to make. Good thing that was his strength. He didn't double the Batista profits by being indecisive. "Here's what we're going to do...continue to bug my brother's apartment. I want the warehouse bugged as well. We should—"

Henry raised his hand, palm facing Cassius. "I have one more thing to tell you. There's no good way to say this." He cleared his throat. "Your brother plans to have you killed."

Cassius's lungs constricted. The air was sucked out of the room. It was the same sensation he had when he reached Mount Everest's summit: oxygen left his brain. *My brother wants me dead. My own fucking brother.* His chest tightened. He was on the verge of hyperventilating. Cassius clenched his fists, digging his nails into his palms. Now was not the time to lose control. If anyone knew how to deal with danger, it was him. He needed to hone those skills now.

"Tell me the details," Cassius said, keeping his voice even.

"I have none. I found out this morning. Damion was at your brother's place, and it was mentioned briefly." His forehead creased. "They said something about Devil's Breath. It was vague…I have a feeling they might try to poison you. Ava asked me to call her after this meeting. Once I leave, I'll give her an update."

He rapped his knuckles on the armrest. "Look, I've been doing this a long time. Most people hire a security detail and go to the cops. You don't seem like the type." A short pause. "Ava told me what happened at Everest. I understand you don't want to bring bad press to your family. My recommendation is that you stall on giving Christian the money for his business. He'll keep you alive because he needs you. Meanwhile, I'll gather more info."

Cassius hid his shock. *Ava told him about Everest.* Part of her job was to bury Batista secrets. To speak to Henry about it meant the two were really close.

Henry was correct about his assumptions. Cassius wouldn't go to the police or hire guards. If Christian wanted Cassius dead, he'd order the hit from anywhere. Even prison. Cassius could only imagine the drama and embarrassment that would cause their family. They'd be the headline of every newspaper and media outlet in the country. Batista Holdings would lose business associates and contracts.

I'm not letting my parents experience this heartache again. His brother already tarnished the Batista name once. The stunt Christian pulled in college was the last straw. That's when their father decided to disown him. In Cassius's opinion, their dad gave him too many chances to begin with. He wasn't going to allow Christian to cause another scandal. The first one triggered an enormous backlash. Cassius spent many sleepless nights consoling his parents and sister. His days were spent rebuilding the Batista Holdings' reputation while juggling college at the same time. He worked too hard to have his self-serving brother ruin everything a second time.

There was only one way to solve the situation. *Christian has to die first.* Their family wouldn't be dragged through the mud. Not if it was done correctly. *A mugging gone wrong, perhaps.* Christian would be portrayed as a victim instead of the criminal he was. Their family would be broken-hearted. But finding out Christian was a homicidal drug dealer would be more traumatic. Yes, Christian had to go. *It's not like it's my first time killing someone.* Cassius condemned his brother, but he wasn't innocent either. *Aren't I a criminal too?*

The thought of murdering Christian made Cassius's stomach roil with self-loathing. His brother—once his best friend—was a mortal enemy. And what about Sera? Did she know about the assassination plot? The truth would come out soon enough. Cassius would make sure of it.

"Bug Damion's and Lorenzo's places too," Cassius said.

"What about the girl?"

He should have Sera's place bugged and be done with her. But it seemed too impersonal. He craved to know more about the aloof woman who secretly read romance novels. The woman who was confident around others, yet easily silenced by her father. The woman who wanted to leave her life behind. The woman whose kisses blazed with passion he'd never felt before. The woman he couldn't get out of his head.

What if it was just an infatuation? *What if it's more?* What if she was lying about everything? *What if I never feel this strongly about anyone else?*

What if...what if...what if?

"Well?" Henry asked.

He wouldn't spy on her. There was a spark between them. One that would either dwindle or expand into all-consuming flames. Cassius had to figure it out. "No, leave Sera alone. I have other plans for her."

"Alright." Henry slid his blazer back on. "Anything else?"

Cassius bit his lip in contemplation. "Tell Ava I want extra security cameras around the Batista estate and my home as well. I don't want my parents to know what's going on. It has to be done discreetly. Find out about this Devil's Breath drug. If the plan is to poison me, then I need an antidote for it." Ava had many connections. If anyone could get him a remedy, it would be her.

"Is that all?" Henry looked at him expectantly. "I know *certain people* if you're interested in their services."

Cassius knew what Henry was hinting at. *A hit man.* "I'm interested." He ignored the way it scalded his tongue. "Don't do anything until I give the go-ahead, but have this person ready." Adrenaline rushed his veins. It wasn't the kind that satisfied him. "I'm leaving for Gillette in two days." Remaining in New York was pointless. He planned on staying for a month to ensure Christian's business took off. Now that his brother wanted him dead, there was no point hanging around.

"Why not leave tonight?"

"I have one thing to take care of first." One person to be exact. *Sera.*

When Henry left, Cassius texted Christian his lie.

I need to go to Gillette for a work issue. I'll be back in a few days. I'm still reviewing your paperwork, but everything looks good so far.

An hour later, his brother answered. *You work too hard. Batista Holdings will be the death of you.*

You'll be the death of me. It was a phrase Cassius had used before when his brother was up to his tricks.

In the past, Christian responded with a sarcastic retort.

This time, there was no reply.

CHAPTER 12

Sera's heart dropped when Cassius entered Maman, the French café she was dining at. She had ignored his texts last night and that morning. Spending the evening with Ruby didn't do a damn thing. Sera thought it would make her forget about Cassius. Instead, he consumed her mind even more. He'd been correct. Sera slept with people to mark it off a checklist—to prove to herself humans were scum. At least sex had been a nonissue before. Now it left her empty and unfulfilled.

Cassius was dangerous. With him, Sera felt things she had no business feeling. It scared her so much that she had to step away. She wasn't avoiding Cassius by any means. He was her mark, after all. She just needed a few days to get her mind right. Her wish wasn't granted. There he was, approaching her table. A table also occupied by Ruby and Raine.

While Ruby sipped her coffee next to Sera, Raine sat across from her with a raised eyebrow and a smirk. Her friend was fully aware of her fascination with Cassius.

More like an obsession. Sera watched him as he strolled toward her. The man was so handsome that it hurt to look at him. How was it possible to be simple and striking at the same time? His outfits were always unpretentious. Today, he wore blue jeans and a gray hoodie. Other than the Rolex on his wrist, nobody would've ever known he was one of the wealthiest men around. That made Sera like him even more. Cassius's confidence took up all the space in the room. He didn't care to flash his riches to prove how successful he was. What anyone thought of him was irrelevant. He only cared about being his genuine self.

"Hi, Sera," Cassius said when he reached her.

It was showtime. "Cassius, what a coincidence." Sera forced boredom in her gaze. "Are you meeting someone here?"

"Why aren't you returning my texts?"

Shit. This was going to be harder than Sera thought. How could she forget that Cassius had no interest in superficiality? She bit back a groan. "I've been busy"—she took a bite of her salad—"I'd offer you a seat, but as you can see, there are none available."

"Actually, there's an empty chair over there." Raine pointed to a table across from them.

Sera was going to murder Raine. When Cassius left to grab the chair, Sera took that opportunity to scowl at her friend. Raine responded with a smug smile. *What the hell is she thinking?* Raine was either desperate for Sera to get the job done, or she wanted Sera to fall for her mark. Of course, Sera would have a better idea of Raine's thought process if she let the woman voice her opinion on Cassius.

"What have you been busy doing?" Cassius set the chair down facing Sera. He slid into it.

"How did you know I was here?" she asked, bypassing his question.

"Christian said you eat breakfast here every day." Cassius's eyes swept the room. "It doesn't seem like your kind of spot. Not *this* Sera anyway. Maybe another version of you."

Sera hated how well he read her. No, it wasn't a seductive nightclub owner's kind of place. It was too warm. The walls were painted light coral, verdant vines covered the entire ceiling, and pastel flowers bloomed in every corner. Next to her table was a vintage bicycle, its basket overflowing with lavender. The café was dainty and delicate. Even the porcelain plates and cups were painted with romantic, pastoral images. Cassius was accurate in his assumption. The *other* version liked it. She wasn't about to admit it. "What are you doing here?"

"I want to ask you something. I'm—" Cassius's focus shifted to Ruby, his gaze lingering on her. Most men drooled over the woman. She was exquisite: cropped chestnut hair, large steel-blue eyes, and thick lips. That's not why he was staring. Sera saw the gears shifting in his mind. "Can you answer my question?"

Sera crossed her legs. "Which one?"

"When you said you were busy, what were you doing?"

"Me." Ruby slung her arm around Sera's shoulder. "We were busy doing each other." The satisfaction in her tone made Sera flinch inside. Ruby wasn't jealous. She was like

Sera in many ways. Both had lots of partners. None they cared about. They also had a knack for cruelty, which Ruby decided to display at that moment.

"You were with someone else after our date." Cassius's face was unreadable. But the tightness in his shoulders exposed his anger. "You're unbelievable, Sera."

"Don't pull some territorial, alpha male bullshit on me." She tossed her hair over her shoulder. "That won't go over well."

Cassius's eyes darkened like clouds before a torrential downpour. "You don't get it, do you? I don't care that you fucked her. The reason you did it is what pisses me off."

Dread scraped its claws down Sera's skin. She didn't like where the conversation was going. He was about to get personal. She didn't do "personal" with anyone but Raine. *Keep your composure.*

Schooling her face, she said, "I do things because I want to. Plain and simple."

"That's bullshit." Cassius leaned forward until they shared breaths. A storm rolled off of him, devouring her whole. "You think all the bodies in your bed will stop you from thinking about me? I promise you it won't." Sera's breath caught as his fingers pressed against the hammering pulse on her neck. "Feel that? Feel how much I affect you? You're scared of getting close to me. You push me away because you know there's something between us." His mouth hovered over her ear. "That makes you a coward."

It took a few beats for Sera to register what he said.

Did this privileged bastard call me a coward? She had crawled out of the gutter, dealt with scums of the earth, and survived Lorenzo's wrath. *How dare he?* The dam holding her emotions exploded.

"You have some nerve." She shoved his chest. "I know plenty of guys like you. Bored country club boys who think it's fun to be with a person like me—rough and gritty. Someone who doesn't abide by the perfect rules the elite set in place. Once their curiosity is satisfied, they move on. And where do people like me end up?" He tried to speak, but she cut him off. "*Alone.* You'll have an entertaining story to tell, and I'll be alone!"

A deafening silence shrouded the table.

Ruby sat stock-still, her coffee mug frozen on her lips.

Raine's fork fell out of her hand, clattering when it hit the floor.

Sera wanted to disappear into the ether. *What did I just say?* She was tempted to take the butter knife off her plate and cut her tongue out. She had to fix this. *Speak. Say something. Anything.* "What I mean is—"

"I'm not the asshole that you think I am," Cassius interrupted. He took her hand, his thumb caressing her wrist. She didn't have the energy to pull away. "I'm sorry I called you a coward. You're not a coward, but I do think you're scared." He stared at her, a plea in his eyes. "All I'm asking for is a chance, Sera. Please give me a chance."

She had no response. Her emotions were too tangled. She needed to smooth them out, reel them in. She remained quiet as she slipped out of his hold. Scooting away from him, she moved her chair closer to Ruby.

Cassius released an exasperated sigh. "Fine, I can take a hint. I'm sorry I bothered you." He stood up. "If you want to talk, you know how to reach me."

Let him go. Raine would figure out how to hack his account. It might take a little more time, but as long as the goal was met, it wouldn't matter. *No, he has to stay.* Sera couldn't lose her target. Her dad would dismember her.

Go.

Stay.

Go.

Stay.

"Wait," Raine said. "Didn't you have a question for Sera?"

"I did…" Cassius gazed at Sera with uncertainty. "I'm leaving for Gillette tomorrow night. It'll only be for a few days. I was going to ask you to come with me. I *still* want you to come with me."

Sera took a sip of water to keep her jaw from dropping. Everyone's eyes were on her. She couldn't believe he wanted to spend time with her after their argument.

"Why?" she inquired, relieved her voice didn't waver.

"I never got to tell you about myself. A secret for a secret, right?" He was talking about her skydiving confessions. It was his turn to reveal something private.

It was a crazy idea. Going to his hometown was too intimate. *It could be an opportunity to extract information from him.* But their altercation rocked her to the core. Her ridiculous outburst was humiliating enough. *How much more can I handle before I break?* She needed to regroup—recuperate. She certainly wouldn't be able to get her emotions in check if she went to Gillette.

"Come with me," he pleaded. "If you don't like it there, my pilot will take you home right away."

The smart thing to do was to say yes. It would move

the plan further along. But her heart couldn't take it. "Have a safe flight tomorrow, Cassius."

His eyes pierced her with unwavering force. Reaching into the waistband of his jeans, he pulled out a book and placed it on the table.

Sera's breath stumbled. *No...he didn't...*

She ran her hand over the title. *Fatal Trap.* "You bought it?"

"I read the entire thing last night." Cassius tapped the cover. "It has a happy ending. She tells him about the things she did in her past, but he doesn't care. He loves her regardless." He shook his head. "At least think about going to Gillette with me."

And he left.

Sera excused herself and went to the bathroom. She had to get away from Ruby and Raine. She feared she'd burst into tears at the table. Leaning over the sink, Sera closed her eyes. *Don't ruin this for Tay. You're better than this.*

A hand touched her back. "That's your favorite book." *Raine.*

Sera opened her eyes and looked at her friend. "Thanks for stating the obvious. I can't believe you were egging him on. You must really want his money."

The corners of Raine's mouth lifted, but there was no humor in her features. "The money doesn't matter to me. I'm not greedy. I'm rich enough. What I want is for *you* to be happy instead of catering to Lorenzo's every whim. You like Cassius. The things he said to you...he's not wrong. And your reaction was so raw and unrehearsed. No one has ever been able to touch that side of you. He asked for a chance, so give it to him. You owe it to yourself."

"Don't." Sera didn't want to relive her conversation with Cassius. "I know you're only doing this job because of me. I'm forever grateful. But can we please not talk about this right now."

Raine held her hands up in surrender. "Fine. How about this. Let's ditch Ruby and watch movies at my house. We have twelve hours till we have to rob the drug lab."

Sera kissed Raine on the cheek. "You have the best ideas."

"I have another great idea..."

"You're relentless." Sera lightly punched Raine's shoulder. "Don't you dare bring Cassius up again. He's my mark."

"That's all the more reason you should go to Gillette."

"Ummm...no," Sera said, feigning annoyance. "I'm relying on you to drain his funds. You're the best hacker in the world, remember?"

"Flattery *will* get you everywhere." She took Sera's hand in hers. "Let's grab some vegan chocolate on the way to my house."

A few hours later, Sera was sprawled on Raine's couch. They'd gone through two movies, and her tummy was full of chocolate. Sera's choice was an action flick. Her *dear friend* chose a romance. Raine was *definitely* on the top of Sera's hit list at this point.

"How many more hours until we have to hit up the drug lab?" Raine asked, popping chocolate in her mouth.

Sera pulled her phone out of her purse. "Six."

She was about to throw her phone back in her bag, but her fingers moved on their own accord. *I'll go with you to Gillette.* She wanted to delete the text the second she sent it.

I promise you won't regret it. Cassius responded.

Sera groaned as she tossed the phone on the coffee table. From the corner of her eye, she saw Raine's satisfied face staring at her. "What?" she asked.

Raine popped another piece of chocolate in her mouth. "Oh…nothing."

Sera tossed a pillow at her friend. "I hate you."

"You better not." Raine caught the pillow and placed it behind her head. "I sat through a cringey romance movie, so I could brainwash you into going to Gillette. If that's not being a good friend, then I don't know what is."

Sera pressed the heels of her palms against her eyes. "I have to kill him."

Raine reached over and squeezed Sera's knee. "You don't have to do anything you don't want to do."

CHAPTER 13

Sera threw up three times next to a trash bin before joining Raine in the dark alley. Standing behind an abandoned building, they blended with the night. Both donned black tracksuits, matching gloves, and sneakers. Underneath their jackets were bulletproof vests. Hopefully, things went well and they'd finish the job with their vests undamaged.

Raine was her usual mask of calm. This was the venomous side of her, one Sera knew well. Gone was the woman who joked and watched romance flicks. A cold-blooded killer took her place. Raine didn't talk to her father anymore, but she held a piece of him inside of her. Elijah—her dad—was a hit man for a local Bronx gang. When Raine was a child, he thought it appropriate to take her to "work." His motivational speeches consisted of telling Raine that she'd be either a prostitute or a killer. She chose the latter. When she moved in with her grandmother, things were better. But her dad had already planted poisonous seeds in her mind. Raine's circumstances strengthened Sera's beliefs that people couldn't change.

"Did you get it out of your system?" Raine asked, patting Sera's back.

"All better." Sera popped a mint in her mouth. "Let's do this."

"Okay, I'll check the other side." Keeping close to the walls, Raine prowled the alleyway, melting into the shadows.

They scoped the place prior to that evening. The information Raine took from Carlo's phone led them to the jewelry store on Ampere Parkway in East Orange, New Jersey, which was an hour away from Manhattan. The store was a front for a drug lab. The ingredients needed for Sera's Devil's Breath recipe were in the basement. They were there to steal supplies and eliminate their competition.

Sera felt a tad guilty; the operation had been Carlo's idea. But he made two mistakes. First, he confided in Sera. He required help when it came to the creation of the drug. She was the best chemist around as far as Carlo was concerned. Second, he asked Christian, Damion, and Lorenzo to do a job for him—hijacking trucks that carried physostigmine and meclizine. Necessary components for Devil's Breath. A few days later, Sera bugged Carlo's office. It didn't take long until they had the details of the entire drug ring. The one thing they couldn't figure out was the lab's location. That issue was resolved when Raine hacked Carlo's phone.

Why do we even need to rob the lab to begin with? Sera asked herself that question many times. *We're stealing four hundred million dollars from Cassius, for crying out loud.* What else did they need? *Fame. Notoriety. To be feared and respected in the criminal world.* That's what Lorenzo and his partners wanted. Sera was starting to understand why greed was one of the seven deadly sins.

We don't want rivals. We shouldn't waste precious ingredients anyway. Let's call it upcycling. You'll take care of it for me, won't you, iha? Lorenzo's wishes were Sera's commands.

Unzipping her tracksuit, Sera pulled a Glock out of the bulletproof vest holster and made sure her flash-bang grenades were secure in their pockets. Zipping her jacket back up, she glanced at her watch. It was one in the morning. They had thirty minutes to get the job done and load the drugs in their unregistered truck. That was the amount of time they gave themselves for big jobs. The longer they stayed, the higher the risk of getting caught. Sera rounded the corner until she saw Raine.

"The guards just walked in. The chemists are probably in there already. Gio is at his mistress's house, so he won't be around," Raine whispered. Based on their research, there should be five chemists, six guards, and thankfully no Gio—Carlo's brother who had taken over the operation.

Raine took a black ski mask out of her pocket and pulled it over her face. Next, she strapped on a six-layer activated carbon mask, covering her mouth and nose. "Eleven people in thirty minutes. Plus, loading the truck with thousands of dollars in drugs. This is going to take a miracle." She unclipped her gun from its holster. "I don't understand why the men couldn't help us. They're useless."

"I won't argue that." Sera took her own ski and carbon masks out of her pocket, put them on, then eyed the perimeter. She couldn't see the truck because it was parked in the back, where the inventory for the shop was brought in. "You disabled the street cameras and cut the power lines, right?"

"What do you think I am, an amateur?" Raine pinched Sera's shoulder. "Now remind me again which drug is which? I forgot."

Sera gave her a sidelong glance. "Physostigmine is going to be in liquid form. Meclizine will come in pill form. Scopolamine is the powder."

"I'm kidding. I remember." Raine clucked her tongue. "Wow, you really do think I'm an amateur."

"I'm glad you find this amusing." Sera softly elbowed Raine's side. "Come on, let's get this over with."

They crept to the edge of the alley where an empty shop was located. One that shared a wall with the jewelry store. Sera removed a wallet-size lock pick set from her pocket and grabbed a small tension wrench and a serrated rake. They could've broken directly into the jewelry store, but those locks were more complicated. *Rightly so.* The place sold diamonds and gold. *And has a basement full of drugs.* Breaking into an empty shop was less difficult.

Sera slipped the tension wrench in the bottom of the keyhole and applied pressure. She slid the rake in next, scrubbing it back and forth until she heard a *click*. "Let's get this party started."

Rained moaned. "*Please,* no corny one-liners tonight."

Sera gave her a playful glare as they entered the store and headed to the shared wall. Sera lifted her left pant leg

146

up and retrieved a five-inch-long pad saw strapped to her calf. Three minutes later, there was a hole in the drywall, and the two women were inside.

The jewelry store was bigger than it looked from the outside. Glass counters with shelving wrapped around the shop, and burgundy carpet covered the floor. Like most jewelry stores, the gems weren't out for display after hours. They were placed in a secure safe. It didn't matter. They weren't there for jewels. Sera and Raine headed to the back room. Based on the information taken from Carlo's phone, the door to the basement was hidden behind a cabinet there.

"Over here," Raine said once they pushed the oak hutch out of the way. "Shit, it has a built-in combination lock."

That was not in Carlo's files. *Why wasn't it there? Don't panic. Think. Think...*

Five minutes passed.

Six.

Seven.

Raine typed in number combinations, hoping to hear a distinctive tick that would let her know which digits were part of the sequence. So far, luck wasn't on their side.

Eight minutes.

Sera glanced at the vent on the floor. "We can get in through there." It was a risk. They didn't know which part of the basement it led to. But they had no other choice.

Using her lock pick kit, Sera unscrewed the vent. She set the cover aside and crawled in. Raine followed behind her. The vent zigzagged down, sharp turns at every corner. Ten feet later, they reached the basement.

Sera peeked through the grille covers and saw that they landed behind a row of steel tables where chemists in hazmat suits were hard at work. Atop the tables was an array of equipment: thermometers, burettes, an assortment of flasks, Bunsen burners, and more. Apparatus Sera was familiar with.

To the right of the room were ten fifty-gallon drums of liquid. Sera was certain they held the Devil's Breath concoction. Straining her neck, she glimpsed metal shelves to the left. They were stacked with boxes of pills, packs of powder, and vials of clear fluid. That's what they came for.

Sera evaluated the room. She studied the chemists first. She wasn't too worried about them. They weren't trained killers, but they were working with dangerous substances. There was no doubt that if they felt threatened, they'd use the chemicals as a weapon. The guards were her main focus. Six of them sat a few feet from the shelves. Their rifles leaned against the table where they were playing cards. Strapped to their waists were handguns. *Well, this is going to be fun.*

She turned her head and nodded at Raine. It was time. Sera pushed the grille open, gripping the sides so it didn't clatter on the floor. She was barely out of the vent when one of the chemists spotted her. Before the woman could make a move, Sera was on her feet. A beat later, a bullet was lodged in the chemist's temple. A whisper of a sound from Sera's silencer. Two more bodies dropped, thanks to Raine.

Three down, two to go.

A scream echoed through the room as a chemist ran

toward the guards. *Great, they have in-suit microphones.* Sera was hoping the biohazard masks would hinder their speech. The traditional ones did. These chemists were obviously not wearing traditional masks.

The guards were up immediately, rifles in their hands.

"This is going to be a disaster," Raine said dryly.

The original plan was a lot smoother than what was happening. If Sera and Raine had taken the stairs, they would've entered facing the guards' backs. It could've been simple and quick assassinations. Why did killing have to be so complicated lately? Sera's jobs were usually straightforward.

Bullets exploded through the air, nonstop and vicious. Sera dropped to the ground and rolled behind a pile of boxes. She saw that Raine had taken cover behind a metal column. With careful motion, Sera stood, aimed, and shot. She hit a guard in his stomach. *Damn it!* She meant to hit his neck. The bullet would bruise him, but it wouldn't penetrate his vest.

He staggered and clutched the side of his ribs. Sera took that opportunity to hop over the boxes and sprint toward him. She was quick, but so was he. Any discomfort he felt had been pushed aside. He lifted his rifle and blasted. Sera crouched down and pulled the trigger on her Glock. The bullet penetrated the man's kneecap. He dropped to the ground, howling like an injured animal. Tossing the heavy rifle aside, the guard pulled out his handgun. Pointing it at Sera, he unloaded while crawling away.

Sera weaved and bobbed, trying to avoid being riddled with holes. She grabbed a dead body beside her. Using it as a shield, she stalked forward. Raine arrived first. Sera had no idea where the woman came from. It was as if she teleported from across the room. With a scalpel in hand, Raine fisted the guard's hair and pulled his neck back. Then, she plunged the blade into his eye.

He wasn't in pain long. Sera put a bullet in his head a beat later. "Where the hell did you get the scalpel?"

"On the table." Raine adjusted her carbon mask. "I ran out of ammunition. I'm improvising."

"You emptied all your cartridges? We have six each." Sera reloaded her gun and handed two of her cartridges to Raine.

"Thanks, chica." Raine tugged the scalpel out of the man's eye, wiping the blood on his shirt. "Be careful," she said, running off to take care of her next victim.

Sera checked her watch. *Crap.* They had ten minutes left. She needed to speed things up. She aimed her Glock at a guard. A blast to the neck. Sera shot another in her temple before jogging over to Raine.

Three lifeless bodies surrounded her friend. They were sliced from neck to belly. Gutted like pigs. "Do I even want to know?"

"What?" Raine folded her arms over her chest. "I told you I was improvising."

Sera opened her mouth to retort, but something caught her eyes. "How did we overlook that?" She pointed to a chemist who was straining to overturn one of the drums. If successful, they'd be swimming in Devil's Breath. The overdose would be immediate. The chemist herself would be fine. Her hazmat suit protected her.

"What the fuck do you think you're doing?" Sera

pointed her gun, but the woman stooped behind the drums. "I don't have a good shot. I'll hit a vat. If I do, it'll light the chemicals on fire."

Raine flashed her scalpel in Sera's face. "I'll take care of her." She charged toward the chemist.

Sera was about to follow when something hit the side of her head and knocked her to the ground. For a second, the room disappeared. Sharp pain ripped through her brain as if it had been struck by a bolt of lightning. She forced herself to stay conscious. *I've been through worse*, Sera reminded herself. *Mind over matter.* Slowly, her focus returned. A male chemist with a metal pole in his hand stood above her. *So much for my lack of concern over the chemists.* She had underestimated them.

"Sera!" Raine yelled.

She rolled her aching head to the side and witnessed the chemist tipping one of the vats over, liquid spilling out with speed. "No! The vats!" Sera yelled back. That was more important.

Raine hesitated briefly, then took off again.

Before Sera had a chance to get up, the man straddled her and pinned her arms with his knees. "Who do you work for?" He wrapped his hands around her neck and squeezed.

"Can't talk…choking…" Sera spat the words out with great effort.

He loosened his grip and snarled. "Tell me."

Sera glanced at her gun a few feet from her. The fall had knocked it out of her hand. "I work for myself."

He slammed his elbow into her nose. Blood gushed

out of her nostrils. The taste of iron dripped into her mouth. "I'm going to ask you—"

The chemist didn't get to finish. Sera bucked her hips, and his body lurched forward. His knees lifted off the ground, releasing Sera's arms. Balling her hand into a fist, she punched his Adam's apple. The chemist sucked back air, his face turning five shades of purple. As he struggled to breathe, Sera went for him again, performing a move she despised. One her father required her to learn.

Sera flexed her fingers, recalling the numerous occasions she broke them in order to gain strength, her digits repeatedly microfractured for this technique. *Here goes nothing.* Curling her fingers into a claw, she struck the man's neck. Ripping into his flesh, Sera tore his trachea out.

Blood spilled out of him, oozing onto Sera. Her gloved hands were covered with carnage. Her masks drenched with her own blood. She must've looked like a nightmare. Now wasn't the time to be concerned about her appearance. She glanced at the vats and noticed a second one had been overturned. Sera pushed the dead chemist off her, grabbed her gun, and ran to Raine.

Her friend stood on one of the metal tables.

The chemist remained in the middle of the spill.

"She dumped the first vat before I got to her. There was nothing I could do," Raine said with a frustrated groan.

They were stuck. Shooting the woman wasn't an option. They couldn't walk over to her either. Unlike the chemist, they weren't in hazmat suits. They'd overdose within seconds. Sera scanned the room. Her left eye was almost shut, compliments of the dead chemist. Her nose needed to be reset...*again.*

Hopping atop the same table as Raine, Sera said, "We have to get out of here. If she dumps more vats, this place will be flooded."

"How are we going to get the drugs out?" Raine asked. "And what are we going to do about her?" She pointed at the chemist.

Sera studied the woman. She wasn't like the chemist who tried to bludgeon Sera. This one wasn't a killer. Her eyes were frozen with fear, like a deer facing off with a hunter. *She doesn't want to hurt anyone.* She just wanted to get out alive.

"Forget the inventory, and forget her. She can't identify us anyway." Not with their ski masks on. "We have to go. I'm starting to feel high." The scent of Devil's Breath swept over Sera, sending tingles through her brain. The carbon mask kept the fumes from completely overwhelming her senses. But it had its limitations. The vapors were too potent.

"Yeah, same." Raine glanced at Sera with pinned pupils. If they spent any more time in the lab, they'd be useless. *No, we'll be dead.*

The two leaped from table to table until they reached the vent. Sera was about to jump to the ground when Lorenzo's voice entered her mind. *Witnesses have to die.* The man was always in her head, even if he wasn't around.

Raising her Glock, Sera aimed it at the chemist and...froze.

"What are you doing?" Raine asked, crouching at the

mouth of the vent. "Don't worry about her. This place is screwed."

"Hold on…listen." Sera's brows furrowed. "Do you hear that?"

Raine cupped her ear. "Cars. Lots of them."

"Why would there be a bunch of cars here at this time of night?"

Sera's question was answered a few seconds later. A crash, followed by footsteps, thundered above their heads. Something was happening on the main floor. Raine's and Sera's eyes widened at the same time.

"Cops." Raine cursed under her breath.

"Maybe someone called about a breaking and entering." Sera wiped her filthy, gloved hands on her pants. "You don't think they know about all of this, do you?"

It was the chemist who answered. "It's not the cops, you morons. There aren't any sirens." The woman waded to a wall behind the drums. She dug her fingers inside the cracks and removed a set of bricks, exposing a window.

"Well?" Sera asked impatiently. "What do you see?"

"It's the DEA." She shuddered.

"Someone ratted us out." Raine spoke Sera's thoughts aloud.

Who? No one knew about the job except for Christian, Damion, and Lorenzo. They wouldn't call the DEA. *Would they?* There was no time to analyze it. They needed to get out. Fast.

"They're going to surround the building if they haven't already." Raine's voice raised in intensity. Sera had never seen her friend panic during a job.

This is bad. Real bad. The footsteps were now by the

door. *They know where the door is.* Someone definitely ratted them out. How else would the DEA know the layout of the place?

The chemist dumped another vat. This one wasn't meant for Sera and Raine. It was a gift to the agents. They'd be done for once they entered the basement. That might've solved Sera and Raine's issue for the moment, but what about the agents posted outside?

"The vent is our only option," Raine said, still crouched before it. That area was dry, but not for much longer. The fluid was inching toward Raine's sneakers. "Devil's Breath is flammable, right?"

"Yeah," Sera replied. They stared at each other, a silent conversation passing between them.

"What do you want to do?" Raine asked as another vat overturned.

The Devil's Breath concoction rushed over the ground like a rapid river. If they didn't make a decision soon, they'd be floating facedown in it.

"Let's go." Sera hopped off the table. Raine squeezed herself inside the vent.

She glanced at the chemist surrounded by fluid, her hazmat suit sticking to her legs. Their eyes met. Sera saw the dread in them. *I could help her.* That wasn't true. *No loose ends.* Another one of Lorenzo's lessons.

Sera ran to the closest table. Grabbing a lighter, she ignited three Bunsen burners and tossed them to the ground. Flames danced over the liquid, weaving into it like a spider lacing its web.

She looked at the chemist one last time as she bolted to the vent. The woman removed her mask and tossed it into the fluid. She'd rather die from an overdose than be scorched by fire. Sera would've chosen the same.

With hooded eyes, the chemist said, "This is it for me. Occupational hazard, I guess."

"I'll catch you in the afterlife," Sera responded. "At the rate I'm going, I'll be there soon." She crawled inside the vent, stopping for a second to watch the fire lick the walls.

The door to the basement burst open as Sera clasped the grille into place. She didn't stay to observe the demise of the agents. Enough time had already been wasted. Sera started her climb up. It was much harder than her descent to the basement. She was spent. The traces of drugs she inhaled and the exhaustion from fighting had taken their toll.

"Are you all right?" Raine asked. She was already a few feet above Sera.

"Fine," Sera lied. "Keep going. I'll catch up."

She analyzed the transverse joints that created small shelves on both sides of the vent. It was barely large enough to hold her, but it would have to do. Spreading her arms and legs wide, Sera positioned her feet on the bottom joints. Using her hands, she gripped the ones above her head.

Sera pulled herself up until she reached the next set of links. And the next. And the next. The metal dug into her palms, cutting through her gloves. Warm blood pooled in the hollows of her wrists. Sweat dripped down Sera's face, drenching her mask. Her arms felt like they were going to snap out of their shoulder sockets.

When she was almost at the top, Sera miscalculated her hold and slipped. She stifled a scream as her knee crashed into the sharp edge of the transverse joint. The metal cut deep into her skin. A wave of horror doused Sera as pain slashed through her like a serrated knife. She'd been wounded enough times to know she was going to need stitches. *Soon.* Gritting her teeth, Sera focused on the rest of the climb. Her vision blurred each time she moved her injured leg.

"What's going on?" Raine asked once Sera caught up with her. "I saw you lose your footing."

"I hit my knee. It's just a bruise."

Raine probably knew she was being dishonest, but Sera wasn't going to complicate their problematic situation by whining. Once they reached the top of the vent, Raine kicked through the sheet metal. Crawling out of the hole, they found themselves on the roof of the shop, twenty feet from the ground. They took a quick peek down and saw pure chaos. DEA agents ran around the building as flames devoured the windows. Sirens from fire trucks could be heard from a distance.

"Let's roll, chica," Raine said.

"Yup," Sera replied, rubbing her knee.

The two slithered on their bellies until they reached the rooftop of the empty store they'd broken into earlier that evening. That's when they bolted. Sera couldn't hide her limp. She felt as if she were sprinting with a claw trap clamped to her leg.

"You're hurt." Raine eyed her.

"Don't worry about it. Keep going," Sera said through clenched teeth.

Raine didn't argue. There was no room for that. Not

with the DEA on their backs. They ran until they reached the end of the building.

Raine peered at the ground and swore. "There's no fire escape. We have to jump." She pointed at the building across the alley. "That building has a fire escape. We drove by it on the way over here." She paced back and forth. "We can lose the tracksuits and masks when we get down. We'll take the subway home and come back for the truck later. It's from a chop shop anyway. And we wore gloves the entire time. We don't have to worry about the DEA lifting our prints."

They were cautious, but there were so many things wrong with the situation. Sera's fear of heights. The sloppy trail they left behind. *My knee.* There was no way she'd be able to make the six-foot jump. Attempting it would be suicide. "You should go. I'll find a different way."

Realization gleamed in Raine's eyes. "You're really hurt, aren't you?"

"Go, Raine." She was grateful her mask concealed the agony on her face.

Raine placed her fists on her hips. "I'm not leaving you."

"You have to. Listen, how many times have I gotten myself out of a bind? I'll get myself out of this one too. We're professionals, remember?" Sera pressed her gloved hand over her mask, soaking up her sweat. "I need you to find my dad. If someone ratted us out, the DEA might be looking for him as well."

"I don't know about this…" Raine tilted her head to get a better view of Sera.

"We've survived worse." Sera wasn't sure her statement

was accurate. They'd been in a lot of perilous situations, but the lab heist might've topped all the others. "I'm begging you, *please*, make sure my father is safe."

Raine shook her head and growled. "All right, Sera," she said with reluctance. "Call me in an hour. If I don't hear from you, I'm coming back."

"Thank you." Sera wrapped her arms around her friend.

"Take care." Raine squeezed Sera tight before releasing her.

The woman leaped like a panther, clearing the distance between the buildings with effortless ease.

CHAPTER 14

Once Raine was out of sight, Sera released an irate sigh. Despite the confidence she portrayed in front of her friend, she had no idea how she was going to get out of her mess. She walked the edges of the roof until she found a gutter spout attached to the corner wall of the building. It led to the garbage dump in the alley. She could try to slide down it. Unlike the vent, there were no joints to grip. She'd have to hold tight and pray she didn't fall and break her bones. Closing her eyes, Sera centered her thoughts. When she opened them back up, she heard footsteps behind her. *Three sets. No, four.*

"Freeze!" a male voice shouted. "Put your hands up and turn around!"

Slowly...

Slowly...

Sera faced them with her palms placed on her head. She was right. There were four agents. And their guns were pointed at her.

Nodding to a female agent, he said, "Frisk the suspect."

The woman was less than a stride away when Sera attacked. Lifting her uninjured leg, she sent a front kick to the woman's stomach. As the woman staggered back, Sera pulled the Glock out of her waistband. She fired one shot. It landed between the agent's eyes. She shot again, blind and wild. The precision she prided herself on was gone. It was about survival at that point. Five bullets hit Sera's vest. Her chest stung. Like she'd been punched with brass knuckles.

Her bullets hit as well. The agent who spoke to her dropped to the ground, a bullet lodged in his neck. The last two agents were closing in, and her cartridge was empty. Theirs were full. Shots pummeled her chest and stomach, relentless and brutal. She had to get out of there before they penetrated a part of her body her vest didn't cover. There was one thing left to do.

She thanked Cassius. Because of him, she was able to commit to her next move.

Sera flew…

Backward…

Off the building…

And landed in the recycling bin.

The impact was fierce. Broken glass cut her skin. Pain shot up her back, like dozens of needles stabbing her spine. Her shoulder was on fire. Sera pressed a hand against it. A dizzy spell engulfed her. She'd been shot.

Breathe. This isn't the first time. When her vision steadied, Sera saw the two agents on the roof with their guns directed at her. One was talking into his radio, the other reloading her weapon.

She only had a few minutes—maybe a few seconds—to get out of there. Sera touched her face, ensuring her ski mask was still in place. Peeling herself out of the bin, she unzipped her jacket. Reaching into the pocket of her vest, Sera yanked out a flash-bang grenade. She tossed it into the recycling bin setting the whole thing on fire. That took care of any DNA she might've left behind.

Then, Sera sprinted. She ignored her throbbing knee, her cuts and bruises, and her bullet wound. She criss-crossed through alleys. If she heard cars coming, she'd hide behind piles of garbage, inside abandoned buildings, underneath parked eighteen-wheelers. *Get to a busy street. That's all I need to do.* She was familiar with North Jersey. She'd been to the bars and clubs around the area numerous times.

Desperation kicked in, along with a fever. Her cheeks were hot, and it wasn't from exertion. Dots formed in her vision. Her stomach tumbled as if she were about to faint. Leaning against a wall, Sera removed the burner phone from her pocket. She couldn't call Raine. She needed her friend to look after Lorenzo. Christian and Damion were an option, but Sera didn't trust them.

There was only one other person.

For reasons unbeknownst to her, she'd saved Cassius's number on the burner phone. *I don't know him. He could turn me in.* Somehow, she knew he wouldn't. *Screw it.* It was either call Cassius or die in some back alley. Sera dialed his number. It rang once before she hung up. There were voices coming from the street. She couldn't be caught on the phone. Sera ducked behind a beat-up couch that smelled of urine. Forcing herself not to gag, she glanced down the alley.

There were six DEA agents on foot. They were stopping people passing by and asking them if they'd spotted a short man wearing a black tracksuit. Sera rolled her eyes. They always assumed the culprit was a man. Because a woman couldn't do quite as good of a job. *Fine by me.* This wasn't the time to be the flaming feminist. Once the agents moved on, Sera dialed the number again. She was barely able to hold the phone. How she would make it to her chosen destination was beyond her. The place was a mile away. It would've been a breeze if Sera wasn't near death.

The phone rang three times before Cassius answered.

"Hello?" His voice was raspy as if she'd woken him up. Considering it was three in the morning, she probably did. "Hello? Who is this?"

"It's me," Sera whispered, not only because she had to be quiet but also because speaking took a ton of effort. "Don't say my name." Cassius wasn't on a burner. Although the DEA would never suspect a billionaire golden boy, Sera didn't want to take the risk.

"All right…"

"I need you." Hmmm…she never said *that* to a man before. *I must be dying.*

"Are you okay?" he cleared his throat. "What number are you calling me from?"

"I need you," she repeated.

"How can I help?" There was confusion and discontent in his tone.

"I don't have much time to talk." She winced as a stabbing ache shot through her shoulder. "I shouldn't be asking you to do this. I don't know who else to call. Can you please pick me up?"

"Where?"

"There's a club called Lounge. It's on Central Avenue in Orange, New Jersey. Meet me in the back." She winced again. Every part of her hurt. "The area is usually packed. It's a strip of bars and restaurants. You should be able to get here in half an hour."

"I'll be there soon." Cassius didn't ask any questions, for which Sera was grateful.

"Cassius." She hesitated. "Thank you. I'll make it up to you."

"There's nothing to make up for," he said before he hung up.

With too much effort, Sera removed her masks, tracksuit, gloves, and bulletproof vest. Underneath, she wore a crimson top and black jeans. She was always prepared for spilled blood. Hers or someone else's. Those colors camouflaged blood the best. She wiped the carnage off her face as best she could. Opening one of the trash bins, Sera threw her clothes in it, along with her gun and pad saw. She grabbed another flash-bang grenade and set the dumpster on fire.

Sera removed the band that tied her hair up and patted down her locks. Tightening her jaw, she ran down the alley. She stopped to walk whenever she hit a main road, only to burst into an agonizing sprint once she reached another alley. Thirty minutes later, she was on Central Avenue. Just as she thought, the strip was packed with drunk club-goers. It was a perfect place to get lost. Walking to the back of Lounge, Sera leaned against the brick wall. She swayed, pretending to be intoxicated. It wasn't a hard act considering she was likely to pass out anyway. A few DEA agents strolled by, continuing their line of questioning. One stopped beside her and spoke to a group of women attending a bachelorette party. Sera held her breath. Her heart pounded in her chest.

When he was done talking to the women, he turned to Sera. "What about you, ma'am? Have you seen a man wearing a black tracksuit?" He looked her up and down. "He's about your height."

Sera stood straight up, attempting to look as normal as possible. "I haven't seen anyone fitting that description." The agent's face was a complete blur, like a Monet painting. *Don't faint.*

"Are you feeling okay, ma'am?" The agent inched closer, taking in her bruises. His eyes fell to her injured shoulder. "I think you're bleeding."

"Oh that?" Sera forced a laugh. "I tripped over a curb and fell flat on my face. Of course, I *also* had to fall on a piece of glass. What bad luck. I'm fine, though."

The agent continued to examine her. "Are you—"

"There you are. Where've you been?" Cassius came up behind the DEA agent.

"She's with you?" the agent asked, turning to Cassius.

An easy smile played on Cassius's lips, and his eyes glimmered with warmth. "We got separated a few streets away. She loves to wander off when she's had too much to drink." His story was simple, but there was something about the man that made you believe him. He had a certain aura—confidence without arrogance, smoothness without slime.

The agent gave Cassius a lingering look. "Have a nice night," he said with a nod.

Sera released her breath once the agent left. "Thank you," she mumbled, barely able to talk. *Tired...so...tired.*

"I'm parked down the street. Do you think you can make it?" Cassius's gaze probed Sera's face.

"Yeah, I'll make it." It took less than a minute to get to the car, but it felt like forever. Sera allowed him to hold her weight. Hopefully, they looked like two people in love. Perhaps she looked like a drunk. She'd pretend to be anybody if it took the focus away from what she truly was. A criminal wounded by DEA agents because she tried to rob a drug lab.

Cassius helped Sera into the passenger seat, delicately buckling her in. The man adjusted her with the gentleness of someone holding a priceless doll. "Are you comfortable?" His cinnamon-scented breath brushed her lips.

"I'm fine." Even in the state Sera was in, she wanted his mouth on hers.

"We'll be back in New York soon. I drive fast."

Sera barely registered Cassius taking off. She *did* register his silence. "Don't you want to know what happened?"

He briefly glanced at her before watching the road again. "All I need to know right now is how you're injured, so I can figure out what to do next."

"No, you've done enough." Sera grimaced as she sat up. "Can you please drop me off at my father's? I have to check on him. His address is—"

"You need a doctor," Cassius growled.

"My father first. I have to make sure he's all right." Sera slumped over, her head almost colliding with the dashboard.

Cassius's hand left the steering wheel. Grabbing Sera's elbow, he steadied her until she was able to lean back in the seat. "Damn it, Sera, take care of yourself. Lorenzo is a grown man. He can handle himself. Tell me where you're injured. Obviously, your shoulder. What happened to it? Anywhere else?"

Sera shivered from her raging fever. She wanted to argue, but there was no fight left in her. She could barely form proper sentences. "Bullet wound on my shoulder… cut on my knee…glass bottles…" The phone in her pocket buzzed over and over again. She didn't have the strength to pick it up. "Raine…calling…need to check on Tay…"

"You're so difficult," Cassius huffed, relaxing his grip on her elbow.

"No…please…" Sera's anxiety spiked. "Don't let go. I need you." *Why do I keep telling him that?*

Cassius's palm slid down her arm to her hand. Entwining their fingers together, he said, "I need you, too, Sera."

Those were the last words she heard before darkness claimed her.

CHAPTER 15

Sera woke up in a warm bed with plush pillows surrounding her. *Where the hell am I?* She blinked twice, attempting to clear the fog in her mind. It didn't work. Her eyes roamed the room, trying to gather clues. Hanging on the wall in front of her was a giant plasma-screen television. Pink roses sat on the nightstand next to the bed. To her left was a panoramic window, a blue chaise positioned at the corner end. Sitting on it was Cassius, his head turned as he stared out into the city. The sunlight hit the curve of his sharp jaw, accentuating his hammering pulse.

Everything came tumbling back. The horrible night she was better off forgetting. "Cassius." She kept her voice low, not wanting to disrupt his respite.

"You're awake." His focus snapped toward her, the line between his brows already on display. There were circles underneath his bloodshot eyes. He looked like he hadn't slept for days.

"What happened?" Sera's shoulder throbbed. It wasn't

as bad as it was *hours?...days?*...ago. The excruciating pain in her knee was now a dull ache. She still flinched when she tried to move.

"Let me help you." Cassius was at her side in a flash. He cupped his hands around her waist and sat her up, propping her head on three pillows. He took a seat on the edge of the bed. "You passed out in the car. I figured you didn't want to go to the hospital. I brought you to my suite instead." He rubbed his forehead. "Your burner phone kept ringing, and you said it was Raine. I took a chance and picked it up. She's the one who brought a doctor here."

"Dr. Z." Sera's face twisted in agony as she tried to move her leg. Cassius frowned but didn't say anything. "She's *our* doctor. She takes care of people like me." A physician that patched up criminals when they got hurt on the job. She didn't report them to the authorities. In return, they kept her wallet padded.

He didn't ask Sera to elaborate. He hadn't asked her a single detail about what happened. Sera was thankful for it. After what Cassius did for her, the man deserved to know. But she didn't want to tell him. She was afraid of his judgment. Afraid her actions would make him sick.

Cassius was nectar, and Sera was spoiled fruit. He was fresh air following a spring rain. She was dust after a volcanic eruption. Cassius was a hero, and she was a villain. He took care of her because it was in his nature. Sera's nature was to hurt others. Like a bee who stung knowing it would die afterward. The bee couldn't help it, neither could she. He'd hate her if he found out who she was—what she was. The realization made Sera want to claw her skin off.

"Are you okay?" Cassius placed the palm of his hand on her forehead. "You don't feel warm."

"No, I'm fine. I'm just tired." She pushed her thoughts aside. "How did you get me up to your suite without scaring the entire hotel."

Cassius gave her a crooked smile. "I sneaked through the back entrance. Ten minutes later, Raine arrived with the doctor." Cassius toyed with the string of his blue hoodie. "The doctor stitched your leg up. The cut is long, from your knee to the top of your thigh. And it's deep, down to the bone." He nodded toward her shoulder. "The bullet wound should heal nicely. It didn't hit any major arteries. Dr. Z gave me an ointment to dab on your cuts. And syringes filled with a local anesthetic that should numb the pain. You can use it a few times a day."

Sera pulled the blanket down so she could see the stitches. She realized she was wearing different clothes. Her jeans and top had been replaced by one of Cassius's undershirts.

"I changed your clothes quickly." Cassius's face reddened. "I promise I didn't do anything inappropriate."

"I believe you." Sera loathed how his bashfulness tugged at her heart. "It doesn't seem like your style. If it were your brother, then I'd be concerned."

Cassius laughed. "I don't blame you."

Sera's sutures were gruesome. She was used to it. It wasn't her first time getting stitched up. It certainly wouldn't be her last. "I'm accumulating a collection of scars."

Cassius's eyes traced each staple on her skin. Her body heated from his gaze. "I'm sure I look terrible. A lot different from the person you went to dinner with last week."

His fingers brushed over her ankle. "You're always beautiful."

Sera's stomach flipped. What was happening to her? She'd been told that many times before. Why did it hit differently when Cassius said it?

His hand moved up her calf, massaging the knots in her muscles. The tension in her body eased. "I want to lessen your pain," he said, giving her a pointed look.

There was a heaviness to his statement. Like he wanted to remove more than her physical pain.

A memory came rushing back to her. *I need you.*

She voiced the sentiment three times.

He said it back.

What did she mean by it? *What did* he *mean?*

It was her turn to flush. "Cassius...about last night..."

He placed her foot on his lap. His fingers made slow circles on her shin. "Yes?"

His calloused hand stroking her skin turned her to mush. *Stop acting like some lovesick schoolgirl. The man is your mark, for God's sake.* Her. Mark.

That was the reality check she needed. Cassius saved her, yet it changed nothing. She had to kill him regardless. "Never mind. It's not a big deal," she said, guilt weaving into her. "Did Raine mention anything about my father?"

"Yes." Cassius's softness disappeared. His eyes hardened like obsidian stones. "She's in the living room. She slept here last night. I'll grab her for you." He abruptly stood up and walked to the door. "By the way, it's two p.m. You slept for almost ten hours. Our flight to Gillette leaves at nine tonight. I can postpone it if you need more time to rest."

Sera forgot she was supposed to go to Gillette with Cassius. There was no way she could leave New York. Not after what happened at the drug lab. Too many things needed to be pieced together. *One, why was the DEA there?* She was about to cancel, but Cassius was gone before she had a chance to reject his offer.

Sera felt his absence immediately. She was cold without him there as if the room temperature had dropped to freezing. The warmth returned when Raine came in.

Her friend grabbed a remote from the nightstand and turned on the TV. Sera knew it was to drown out the conversation they were about to have.

"How are you feeling?" Raine kicked off her shoes and hopped on the bed.

"Terrible," Sera grumbled.

Raine's bottom lip was raw—a sign she'd been chewing on it. The woman was clearly stressed. "I shouldn't have left."

Sera rolled to her side, facing her friend. That slight movement made her body scream. She refused to show it. Sera didn't want Raine to feel worse than she already did. Not that the woman had anything to feel bad about. "I *asked* you to leave. It was important you reached Tay. He can't get caught." Her father had a lengthy criminal record. This drug operation would land him in jail for life. "Is he all right?"

"Yeah." Raine placed her hand lightly over Sera's. "I

found him in his penthouse. I told him what had happened. He had spoken to Christian and Damion earlier that day, and nothing seemed out of place. As of now, the DEA hasn't come knocking."

Sera released a relieved breath. "Maybe the DEA showed up to bust the lab. We just got caught in the crossfire." She doubted her own words. The expression on Raine's face revealed that she doubted it too.

"There is something strange." Raine rubbed the back of her neck. "I went to the warehouse after I brought Dr. Z here. I had this nagging feeling I couldn't get rid of. When I got there, I saw Damion and Christian walking down the street. I followed them on foot." Raine wrinkled her nose. "You know how the warehouse is in a secluded area, but three streets up there's an abandoned-looking house?"

"Yes." Sera didn't like where this was going.

"They went inside the house. There was a small truck parked out front that they were loading with boxes. It was almost six in the morning. What the hell were they doing? It doesn't make sense."

Sera frowned. "There haven't been any shipments coming in. We didn't get any money from Cassius either." Sera would've known ahead of time if Devil's Breath gems had been delivered. Even if there was inventory Sera wasn't aware of, why would it be stored in an abandoned house? "Do you think they're working with the DEA?"

"It's hard to tell." Raine leaned back, resting her weight on her arms. "I went inside the house after they left. There was nothing there. I'll keep investigating. In the meantime, we should lie low. I told Lorenzo to do the same."

"Does Christian and Damion know about the DEA bust?"

Raine stretched her legs out. "Your dad called me an hour ago and said that he told them. Apparently, they're shocked."

Sera was exhausted again. "I don't trust them. We should keep our distance for now. I'll call Tay to let him know."

"I'll tell Lorenzo. You should rest."

"It's okay. He's probably worried about me." Sera pulled the covers up to her chin. "I'll ask him to pick me up so you and Cassius can relax. You both have done enough."

Raine pressed her thumb and index finger above the bridge of her nose. "Sera, I invited him here. He didn't want to come."

"Oh...did he say why?" She kept her expression blank, but her chest constricted.

"He doesn't want to get involved in this mess." The disgust in her voice was a living thing.

Sera's spirit crumpled like a dead flower. She *knew* how her father was. She *knew* he'd react this way. But the sting was still potent every time he disappointed her. Schooling her face, Sera said, "Tay is right. He has a long criminal record. Coming here would be a bad move for him."

Raine's anger loomed like a dark wave ready to crash. "Lorenzo is a selfish—"

"Back to our plan." Changing the subject was Sera's best option. "I'll stake out the abandoned house in the evenings. I have a friend in the NYPD. I'll see if he can get any information. He's not DEA, but it doesn't hurt to try. I'll start surveillance tonight."

"No." Raine set her jaw, ready for a challenge.

"No?" Sera repeated, her temper unraveling with each passing second.

Raine ran her hand through her faux-hawk. "We need a break."

"A break?" Sera snarled. "What the fuck do you mean *a break*? The DEA might be on our asses. God knows what Christian and Damion are up to. We are either going to get locked up or screwed over by two morons. I honestly don't know what's worse."

Raine smirked. "Do you trust me?"

Sera gazed at her best friend. Her anger evaporated. It wasn't Raine's fault they were in this position. She never had to get involved in the operation. She did it for Sera. Raine was the only one Sera could rely on. Lorenzo wasn't always there, as much as it pained Sera to admit it. *He's not here now.* "What kind of question is that? Of course I trust you—with my life."

"Good. I'd have to kill you if you said you didn't," Raine teased.

Sera shoved her friend's leg. "How about I push you off this bed?"

"What if I fall facedown on these covers?" Raine's eyes glittered. "You wouldn't want me to get red lipstick on your lover's pristine sheets."

"He's not my lover," Sera said with a glare. A very weak glare.

Raine tousled Sera's hair. "Then why did you call him?"

"I don't know." She groaned, burying her face in a pillow.

"Because you trust him. Why is that?"

Sera's head throbbed. Why did Raine insist on digging into her vulnerabilities all the time? Sera flopped on her back like a fish out of water. It was a bad move. Pain seared her shoulder. "I have no clue." Sera winced. "I also have no clue why I don't want to kill him." *There...*she said it.

Raine's perfectly arched brow lifted. "Chica, you obsessed over Cassius when you were researching him. You fell for him before you met. I've told you before: he's similar to that man in your favorite romance novel."

Sera's cheeks heated. "Stop making me sound like some infatuated teenager."

Raine tilted her head in consideration. "Have you ever thought about getting out of this life?"

Damn it, the woman didn't let up. "Nope," Sera said. That wasn't true. She had thought about it. But there was no reason to fantasize about things that would never come to fruition.

Raine peered at Sera as if she were a computer. One she planned to hack. "I've been thinking about it a lot recently."

Sera's jaw dropped. *"What?"* Of all the criminals she knew—and she knew plenty—Raine was the least likely to get out...or so Sera thought. "Why? What would you even do?"

Humor danced over Raine's face. "You sound surprised. Is it because you think I'm a psychopath who enjoys this line of work?"

Sera rolled her eyes. "We're both a little strange. How else would we be able to stomach what we do?"

"I've been talking to my therapist." Raine toyed with the chain of her necklace. "Don't worry, I didn't tell her about our business. We discussed my goals and feelings. The sessions made me realize that this life isn't for me. I became a criminal because it's what I had to do to survive. Now I do it because it's comfortable—it's all I know. I'm sick of it, Sera. I've made a ton of money off other people's pain. It's not something I want to do anymore. I need to step out of my comfort zone and create healthy habits. Ones that serve my highest self."

"Your highest self?" Sera couldn't believe what she was hearing. "I didn't even know you were going to a thera-pist. *Who are you?"*

Raine pulled her knees to her chest and wrapped her arms around them. "How long can we keep living like this? Most of the people we know are either in jail or dead."

"What would you do if you gave up this life?" Sera asked, concealing her sadness—her jealousy.

Raine rested her cheek on her knee. "I've been looking at houses in the Dominican Republic. I've been wanting to get in touch with my roots, so I was thinking of opening a few beach bars there. Can you imagine how fun it would be to scuba dive all day and drink *Mamajuana* at night?" Raine smiled. It was the softest smile Sera had ever seen on her face. "Come with me."

"I can't." Sera's heart ached. She was about to lose her one true friend. Moving to a different country with Raine wasn't an option. Her place was with Lorenzo. "You should go, though. You'd look hot in a scuba suit." Sera grinned, burying her grief in a place she couldn't access easily.

Raine sighed through her nose. "I won't leave if you don't want me to. I wouldn't flat-out abandon you. But *please* think about it. This can be our last job. Your dad will be set for life. He won't need you anymore."

Last job. Robbing Cassius and killing him. Sera's heart crawled up her throat. "Raine, I want you to be happy. I'm serious, you should go. But I have to stay." Sera was who she was. *People don't change.* Okay, maybe Raine changed. She was a rare exception. "You don't have to finish the job. I'll still give you a cut." Sera forced a smile even though tears pooled in the corners of her eyes. "Get out of this city and follow your dreams. Send me postcards with palm trees on them. Don't worry about me. I'll be less stressed since I won't have to deal with you constantly prying into my life."

Raine nudged Sera on her good shoulder. "You love when I pry." She sighed through her nose again. "You shouldn't kill him, Sera. I got to know him a bit last night. He's good. Genuinely good. And he cares about you."

Sera scrubbed a hand over her face. "I don't have a choice."

"You always have a choice, chica." Cassius had said the same thing to her during their first date. "He saved you. He didn't ask questions, nor is he asking for anything in return. How often does that happen to people like us?"

"I'm so confused." Shame jammed into every nook of Sera's body until she was bursting with it. "I don't know what to do anymore."

"Don't change your mind about Gillette. Go with Cassius." Raine lay down next to Sera. "Decide what to do when you come back. I'll take care of things while you're gone. If it makes you feel better, your dad thinks you should go too. His motives are different from mine. Big surprise there." Raine's voice dripped with sarcasm. "Your dear tay wants you to gather more information on Cassius."

Sera's throat went dry. "Yes…information…good idea."

"Oh for God's sake, Sera. Stop being your father's robot." Raine blew out a frustrated breath. "Go to Gillette. I'll keep trying to hack Cassius's account. Deal?"

"Why are you so pushy about this?"

"Look, I joke about Cassius being some romance novel hero. But he's not an idea anymore, Sera. The man is *real*. And he *sees* you—*really* sees you. He validates you as a person, not just something to be used for violence or sex." Raine ran her fingers through Sera's hair. "You deserve a chance with him."

Sera frowned. "What if he doesn't actually want me?"

"You're so damn stubborn." Raine stretched her arms above her head like a lazy cat. "What do I need to say to convince you that the man is mad about you?"

"What about his sensation seeker diagnosis?" Sera stared at the ceiling. "What if that's the only reason he's enamored with me. I trigger his brain. I bet his adrenaline rush last night was similar to what he feels when he participates in extreme sports. That's why he decided to help me."

"Part of his attraction to you is due to how his mind works, but what does it matter? You're exciting and dangerous. That's your personality. He's exciting and dangerous as well. You two are the perfect match." Raine clicked her tongue. "Who's this doctor he sees. I want to scan our brains." She tapped her temple. "I'd love to know what goes on up there."

Sera huffed. "We'd probably traumatize the poor neurologists." They burst out laughing until they heard a knock on the door.

"Come in," Raine said.

Cassius stepped into the room. "I hate to interrupt this party, but Raine's phone keeps buzzing on the coffee table."

"Shit, I forgot that I had to pick my cousin up from JFK." Raine leaped out of bed and straightened her shirt. "She's flying in from California for a job interview." Strolling to Sera's side of the bed, Raine kissed her forehead. "Lylas."

"Lylas," Sera repeated, squeezing her arm.

The air felt thin after Raine left. Unease settled like smoke around Sera, rendering her speechless. Cassius, on the other hand, leaned against the doorframe, his laid-back confidence never failing him. The man was a mountain. Prominent and strong. When he was around, everything else faded in the background.

"How are you feeling?" he asked.

Sera sat up and attempted to be graceful—attempted to be the woman he met at 1 Oak. She wanted to rewind to when he thought of her as a sexy and fierce siren. But her pain was too heavy to hold the meticulously crafted mask in place. "I've had better days. I'm guessing you want to know what happened last night?"

Cassius shrugged. "Do you want to tell me?"

"Not particularly."

Cassius watched her through his thick, dark lashes. "Then don't."

"Aren't you the least bit curious?"

Cassius tilted his chin and bared his teeth. It reminded Sera of an animal sniffing out its next meal. "Whatever your problems are, I can make them go away," he said in way of response.

Sera met his eyes. "Because you're richer than rich?"

"Yes. I've made issues disappear before." Cassius's confidence remained, but a muscle feathered in his jaw. Whatever he had done didn't seem to sit well with him.

"Money doesn't solve everything." She pressed the pad of her finger against a stitch on her thigh, despising and welcoming the pain it brought her. "It can't make your personal demons disappear."

"I know. Trust me, I know." His throat bobbed, and his neck muscles twitched. The man was visibly trying to exorcise his own demons. Sera wondered what he could have done in his past to trigger such an intense response.

"Why did you help me?" she asked.

"You asked me to."

"Would you do it for anyone?"

"No." Cassius blinked with leisure. The blood in her veins heated. Warmth exploded over her skin. "I helped you because it was *you*." He ran his thumb absently over his bottom lip. "It's no secret that I have feelings for you. I just didn't know the full extent of my feelings. But something occurred to me when you fainted in my car last night." He cleared his throat. "Remember when I told you

I couldn't see a future with any of the women I've been with?" He didn't wait for a response. "Well, I couldn't *not* see a future with you. The thought of losing you put fear in a different perspective. I'd never been so afraid in my life. It takes a lot for me to get scared. I fucking volcano surf, for God's sake. It's not like I haven't lost people before. This felt different, though." A beat passed before he spoke again. "You know...we're the same in a lot of ways. I've always wondered what it would be like to meet someone like me. Sera—"

"Stop." She wasn't prepared to hear the rest of what he had to say. His frankness was chipping away at her. *Why does he always have to be so candid?* "Your perception of me is off. We're not the same. I'm not a good person, Cassius."

"Just because you think it doesn't make it true," he said, matter-of-factly.

Sera swallowed. "You barely know me."

"You keep saying that, yet here we are." Cassius slipped his hands in his pockets, his entire body relaxed. The man wore ease like a tailored suit. "There are people in relationships who have known each other for years. A lot of them get married. Most end up divorced. So, what's the difference?"

Sera huffed. "Are we talking about relationships again? Is that what you want from me?"

Cassius's lips curved upward, slow and smooth as drizzled honey. "Isn't that what you want?"

Yes. The thought slid into her mind like an unwanted houseguest. It took up space she didn't have to give. Instead of answering his question, she avoided the topic.

He's right. I am a coward. "Can you take me home so I can pick up some clothes for Gillette?" she blurted out.

Cassius's eyes sparkled with laughter. "Of course, Sera."

She was thankful he didn't probe further. He must've understood that she had the emotional maturity of an eight-year-old. He clearly decided to cut her some slack.

"Are you going to be okay to fly?" Cassius walked over to her.

"I'm used to this." She scooted her battered body off the bed. "A few shots of Dr. Z's anesthetic and I won't feel a thing."

Cassius cupped her hips, helping her get up. "By the way, it hasn't been two weeks yet. I have more time."

"What?" Sera tried to ignore her desire to close the distance between them.

"Don't you remember telling me that I have three weeks to find a way to make you *really* want me?" His gaze darted between her mouth and neck. "I said I'd do it in two." He tipped his head down and planted a hint of a kiss on her lips. "I always keep my promises."

CHAPTER 16

Sera and Cassius arrived in Gillette close to one in the morning. A driver named Mason picked them up in a Rolls-Royce Sweptail. The one-hundred-twenty-million-dollar Gulfstream jet was the first sign of how truly wealthy Cassius was. The thirteen-million-dollar car was the second. In New York, Cassius stayed at a fancy hotel, dined in expensive restaurants, and drove around in a rented BMW. All of which Sera could afford. Other than his understated attire, it was obvious the man had plenty of money. Sera had plenty of money too. *But now...*

There was rich, and there was wealthy. Cassius was the latter. Further proof of his ridiculous affluence was uncovered when they reached his home. It was hidden behind ten miles of tree-lined street and situated on sprawling green land. Lots and lots of land. Five hundred acres to be exact. Sera knew it based on her research.

When the car pulled into the circular driveway, Cassius asked if she wanted a tour. She said yes without hesitation. He walked her around the property for a few minutes—just long enough for Sera to observe the thicket of trees surrounding the estate. The fall season had turned the leaves into hues of ambers and reds. It was too dark to see their full shade, but Sera was certain in the daytime they resembled freshly lit flames licking a cornflower sky.

A giant garden sat behind lit fences on both sides of the home—neat rows of vegetables and flowers peppered the pristine lawn. Behind the house were two infinity pools, a hot tub, a patio equipped with a professional grill, a fire pit, and a bar. Although it was too far of a walk at night, Cassius pointed out the location of the horse stables, along with the tennis and basketball courts.

The house itself was beyond impressive. It consisted of white stone, large bay windows, and columns that connected to a wraparound balcony on the second story. The inside was comprised of soaring ceilings, pillars that framed winding staircases, marble fireplaces, marble bathtubs...*marble everything*. It wasn't cheap marble either. It was the Italian kind that cost thousands of dollars per square foot.

As if that weren't enough, the home had ten bedrooms, ten bathrooms, two kitchens, a movie theater, a library, a wine cellar, a bowling alley, and a pool hall. *Fourteen thousand feet of pure luxury.* Again, it was something Sera learned during her research. What she hadn't been aware of was the simplicity of the furniture. It was similar to her penthouse decor—grays and whites with clean lines and no clutter. Understated elegance. *Like Cassius.*

"What do you think?" Cassius asked, leading her to one of the rooms.

Sera blew out a breath. "It's amazing. Do you live here alone?" She already knew the answer.

"No." His eyes shone like black diamonds. "My wife is out of town. I decided to bring my mistress here while she's gone."

Sera shoved him lightly. "I'm no one's mistress."

They stopped in front of a closed door. "Fine, you can be my wife then." He winked.

It was a joke. But Sera couldn't help but let her mind linger on his statement. What would it be like to be his wife? To live a normal life. She never once thought about marriage. To her, it was as likely as flying to the moon. "I'm not wife material, but I've heard I make a great friend with benefits. Well…maybe not friend. An acquaintance, perhaps."

Desire flared in Cassius's eyes. Thick and suffocating. He leaned toward her, his eyes on her collarbone. His arm swiveled around her waist.

Sera inhaled, her heart flying out of her chest.

It was *finally* going to happen.

They were *finally* going to have sex.

Then…

Cassius turned the knob and opened the bedroom door. "This is where you're sleeping." His lips quirked as he tried not to laugh.

Sera *did* laugh. "You're an asshole. Is this how you treat your guests?"

Cassius shrugged. "Don't worry, I'll make sure you have a good time." A savage smile spread across his face as he walked backward, away from her. "I'll be in here." He stopped when he reached the door across from where

Sera stood. "If you need anything, let me know. Your suitcase is in the closet. Mason brought it up."

Sera was about to walk into the room when a thought hit her. "Wait, what about the secret? You told me if I come here, you'll tell me your secret."

"Tomorrow," he replied.

Before Sera could respond, Cassius entered his room and closed the door.

Sera changed into shorts and a fitted button-down tank top, so she wouldn't irritate her gunshot wound by pulling a shirt over her head. Grabbing two syringes from her bag, she administered an anesthetic shot to her shoulder and thigh. Sera was an expert at it. She'd used the medicine many times before. *Thank goodness for Dr. Z.* The woman was a godsend. The ache in Sera's wounds subsided immediately. She wished it could do the same for her brain.

Her mind raced as she collapsed on the bed. What was she doing there? She wasn't going to kill Cassius in Gillette. She didn't know if she could kill him at all. With a deep sigh, Sera looked around her. The space was huge. There wasn't a single part of the house that could be considered small. Even the laundry room was the size of a studio apartment. Sera was living every woman's dream. She was vacationing in a giant estate, and the sexiest man alive was a stone's throw away. Not to mention, he happened to be a billionaire. *One that has feelings for me.*

But she wasn't "every woman." She was Sera. A gutter cat masquerading as a lion. She crawled under the covers as her thoughts exploded, spreading like fireworks gone awry.

The standoff with the DEA.

Christian and Damion's suspicious activities.

Her father's safety.

Raine leaving.

Cassius.

She didn't deserve him, but because she was selfish, she wanted him. Sera tossed and turned, unable to fall asleep. She glanced at the clock on the nightstand. It was almost five in the morning. *Fuck it!* She left the room and knocked on Cassius's door. A few seconds later, it opened. Sera tried not to gawk. The man was wearing black boxer briefs. And nothing else.

His body. She didn't know anyone could look the way he did. His muscles were carved as if a sculpture personally chiseled each one with detailed concentration. His amber-brown skin shone as if he were dusted in sunlight.

"Are you all right?" he asked, his eyes hooded with sleep.

Why the heck did I wake him up? She was *not* this person. *I'm not weak and needy. I'm cold and ruthless.* A femme fatale, as Cassius called her. "Sorry, this was a bad idea." Sera turned to go back to her room.

Cassius grabbed her good arm. "Wait, talk to me. What's going on?"

Her face burned. She hated herself for being fragile. Lorenzo would disown her if he saw how she was acting. "I...ummm...I can't sleep. I was wondering—"

"Come in." Cassius stepped aside so Sera could enter. She didn't have to finish her sentence. As usual, Cassius knew what she needed. Taking her hand, he led her to his bed.

Sera crawled under the sheets, partly relieved and partly mortified. "I don't do this, okay. I'm not like this. It's because—"

"It's okay." Cassius's voice was soft and soothing. He slid beside Sera, rolling on his side to face her. Moving his palm to her cheek, he kissed her. A slight brush of his lips over hers. The sensation sent a shiver through Sera's body. She wanted more, but her mind was too much of a mess. Again, he knew that. "Go to sleep, Sera."

She curled into Cassius's chest, molding their bodies together. He wrapped his arms around her, careful not to disturb her stitches or bullet wound. She inhaled the scent of him. It was crisp and clean, like fresh soap. A smell she wanted to remember forever.

Cassius caressed her back until her eyes drooped. His hard length pressed against her stomach. But he didn't act on his desire. "I'm sorry I can't help it."

"Are you seriously apologizing for being aroused?" Sera mumbled. Her cheek pressed against his heart, the sound comforting her. "Don't worry, I like how it feels."

He buried his face in her hair. "Sera, you have no idea what I would do for you."

Do *for* you. Not *to* you. An offer to give rather than take.

Would he die for her? That's what it would come to. Blinking back tears, Sera closed her eyes and focused on his fingers caressing her back. For the first time in months, Sera fell into a deep sleep.

When Sera awoke, Cassius was no longer next to her. She glanced at the clock hanging across the bed. It was three in the afternoon. She never slept in late. *Sleep is a waste of time*, her father's motto. *It always goes back to you, Tay.* Sera's entire life was Lorenzo. She used to think that was a good thing. Now she wasn't so sure.

She left Cassius's room, stopping at her own to inject another shot and check her phone. There were no messages. *Good.* Making her way down the stairs, Sera veered to the left and looked for Cassius in his office, then in one of the living rooms, finally she found him in the kitchen.

"What time did you get up?" Sera asked, walking to the breakfast bar. *Marble, of course.* She looked around the kitchen. White cabinets and stainless-steel appliances—no frills, clutter, or decor. During her research, Sera found out the estate was a family heirloom. He moved into it when he was of age. That explained the simple furniture. Sera predicted that if it were up to Cassius, he would've moved into something less flashy.

"Around eight. I had a few things to take care of. I wanted to let you sleep in." He grabbed the kettle from the stove and poured her some tea. "No coffee, right?" He handed her the cup. "You don't put poison in your body."

Sera slid on the stool across from where he stood—the breakfast bar separating them. She took a sip of the tea, savoring the warmth gliding down her throat. "You have a good memory. Thanks for letting me sleep with you last night. It was...*different*."

Cassius flashed his perfect white teeth. "Your prose is so romantic."

Sera put her cup down. Placing her forearms on the

counter, she leaned forward. "I have many other talents." She gave him a once-over. He was wearing a white T-shirt and gray sweatpants. He looked amazing, but she preferred him half naked. "I'm disappointed you put more clothes on."

Cassius also placed his forearms on the counter and leaned forward, his face inches away from hers. "Last night was foreplay."

"What will today bring?" Sera cocked one brow.

Cassius's smile turned lethal. His eyes flicked to her mouth. "Are you hungry?"

"For what?" Sera could've devoured him whole.

Cassius stood abruptly. "Mason got us breakfast." Turning to face the stove, he retrieved a couple of boxes from a brown paper bag. "Tofu scramble, fruits, roasted potatoes, and nondairy pancakes. It's technically lunch, but breakfast food is good any time of day. Don't you think?" The amusement in his tone was blatant.

"I agree. How nice of Mason. I like a man who knows how to please. Where is he, by the way?" Sera asked with nonchalance. "I'm curious to see what other forms of pleasure he's willing to dole out."

Cassius laughed. "He's with his wife and kids." He plated the food and placed it in front of her. "I'm kidding. Mason is single. If it were up to me, I'd be the only one pleasing you. Not Ruby, not the man at the Mandarin. Just me."

"That's called a relationship. I don't do those, remember?" Sera took a bite out of the tofu scramble. It was divine. "Besides, who'd be pleasing you? Most men aren't satisfied with one woman."

Cassius took a sip of coffee and licked the small drop that dripped on his bottom lip. Sera tried hard not to stare. "You must be confused about my love life, or lack of one. I barely go on dates anymore. I'm super busy, so I end up neglecting that part of my life. It's like forgetting to eat because you get caught up with projects and activities."

Sera's unexpected laughter almost made her choke on her food. "Did you compare finding love to eating? I thought I was the one with the romantic prose."

Cassius's mouth twisted to one side. "What I'm trying to say is that dating is the least of my priorities. When I tell you I want you…it means I want *you*. Only *you*. I've already admitted that I can't *not* see a future with you."

He didn't wait for a reply before he continued. Sera was relieved. She wouldn't have known how to respond. "There's something I want to ask you. My parents know I'm back, and they're hosting a family dinner tonight. We usually do it on Sundays. Since I've been gone for a while, they want to get together this evening at six." He swirled the coffee in his cup. "It'll be my mom, dad, and sister."

"That's fine." Sera polished off her plate. "I understand." She didn't understand. Lorenzo wouldn't visit her after she got shot doing a job for *him*. Cassius's family was dying to see him. He hadn't even been gone a month. "I'm sure they missed you. If it's okay with you, I'd love to peruse your library. I can sit on your veranda and read."

Cassius grabbed her empty plate and put it in the sink. "Sera, I'm asking if you want to come with me. I told them I have a friend visiting."

Sera's heart skipped a beat. Meeting Cassius's parents

put her on edge. What if they didn't like her? *Why do I care?*

"I can tell them I'm busy," Cassius said quickly. "I know you might not feel comfortable going since you're hurt."

"No, I'd love to go." The thought made her nauseated, but she owed Cassius. He'd done so much for her. "I'll give myself extra shots tonight so I won't be in any pain. I can cover my bruises with makeup." Sera had done it many times before. With all the injuries she had endured due to her line of work, plus having a father like Lorenzo, her cosmetic skills were perfect. "What do I wear?"

Cassius gulped down the last of his coffee. "Wear whatever you want."

"Should I tell them how you looked up my dress the night we met?" Sera batted her lashes.

Cassius stretched his arms over his head. His muscles rippled beneath his shirt. "I already told them how you took your clothes off during our first date. *And*, like the good western boy that I am, I turned you down."

"I wouldn't brag about rejecting me. It'll show people what a horrible decision maker you are." Sera stood up, nice and slow. She wanted him to take in her scantily clad body.

And he did. Cassius's eyes roamed her curves. His expression revealed that he was done waiting. He walked around the breakfast bar. "Is the opportunity still available?" The intensity in his stare made Sera's pulse sprint.

Sera nodded, not trusting herself to speak.

"Good." Cassius wrapped an arm around her waist and pulled her to him. Sera stood on her tiptoes as he parted her lips with his tongue. His length pressed against her stomach, hard and ready.

Sera ignited. Every nerve—every fiber of her being—craved him. Cassius's touch, his scent, his breath felt familiar. Like he was always meant to be hers. It frightened her. She wanted to curl into him and pull away at the same time.

"Do you want to stop?" Cassius asked as if he sensed her hesitation. "Is your shoulder or leg bothering you?"

"No, I'm fine." Sera ground her hips against him. She'd wanted Cassius before she met him. Her fears weren't going to hinder the moment.

"You have no idea how many times I've dreamed of being inside of you." Cassius's kisses turned rougher—more urgent.

Sera welcomed it. The longing in her belly stretched lower, the pressure unbearable. "Show me." Careful not to bother her stitches, Cassius lifted her onto the counter. "Take your shirt off."

Cassius abided, sliding his top over his head and throwing it to the ground. He removed her shirt next. His knuckles brushed over her bare breast. "Beautiful," he whispered, taking her hardened nipple in his mouth.

Sera tossed her head back and moaned.

"I want to taste you," he murmured. "I'm going to spread you on this counter and lick you until you come. Then, I'll do it again."

"Okay." It was a lame response, but her tongue wouldn't cooperate. Sera had never come with anyone before. She also never cared about anyone before. *Maybe this time I can.* She wanted to. Her body demanded it.

Gripping Sera's waist, Cassius's mouth moved down her stomach. He started to slide her shorts off.

Then, his phone buzzed in his pocket.

"Ignore it," Sera panted.

"I plan to." His teeth nipped the skin of her belly.

The phone was silent for a few seconds before it rang again.

And again.

And again.

"Shit." Cassius stood up. "I'm *so* sorry. I need to see who it is. It's probably important." Sera tamped down her frustration as Cassius checked who called him. "It's my company's lawyer, Ava," he said with a frown. "I have to take this."

Sera groaned as she slid off the counter. When they went skydiving, Cassius cut off their heated moment because he had a meeting with Ava. Sera was going to murder this lawyer. "Fine, I'll wait until you get off the phone." She put her top on and buttoned it up.

"I have to get ready to go to my parents. I'm assuming you need to get ready too." Cassius kissed her forehead. "Don't even say we can do it fast. I'm going to take my time with you."

Sera placed her fists on her hips. "Better be worth it."

"It will be, sweetheart." Cassius ran his thumb over the curve of her jaw. "I'm going to take the call outside since I have to talk to Mason as well. He's tending to the horses right now. I'm *really* sorry, Sera."

She waved a dismissive hand in the air, ignoring the hot tension between her legs. "I have to check in with Raine anyway."

Once Cassius left, Sera headed to her room and dug the burner phone out of her suitcase. Raine picked up right away.

"Hey," Sera said. "How's everything going?"

"No news so far. You've been gone less than twenty-four hours." Raine's voice was muffled as if she were eating. "Lorenzo's good, and the DEA hasn't shown up. The abandoned house is still empty." Raine's chewing sounded through the phone. "How's it going over there?"

Sera sat on the floor of the walk-in closet and leaned her head against the wall. "Cassius is perfect. Oh, and I hate my life."

Raine was quiet for far too long. Finally, she spoke. "Drop the job, chica. Who the fuck cares what Lorenzo wants? He's been mooching off of you for years. Your dad is a greedy bastard."

"This job has to happen, Raine." Sera rubbed her temples. Everything hurt, and it had nothing to do with her injuries. "I just want to get this over with. When we have the money, and he's..." She couldn't bring herself to say *dead*. "It'll be painful, but this is worse. It sucks to be with him, knowing it has to end."

"You really want to do this? Fine. Let's get this done as soon as possible." There was a challenge in her tone.

"As soon as possible?" Sera repeated. Raine was calling her bluff. But there was no bluff to be called. "How?"

Raine exhaled. Her agitation whooshed through the phone lines. "I'm assuming he has a desktop computer. Do you think you can access it at some point without him seeing you?"

Sera bolted up. "He's not in the house. I can do it now."

With Raine on the line, Sera went to Cassius's office. Passing a couch and a bookcase, she sat behind his desk. Her palms perspired as Raine walked her through the process.

"It's easier to hack computers when you're in the user's actual Wi-Fi." Raine was chewing again. Sera couldn't believe her friend was eating while she was in the midst of a panic attack. "Let's check what systems are on his network using the ARP protocol. Before we attack, we should do a Nmap connect scan, a TCP—"

"Raine," Sera growled. "I don't know what you're talking about. Tell me what to do. *Step by step.* We need to hurry. I don't know how long he's going to be gone for."

"Okay, Okay. Sheesh." Raine huffed. "I have my laptop in front of me. I'm going to connect on my end."

Raine spouted off a bunch of different numbers and letters sequences. Sera's hands shook as she typed it in. It seemed like hours had passed when it had only been a few minutes in reality.

"How much longer?" Sera asked.

"Give me a second. I think I have…" Raine paused. "Oh shit, I'm in. I have access to all four accounts." Raine giggled…*actually giggled*…like a schoolgirl giddy over her first crush. "Here's the deal: I'm going to use an algorithm based on a random number generator. It'll send dollar amounts between one and one thousand to *two hundred* offshore accounts. Cassius won't notice until it's too late. When that's done—"

"Then it's my turn." Sera clicked to close out of the computer. She never despised herself more than she did at that moment.

"Yes, ma'am." Raine giggled again. "I can't believe I got into his account. I doubted myself for a while there."

"That's great," Sera said, her throat closing up.

"Give me the thumbs-up, and I'll hit the button." Raine seemed less enthused than she was a second ago.

"Might as well do..." Sera's ears perked up. Footsteps were coming toward the office. Two men were speaking to each other. One sounded like Cassius, the other like Mason. "Shit, he's coming. I have to go." Sera hung up the phone and closed the rest of the tabs with speed she didn't know she possessed.

She barely made it under the desk before Cassius entered the office. *Please don't come here.* He wouldn't have seen her. Sera was tucked in a crook behind one of the cabinets. But it would've been a close call.

She peeked between the slither of a crack, where one part of the T-shaped desk connected to the other section. Sera caught a glimpse of the two men by the bookcase. Cassius stood next to Mason, who was placing a manila envelope on one of the shelves. Unlike Cassius, he was the epitome of what Sera assumed Wyoming men looked like. A brown cowboy hat sat on his head. It matched his snap-up shirt and cowboy boots. A silver belt buckle held up his fitted blue jeans.

"Thanks for taking the papers to Ava and picking up the antidote," Cassius said.

Antidote? For what? Sera's phone screen lit up. *Raine.* Thank goodness her ringer was silent. Sera ignored the text, but another came through.

What do you want me to do? Should I start draining his account?

Sera wiped her palms on her shorts. *Say yes. Say yes. Say yes.*

"I can see why you can't stop talking about this girl. Sera is gorgeous." Mason's voice distracted her train of thought.

Cassius laughed. "I don't always talk about her."

"I've known you since we were young'uns. I've never seen you this captivated with any woman. I know it's not how she looks either. Beauty never held your attention."

Cassius didn't say anything for what seemed like forever. On an exhale, he said, "Sera told me on our first date that she'd end up breaking my heart. She's not lying, but I'd still risk it. I'll take what she'll give me. Pathetic, huh?"

Mason patted Cassius's shoulder. "There's nothing pathetic about you."

Hello? What do you want me to do?

Hi?

No need to answer. This isn't important at all.

Hellllloooooooooo?

Sera wiped away a tear that slid down her cheek. With shaky fingers, she wrote Raine back.

CHAPTER 17

Cassius sat in his car, waiting for Sera to finish getting ready. He told her he needed to make more business calls, which was true. Mainly, he wanted a few minutes to digest the conversation he had with Ava. The private investigator hadn't been able to dig up much. At least not yet. The only new information he received was that Lorenzo stayed at his friend Butch's house quite often. When he was home, no one came by, nor did he speak to anyone on the phone. The bug Henry put in Lorenzo's penthouse proved to be pointless, so Cassius asked for the man's car to be bugged and tracked. He asked that Christian's and Damion's cars be tracked as well.

The good news was that Ava did a wonderful job executing Cassius's requests. *Like she always does.* He wouldn't know what to do without that woman. Ava had Mason deliver the Devil's Breath antidote to Cassius that morning. The sugar glass vials filled with the liquid cure were in his trunk. Unbeknownst to his parents, their estate had additional cameras and security systems in place. Cassius's house was secured as well.

She did chew him out for bringing Sera to Gillette. *How high do your dopamine levels have to be until you're satisfied? You put your life at risk whenever you participate in those crazy sports, but this is even more insane. If you want a rush, get a dominatrix. Not a woman who might be an accomplice to your murder.*

Cassius agreed that Sera staying at his estate wasn't the smartest idea. He had no clue what role she played in the assassination plot. *She told me about the drugs*, he reminded himself. But that could've been part of the scheme.

He didn't know what to make of Sera. She came to his bed for comfort, yet that morning her walls were up again. The woman used seduction and sex to deflect her vulnerability. Cassius bet if he asked her why she went to him at five in the morning, she would've asked him to take her to the airport. Cassius couldn't let her go. He wasn't some deranged stalker. If she wanted to leave, he wouldn't stop her, but it would hurt a lot. He truly couldn't see a life without her.

Cassius made up his mind. He had to talk to her and get to the bottom of everything. He was planning to wait till Sera came to him, but time wasn't on his side.

He'd ask what transpired the night she got shot. He'd ask about the drugs Christian and Lorenzo were smuggling into the country. She revealed the information to him days ago. It hadn't been brought up since.

There was something else, too—one other thing the investigator found. This piece of data had to do with his brother. It made Cassius want to retch. He knew Christian's moral compass was skewed, but not to *this* extent. It strengthened Cassius's resolve that Christian had to die. He was a danger to society.

Cassius wondered if Sera was a part of Christian's repulsive venture. He realized by now that she wasn't the most upstanding citizen. Her virtues were questionable. *She wouldn't do this, though. Would she?* Maybe he had a blind spot when it came to her. Cassius scrubbed a hand over his face. *Christian, you sick bastard.* To think he was at the warehouse, only blocks away from an abandoned house where his brother stored the—

Sera stepped out of the front door and whistled. "You might not be flashy with your clothes and furniture, but you sure love your toys." She hopped into the passenger's seat of Cassius's car. "Bugatti Veyron Super Sport. Impressive. I love the matte gray color."

Cassius cocked a brow as he put the car in drive. "What do you know about Bugattis?"

Sera ran her hand over the dashboard. "I know it goes from zero to two hundred seventy miles per hour in thirty seconds. I know it was once recognized as the second-fastest car in the world. I used to attend car shows with my dad when I was little. I've always wanted one of these. What can I say? I like fast things."

Cassius pulled the car onto the private tree-lined street that ran ten miles. "Want the experience?"

Sera grinned. "What are you waiting for?"

Cassius didn't need any more encouragement. He took off. Thirty was for amateurs. Cassius hit two hundred seventy miles in twenty seconds. "What do you think?" He looked over at Sera. Her jaw was clenched. She gripped the sides of her seat so hard her knuckles had turned white. "Shit, Sera, I'm sorry. Are you all right?"

Her gray eyes flickered with lightning. "Do it again. This time go faster."

Cassius abided. He reached the target speed in eighteen seconds. "Better?"

Her face was savage and feral, like a storm cloud ready to burst. "Can I drive?"

Cassius hesitated for a moment before changing seats with Sera. He barely finished giving her instructions when she gunned the engine. She hit the target speed in sixteen seconds. Cassius almost proposed to her right then and there.

Cassius took notice of Sera's attire when they arrived at the Batista estate. Gone were the six-inch heels and tight outfits he adored. Instead, she donned a button-down jean shirt with rolled sleeves. It was haphazardly tucked into skinny black jeans. And she wore flats. He'd never seen her dress so modestly. Was she trying to impress his parents? Not that they would've cared what Sera wore. The thought that she tried to make an impression was endearing. Of course she'd deny it if he brought it up.

"What?" she asked, closing the car door.

"Nothing." He shoved his keys into the pocket of his jeans. "I'm just admiring how beautiful you are."

Did her cheeks turn pink? *Interesting.* He was certain

many people had told her the same thing, probably in a more poetic manner.

"What's your family like?" Sera fiddled with the diamond bracelet around her wrist. *She's nervous.*

"They're not uptight and snobby," Cassius said as they walked up the short flight of stairs to the door.

He couldn't blame her for feeling intimidated. He, who grew up on the estate, understood how decadent it appeared. It was set on three hundred acres of land and had a spectacular view of the mountains. It was similar to Cassius's home: white stone, columns, balconies, and massive windows. A ten-car garage stood to the left of the house. A few feet away was a full-size cottage his parents used as a guesthouse. On the right was a koi pond with a waterfall. Beside the waterfall were steps leading to a sculpted garden filled with flowers and fruit trees.

Before he could unlock the door, Sera grabbed his wrist. "I'm not used to this. I don't know if I'm any good at it." In the short time he'd known her, she'd never looked afraid. Not even when she had a bullet lodged in her shoulder.

"Hey." He cupped her cheek. "Don't let the house fool you. My parents and sister are the most laid-back people you'll ever meet. I bring a different girl here every family night, and they all feel at ease," he jested.

That got her to relax. Pushing him lightly on his chest, she said, "All this time I thought I was special."

"You are special." Cassius opened the door, not wanting to give Sera time to dwell on the comment. She was fragile. Physical injuries couldn't break her, but emotions could.

Sera's eyes widened when she stepped in. "Shit, this is gorgeous."

It was, and Cassius knew it. The manor resembled an eighteenth-century Neoclassical home. It had twenty-thousand square feet of living space. Unlike his simple furnishings, Cassius's parents opted for a highly embellished Rococo style. The wood on every piece of furniture was imported Brazilian rosewood. He couldn't wait until Sera saw the ballroom. At thirty years old, he still couldn't believe he grew up in a house with a ballroom. Not to mention the fifty-foot swimming pool in the back.

"The house is decent," he teased, leading her from one room to the next. His parents and sister were probably out on the veranda. That's where they held their weekly dinners. Cassius wanted to show Sera around before introducing her to his family.

"It looks like a castle," Sera whispered. "I can't believe you grew up here. When I was a kid, I would've sold my soul to live in your garage." She laughed. There was no humor in it. "I bet each bedroom is bigger than the apartment my dad raised me in."

Cassius wondered if Sera realized how much her icy facade had melted. The more time he spent with her, the more she showed her true self. From her outburst in Maman to her confession the night she got shot. Sera didn't resemble the shielded woman he'd met at 1 Oak anymore. Her walls weren't fortified like they were at Kusina. There were cracks in it. Cassius was determined to peel them open.

They entered a parlor decorated with gold brocade ottomans and baroque-style settees. Balloon-back throne chairs were strategically placed around the room. Slipper seats surrounded dapper card tables holding fancy chess sets. And ridiculously expensive paintings hung on the eggshell-colored walls.

Sera stood in the middle of the room, her hands wringing together. She looked like a deer that had accidentally entered a lion's den. Cassius speculated on how many people had seen her that way before. Maybe her dad. Maybe Raine. *And me.*

Cassius sat on a slipper chair and played with a piece on the chessboard. He was suddenly aware that he didn't know much about Sera's childhood. Her adoration for her father was obvious, and she did tell him about her mother's absence, but that was it. As an adult, the woman was rich and confident. *Was she always like that?* "Sera, how *did* you grow up?"

She was silent, taking in a Picasso on the wall. When he thought she wasn't going to answer, Sera said, "We were dirt poor. We lived in Section 8 housing. Rats and roaches were my friends." She laughed another humorless laugh. "Tay and I were always starving. When our food stamps ran out, we'd wait until the grocery stores closed, then we'd go dumpster diving. Tay gave me most of the food. He refused to eat until I was full." She glanced over her shoulder at Cassius. "There was one store in particular that had the best fruits and vegetables. We'd break their fence and grab as much as we could."

Cassius maintained a flat expression, although his mind was reeling. He never imagined the woman standing in front of him—manicured nails, Louboutin flats, and a Hermès purse—had scoured trash bins for food. "I'm sorry, I didn't know."

She shrugged and walked over to the next painting. "No one does, except for the people I grew up with. I'm not keen on divulging information about my life to others."

She told me. "Thanks for trusting me," Cassius said.

Sera's shoulders stiffened as if she hadn't realized she'd confided in him. "*Nu Couché* by Amedeo Modigliani, 1917." She nodded toward a painting. It was a clear attempt at redirecting the topic.

Fine. He wouldn't push her. Not when it came to her upbringing. Cassius glanced at the portrait of a nude woman lying on her back. "My sister bought it for my parents on their twenty-fifth wedding anniversary. You know a lot about art?"

Sera faced him, her hands clasped behind her back. The dead eyes he hadn't seen in a while were back. Decades of a hard life seeping the color out of them. "I know how much certain paintings cost. *Nu Couché* is worth one hundred seventy million."

Cassius already figured Sera wasn't *just* a business owner. People that ran legitimate companies didn't have gunshot wounds. Unless they were unfortunate victims of a crime. Sera was no victim. Ruthlessness lingered on her skin like strong perfume. There were times when she was with him where it evaporated, but it never fully dissolved. Most people would run, but it turned Cassius on instead. "Do you steal paintings for a living?"

Her lips quirked as she walked toward him. Cassius slid his chair out, allowing her to stand between his legs.

"I don't steal paintings." Sera cupped his cheeks. "Anymore. I don't steal paintings anymore. Even if I did, I wouldn't steal from you or harm you in any way." Her right hand stayed steady. A sign that she spoke the truth.

Cassius slid his fingers into the waistband of her jeans and pulled her close. He kissed her, deep and slow. Sera's shoulders softened. He sensed her barriers crumbling once more. He wished Sera realized how much she cared about him. Her body exposed the intensity of her emotions, and he longed for her mind to stop fighting it.

With reluctance, Cassius broke their kiss. "Time to meet my family." Taking her hand, they walked out of the parlor and toward the veranda.

Sera's awe was apparent when they stepped outside. Past the patio was an enormous swimming pool with a diving platform that held boards of different heights—the highest being thirty-five feet. Cassius's parents had it installed for him. By the age of seven, he was performing backflips off it. The other side of the pool contained waterslides that rivaled those at a water park. And behind the pool was a marigold garden framed by Autumn Blaze maple trees.

"Hey, everyone," Cassius said in a way of greeting.

Sera's hand squeezed his. An involuntary, nervous act. Cassius gave her a reassuring smile. She gave him a tight one in return.

He was well aware of how formal his family looked. His mother, Antônia, loved her skirt suits and pearls. His father, Lucas, adored collared wool cardigans and slacks. Jacey, his sister, had a face that appeared contemptuous at all times. Cassius had been told that the woman looked unapproachable. In truth, she was the warmest person he knew.

Right when he thought Sera was about to make a run for it, his mother stood and walked over to them. "Cassius." She hugged him. "This must be your *friend*." The way she said it made him groan internally. He felt like a teenager bringing home a girl for the first time. In a way, he was. He hadn't brought a woman to his parents' house in years.

"My goodness, you're *gorgeous*," Antônia said to Sera, hugging her as well.

Sera flinched. Cassius predicted it had nothing to do with her injured shoulder and everything to do with the fact that she wasn't used to affection.

"Thank you for the invite, Mrs. Batista," Sera said. He was awed by how quickly she found her composure. "You have a beautiful home. Cassius told me wonderful things about his family. I'm grateful to meet all of you."

Cassius hid a smile. How could he forget that Sera was a chameleon? She pretended to be who she needed to be. *Except she's not pretending.* She *was* grateful to meet them. Her right hand didn't quiver, and the clouds in her eyes parted a bit. For someone like Sera, it was progress.

"Oh please, call me Antônia. We're happy to have you." She squeezed Sera's wrist and stepped aside so Cassius's father could greet her.

"You can call me Lucas," Cassius's dad said, striding up to Sera. He wrapped his strong arms around her. "We're huggers in this family. I hope you don't mind."

"Not at all." Sera laughed. A genuine laugh.

Jacey was right behind Lucas. "Mãe is right. You are

gorgeous." She embraced Sera. "Why are you hanging out with Cassius again?" She flashed a wide smile, her expression softening. The unintentionally disdainful look faded from her features. "I'm kidding. My brother is the best." She waved them over. "Come and sit. We have so much food."

Sera started to follow, but Cassius hooked a finger in the belt loop of her pants. "Are you all right? I hope you're not overwhelmed."

"I've never been hugged this much in my life." It wasn't an insult. Her tone was flat, but Cassius heard the appreciation in it. He had a hunch Lorenzo wasn't the most doting father out there. *He wouldn't even visit her when she was hurt.* He used her to fund his share of the drug operation. And he brought her along on dumpster-diving sprees when she was a kid. Cassius wondered how many other heinous crimes Lorenzo exposed her to.

"Thanks for coming here with me." Cassius's eyes bored into hers.

Sera didn't break his gaze. Something took shape between them.

Something that made him realize that even if he never saw her again—even if decades had passed—his heart would always belong to Sera.

CHAPTER 18

"Sit next to me, Sera," Cassius's sister said.

Sera silently thanked Jacey for interrupting the wordless exchange between her and Cassius. It was too intimate for her liking.

She didn't know what she was doing anymore. She'd lost complete control of herself. The text to Raine played in her head. *Why did I tell her no?* When Raine asked if she should drain Cassius's accounts, Sera told her to wait. *Tay is going to hate me. There has to be another way, though.*

When she went home, she'd convince Lorenzo they didn't need Cassius. She couldn't stop Christian from hiring someone else to take care of the hit, but Sera wasn't doing it. How could she assassinate the man she...*what?*

Sera wouldn't allow herself to finish the sentence. She and Cassius could never be together. He was better off with someone like himself: classy and good-hearted. Someone who didn't commit crimes and fuck random strangers on a Friday night. Although...the idea of Cassius with someone else made Sera want to vomit. *If I can't be with him, the least I can do is not kill him.*

"Here you go," Jacey said, pulling a chair out for Sera.

"Thank you." Sera brushed her tremulous thoughts aside as she took a seat next to Jacey. Tonight was not the right time to break down.

Cassius slid beside her and rested a hand on her knee. "Don't be nervous. My family will love you," he whispered.

"Of course we will," Jacey said with a smile. Apparently, his voice wasn't as quiet as he thought. "Now, would you like some orange juice?"

Embarrassment heated the air around Sera. Thankfully, she was well versed in the art of nonchalance. "Oh, yes, please," she said, keeping her tone light. "It looks amazing."

"It's freshly squeezed." Jacey poured Sera a glass. "We grow the oranges in our greenhouse."

They have a freaking greenhouse? What did these people *not* have? Sera took a long drink. It tasted like pure sunshine. "My goodness, this is amazing."

"I'm glad you like it. Cassius drinks gallons of it when he's here," Jacey said, passing Sera a breadbasket.

She grabbed a piece of bread and dipped it in a porcelain canoe dish filled with olive oil. Sera discreetly studied the Batistas as she nibbled on the crust. She was an assassin, after all. Observing people was what she did for a living. Habits like that weren't easy to break.

First, Sera scrutinized the woman sitting across from her. Cassius's mother was stunning. She wore no makeup, except for red lipstick, which flattered her glowing brown skin. Her black hair was tied in a tight bun, and pearls draped her long neck. Gracing her tall, lithe frame was a tweed Chanel skirt suit. In the Philippines, there was a mythological dancing deity who was rumored to be one of the most beautiful women on the planet. There were no pictures of her, but Sera imagined she looked something like Antônia. Cassius's mother had the willowy elegance of a ballerina and a graceful face that could only belong to a goddess.

Lucas, on the other hand, was the embodiment of old money. He lounged next to his wife, lazily sipping his brandy. Wealth oozed out of the man's pores, spilling onto his clothes. There were no labels on his outfit, yet he still managed to convey his affluence. He didn't seem to do it on purpose. It was just who he was. His silver-collared sweater and black pressed slacks complemented his salt-and-pepper hair, the snifter in his hand completed the look. All he needed was a high-back chair, and it'd be like he stepped out of a *Forbes* photoshoot.

Then, there was Jacey. She was the spitting image of Cassius. They had the same curly hair, amber-brown skin, and night-black eyes. They could've been twins, except Cassius's face was open and encouraging. Jacey's features were cold and distant—much like Sera's. She'd been prepared to grit her teeth during dinner while Jacey threw out haughty remarks. It turned out, Cassius and Jacey had more in common than Sera thought. The woman was as welcoming as her brother. Her geniality took Sera aback. The whole family took her aback.

They seemed so...*sincere*. They also intimidated her. The Batistas were the epitome of sophistication. The top of the food chain. Sera felt small next to them. Like a fraud, they'd be able to see right through.

"Cassius told us you're vegan," Antônia said, interrupting Sera's musings.

Thank God. She was getting ready to excuse herself and find a bathroom, crawl out of the window, and hop on a plane back home. "Yes, I've been vegan since college," Sera said, clearing her throat.

"That's wonderful." Antônia folded her hands on the table. The engagement ring on her finger was the size of a rock. The glimmer in it was blinding. "I asked our chef to make a Brazilian-inspired vegan meal. We wanted to give you a taste of our culture."

Lucas took a bite out of his bread. Wiping the corners of his mouth with a napkin, he said, "Wyoming is famous for steak, steak, and more steak. It gets a bit boring. I'm glad we're trying something new."

Sera was stunned yet again. A family who just met her, prepared an entire meal to suit her needs. No one besides Raine had ever done anything for her without their own self-interest in mind. "You didn't have to do that. I don't want to be an inconvenience."

Lucas waved his hand in the air. "It's not an inconvenience at all. We like being pushed out of our comfort zone."

"Absolutely." Antônia unfolded the napkin next to her plate and placed it in her lap. "And the food smelled heavenly."

"Yes, it does." Jacey spooned olive oil onto her plate. "Sera, I'm so glad you're here. I thought Cassius was going to be single the rest of his life."

"Oh, I...ummm...we're not..." Sera looked at Cassius, hoping he'd have the proper response.

"We're not what, Sera?" Cassius asked, his eyes gleaming with laughter.

Luckily, the food came out before she made a fool of herself.

Sera's stomach rumbled when she saw the selection. The main dish was vegan *Feijoada*—black bean stew served in a clay pot. The table was also stacked with plates of banana empanadas, yuca fries, spinach in coconut milk, okra tomato salad, jeweled rice and lentils, tofu moqueca, and much more. Sera had never tasted Brazilian cooking before. She was eager to dig in.

After they piled their plates, Lucas turned his focus on Sera. "So, what do you like to do for fun?" he asked.

Sera thanked the heavens he didn't inquire about her businesses or family. She didn't want to taint the night with lies. "I like to read, and I like..." *Shit.* She couldn't think of anything else. *That* was her only hobby? The revelation made her flush. She never considered herself boring until now.

Cassius placed a hand on her upper back, rubbing the spot between her shoulder blades. "Sera likes to drive fast cars," he said, saving her from further humiliation. "She drove my Bugatti today. Zero to two hundred seventy in sixteen seconds."

Jacey whistled. "Damn, Cassius, you have some competition. Did you show Sera your dirt bikes and the super-cool track you built?"

"You have *dirt bikes*?" Sera's eyes widened, her nerves

calming as the discussion continued. "I want to try riding one."

"Nooooo." Antônia placed a palm on her forehead. "I'm going to have a heart attack. My *darling* son traumatized me with those bikes."

Lucas laughed. "I don't suppose Cassius has told you about his dirt bike fiasco?" He reached for his wife's hand and squeezed it.

"No...he hasn't. I have to hear about this." Sera smiled, all teeth and humor. *What's happening to me? Am I seriously enjoying this wholesome family dinner?*

"Now we're sharing stories about me?" It was Cassius's turn to flush. "Please don't bust out the baby pictures next."

"When did you become so shy, big bro?" Jacey rolled her eyes. "When Cassius was eight, Mãe and Pa bought him a dirt bike. Instead of easing into it, he decided to try some tricks. He broke his arm doing a flip on it. We took him to the doctor to get a cast. The following day, he cut his cast off and attempted another trick. I personally think my big bro is a badass for doing that. Mãe and Pa are traumatized."

Sera's jaw dropped. "Our skydiving date makes *so* much more sense now."

"Skydiving date?" Antônia cut into her empanada. "You drive fast cars, skydive, and want to ride dirt bikes. You are Cassius's dream come true."

Sera almost choked on the yuca she was chewing on.

She was saved from responding when Lucas said, "My son has some interesting antics, that's for sure. Cassius, did you tell Sera about the time I was sleeping, and you tried to poke my eye out? You said you wanted me to be a pirate."

Cassius chuckled. "In my defense, I was five and thought pirates were the coolest people in the world. I felt terrible after."

"Really?" Antônia huffed. "I remember you stole chocolate out of our hidden candy jar ten minutes after your attempted assault."

The whole table broke out into a fit of laughter.

"What's your favorite story about Cassius?" Sera asked once everyone calmed down. She surprised herself with her own question. *Why do I care to know?*

Lucas tapped his chin. "Christmas...I believe..."

"Is it, honey?" Antônia rubbed the top of her husband's shoulder. "Are you sure?"

"I don't know about that, Pa." Jacey's lips twitched as she tried to suppress a smile.

"I have a feeling I'm missing some information. Someone give it up," Sera teased. *Who am I right now? Why am I acting like this? Why can't I stop?*

"Well, since you asked..." Antônia filled her glass of wine. "When the kids were little, they'd try to stay awake on Christmas to catch Santa Claus." She looked at Cassius, her eyes overflowing with fondness. "They even rigged traps using bungee cords and butterfly nets. When they fell asleep, Lucas and I would mess with the traps so it looked like Santa got away." A soft smile graced her face. "One Christmas, Lucas climbed the roof of the guesthouse to stamp fake reindeer hoofs on it. The kids were in bed, or so we thought. It turned out that Cassius was awake. He came outside and found Lucas on the roof. My husband had to act like he was fixing shingles at midnight. He spent an hour pretending to hammer random edges of the roof."

Another burst of laughter rose over the table. As the night progressed, Sera felt more at ease. In fact, she was more comfortable with the Batistas than she was with her own father. She couldn't remember a time where she smiled so much that her cheeks hurt.

The conversation flowed for hours. Lucas and Antônia talked about their kids as if they were precious gems, but they didn't speak of Christian often. When he was brought up, the pain in their voices was undeniable. They raved plenty about Jacey's and Cassius's accomplishments. Jacey's science experiments were one of their favorite topics. And they apologetically mentioned Cassius's target shooting medals. Cassius and Lucas had once been hunting enthusiasts. Sera thought the sport vile, but she envied the camaraderie between Cassius and his dad.

Sera tried to remain detached, but she found herself opening up to the Batistas. They were inviting, like a cozy fire on a winter night. You couldn't help but want to get a little closer—eager to feel its warmth. Before she knew it, Sera was telling them about herself. She mostly spoke of her college experiences and Raine, avoiding the topic of her father at all costs. It was the first time in her life that Sera felt safe around others. The first time she didn't feel the need to wear armor.

As cheerful as the gathering was, Sera's heart crumpled a bit. How she wished she'd grown up with the Batistas. Their life seemed like a fairy tale. And it had nothing to do with their wealth. Lorenzo had bought Sera presents for Christmas, but he left them under the tree for her to open alone while he went out with his friends. In the evenings, he'd stumble home drunk with a woman on his arm. Sera spent those nights trying to drown out sounds of them having sex.

Instead of making traps for Santa, Sera disabled alarm systems to break into homes. Like Cassius, Sera broke her arm, too—twice. Lorenzo flipped a car they'd stolen because he was high. Sera smashed her arm against the passenger door, the impact brutal enough to break her bones. The second time, Lorenzo broke Sera's arm himself. He claimed it was due to her disobedience.

Sera had never come across a family like the Batistas. She thought they only existed in those feel-good movies. The kind that people watched during the holidays. Christian made them out to be wicked—elitists and snooty and selfish. They were nothing of the sort. Jacey was hilarious, constantly cracking jokes. Antônia and Lucas were vibrant and vivid. When they gazed at each other, it was as if there was nothing else in the world they'd rather look at.

It reminded Sera of...of...

Of when Cassius looks at me.

Realization slammed into her solar plexus. She found it hard to breathe. Sera took a swig of water, gulping down the taste of terror. Did Cassius love her? He claimed he had feelings for her—that he needed her. He even confessed he wanted her in his future. *Do I love him?* She tried to swallow the notion—push it past her stomach. It got lodged in her throat.

As if Cassius detected the chaos brewing inside of her,

he reached over and brushed her wrist. The sensation calmed her instantly. His touch felt like home—a plea she didn't know she made. Against her will, Sera's entire heart bowed to him. And something she didn't have a name for came to fruition.

"Is everything okay?" Cassius asked, low enough so no one else could hear.

"Yes, I'm fine," she said with a shaky smile. She hated how in tune he was with her. "Your family is great, by the way."

"I'm sure they think you're great too," Cassius said quietly. Leaning over, he kissed the curve of her jaw. A shiver ran down her spine. "Are you still hungry?" he asked a little louder.

"Yes, dear." Antônia pushed a platter toward her. "Eat as much as you like."

"I don't think I can take another bite." Sera put her hand on her belly. She must've eaten five plates of food. It was the best meal of her life. "Everything was delicious. Thank you for accommodating me."

"We would've never tried vegan food if it weren't for you. We'd be missing out." Antônia set her fork and knife on the plate.

"Do you two have plans tonight, or are you staying to watch a movie with us?" Jacey asked. "Pa wants to watch some history flick, Mãe and I want romance."

Cassius faced Sera. "We end family nights with a movie." He tucked a piece of her hair behind her ear. "I figured you'd be too tired to stay."

"I'd love to watch a movie." She wasn't just saying it either. The idea of leaving the Batistas made her sad. She wanted to stay there forever. With them, she felt secure. *Normal.*

"Perfect." Lucas slammed his palm on the table. "Our guest can decide."

Sera didn't want to reveal the fact that she thoroughly enjoyed romance flicks. She also wasn't sure if immersing herself in a love story was a good idea. Not while she was sorting her feelings out for Cassius. She picked an action flick.

Antônia pushed her chair back and stood up, a glass of wine in her hand.

"It's settled. Let's head to the theater room."

Sera got up to follow Cassius's mother. A sensation skimmed over her—a memory of an emotion that had been stored away in a dusty attic. The Batista family pulled it out that evening and polished the grime off.

Sera dug inside of her until she recalled what it was. *Happiness.*

Cassius's phone buzzed as they were leaving the veranda. Sliding it out of his pocket, he glanced at the screen and frowned. "I have to take this call. It's work-related." He gave Sera an apologetic smile. "Do you want to go to the theater with everyone else? I'll be there soon."

"Sure, I'll see you there," she said.

Jacey tossed her arm over Sera's shoulder. "We'll take good care of her."

Cassius made sure they were gone before he picked up the phone. "Hey, Ava, what's up?"

"I found out some more things." There were no formalities when it came to Ava and Cassius's relationship. They cut right to the chase.

Cassius glanced around the corner, ensuring no one was there. "Make it quick. I'm with my parents for family night."

"You brought Sera?" Ava's voice raised.

"I don't have time for one of your lectures." Cassius leaned against a column. "Get to the point."

"Are you sitting down? If not, then you need to."

"Ava, get to the damn point," he repeated. His patience was wearing thin, but he did as he was told and sat at the table.

"I've been the family lawyer for twenty-seven years. It's my duty to protect the Batistas." A clicking noise ensued. The woman was lighting a cigarette. "It didn't take long after we bugged your brother's car to get additional information. Henry found out that Christian holds his private meetings in his Benz. I guess he believes it's a safe place." Ava inhaled and blew out. "There's a woman named Raine. Henry is looking into her files. She's some sort of genius hacker."

Cassius picked up a fork and twirled it between his fingers. "I know who she is." Sera's closest friend is a hacker. Her father was a drug dealer. What kind of shit was this woman into?

"Do you know Raine grew up in the slums with your little girlfriend?" Ava's voice was dry as sandpaper. This time it wasn't from the years of smoking. "She crawled out of that dump and got a scholarship to Yale. She chooses to use her computer science degree for criminal activities."

Sera told Cassius that Raine owned businesses in the city. *Don't they all.* He knew better, though. It was too bad. Raine seemed like a sincere person after she dropped her icy charade. She tossed it aside the night Sera got shot. Her concern for her friend overpowered her performance. "Go on," Cassius said.

"I don't know how to tell you this." Ava's grief echoed through the phone lines, louder than a cannon's blast. "Christian concocted a plan months before you came to New York. Getting you to the city was part of the plot. He doesn't truly care if you funded his operation because Raine plans to hack your bank accounts anyway. The money will be split five ways: Christian, Damion, Raine, Lorenzo…"

The forked dropped out of Cassius's hand, clattering on the ground. "Who's the fifth person?"

"You know," Ava said quietly. Her sharp tongue and quick wit were gone.

"Yeah, I do." He couldn't bring himself to say her name. The woman in the theater with his family planned to rob him. *I wouldn't steal from you.* She said those words less than two hours ago. And her hand didn't shake. *Why didn't her hand shake?*

"That's not all." Ava cleared her throat. "First, I want to reassure you that you're not in danger right now. Raine hasn't been able to hack your accounts. The encryptions we've put in place are strong." She cleared her throat again. "Your killer won't execute the order until they have the money. They know if you die before they gain access to your funds, the money will go to your family. That'll create a new problem for them. On top of that, there will be an investigation for your murder. Bottom line: as long as they can't get into your accounts, you're good. Don't give Christian anything, not even the fifteen million you promised him. I'm going to call the bank and your accountants. We'll get your funds locked down by this evening."

"Good." His pulse raced. "What about the killer? Did Henry find out who this person is?"

"Yes." *The way she said it...*

Foreboding slithered down Cassius's spine like a wolf spider. Its pointed fangs pressed against his skin, waiting to sink in. "Who is it?" He knew before she spoke the name aloud.

"Sera."

Sera was his assassin. *How?* Cassius prided himself on reading people. Why didn't he see this coming? *Because she's not going to go through with it.* Sera had a stellar act everyone fell for, but she wasn't able to hide her true self with him. Like a snake who couldn't help shedding its skin. The woman loved him. He knew it even if she didn't. When Sera looked at him, it was as if she found something she'd been searching years for. She sought him out when she was hurt and went to him when she couldn't sleep. She held on to him as if he were her lifeline.

"Damion has a concern." Ava broke his reverie. "He's worried Sera will back out of the hit. He thinks that she's developed feelings for you. Lorenzo eased his worry. He claims his spawn—his endearing term for his daughter—won't ever betray him."

Ahhh, there is that issue. Sera was loyal to a fault when it came to Lorenzo. He was her Achilles' heel.

"Do you want me to take care of Sera and your brother? Henry's man is waiting for our call."

Cassius should say yes. Except... "I'll take care of it myself. Get me the details on how she works. What's her most common method of assassination?"

"What are you planning to do?" Ava asked, her tone heavy with disapproval.

"Don't worry about it. I've got this under control." Cassius stood up and paced. "She won't kill me yet. You said so yourself. They need my money first."

"Cassius." There was a clicking noise followed by an inhale and an exhale. "You're playing with fire."

"Aren't I always?"

"This is different." Ava groaned. "This isn't one of your adventures. This is *murder*. They are going to *kill* you."

Adrenaline rushed through his veins like a waterfall, almost knocking him over. "I'll be fine."

"I don't know who's worse, you or your brother," Ava snapped. "If your brain wasn't so screwed up—" She cut herself off. "I'm sorry, I didn't mean that. This whole thing is so fucked up. If anything happened to you..."

"I know." Cassius wasn't offended. It wasn't the first time he's heard the remark. His family never degraded him, but others had. He learned to brush it off. "You have nothing to worry about. Don't forget, this brain of mine is the reason Batista Holdings doubled its profits." Cassius's risky yet strategic moves were an asset to the family business.

"Yeah, yeah." Ava sighed. "I'll trust you with this situation for now. If things go awry, I'm stepping in. You might be my boss, but there's no way I'm letting you get killed."

"Deal," Cassius replied.

Another sigh. "Let's say she doesn't kill you. What are you going to do? Marry her and live happily ever after, knowing she intended to assassinate you at some point?"

"Why not?" Cassius smirked. "You know I like those who haven't had all the rough ridden off them." He repeated what he had said to Sera on their first date.

"You're impossible." Ava snorted. "Goodbye."

She was right. He was walking a tightrope when it came to Sera, but he'd been through plenty of perilous adventures. *I survived them all.*

Cassius would find a way to keep himself alive. He was sensible enough to know it might not work out.

Someone might have to die, but it wouldn't be him.

CHAPTER 19

Sera and Cassius left the Batista estate close to midnight. *Please visit us again.* That was the last thing they said to her. Too bad there would never be an "again." Sera would return to New York, and whatever was going on between her and Cassius would be over. She'd continue with her criminal ways. He'd get married, have two kids, and adopt a Labrador retriever. *At least I'm not going to kill him.* She wouldn't have that on her conscience.

Sera wanted to scream. She spent the evening with the most amazing family. And the man in the driver's seat of the Bugatti...*a fucking Bugatti*...was a godsend. She wondered how the Batistas would feel if they knew about the millions of dollars she laundered each year. Better yet, the forty-two kills she had under her belt. There'd be no "please visit us again" if they found out who she was.

"You're quiet. What's up?" Cassius asked as he steered the car out of the gates.

"I'm just thinking about tonight. You have a wonderful

family." Sera was too tired to act cold and disinterested. She didn't want to anymore, not around him. "Thanks for introducing me to them. I don't think I've had that much fun in years."

"They thought you were wonderful too." They stopped at a light. Silence enveloped the car. The only sound was the clicking of the turn signal. Finally, Cassius spoke. "Remember when I said I had a secret to share with you?"

Sera nodded. "A secret for a secret."

The traffic light turned green, and Cassius made a right turn. "I want to take you somewhere." There was an edge to his voice that Sera had never heard before.

Cassius drove until the highway veered off to a narrow paved road that transformed into a windy dirt path that climbed a mountain. All of a sudden, there was nothing but trees and the night sky. Civilization was left behind. Absence of light pollution exposed the millions of stars—balls of fire that glimmered like diamonds—embedded in a sea of black velvet. The moon hung above them like a white pearl.

"Where are we?" Sera asked.

Cassius glanced at her sidelong. "Bighorn Mountains. Right now, we're at three thousand feet. The mountain goes up to thirteen thousand feet."

"Thirteen thousand feet?" Sera had never been to the mountains. She'd never been outside of New York City. As rich as she was, Sera had only traveled once—to Colombia. She went for a few days and conducted business the entire time. Sera didn't have time to travel for fun. There was always so much to do for herself and Lorenzo.

"Don't worry, city girl." Cassius flashed a sweet smile meant just for her. "We're not going up that high." He made a sharp turn. "We're almost to our destination." He made another sharp turn.

They ended up in a clearing, surrounded by thickly settled trees. In the middle of it was a tiny log cabin. Cassius reached over Sera, opened the glovebox, and retrieved a small controller. He pressed a button, and the porch light turned on.

The cabin was simple, much different from Cassius's home and the Batista estate. The outside—made entirely of wood—had giant windows, a chimney, and a wrap-around porch. There was nothing fancy about it. The entire structure could fit in Cassius's kitchen.

Sera loved it. The place had a rustic charm. "What is this?"

Cassius stepped out of the car and strolled toward the house. Sera followed his lead. "It's one of my houses," he said.

One of his houses. How many did he have? When they reached the porch, she saw that there was a swing bed. How comforting would it have been to sit there and stare at the night sky? Sera wondered how many women Cassius had done that with, possibly on the same swing bed she was staring at.

Shutting out the vision, she entered the home. Sera was shocked to find that the inside consisted of one small room. To the left was a king-size bed with a gray duvet cover. To the right was a small kitchen with granite counters, a few cabinets, a small fridge that reached Sera's thigh, and a wood-burning stove. The bathroom, next to the kitchen, contained a toilet and a sink.

"The shower is outside," Cassius said, leaning against the kitchen counter.

Sera opened the sliding glass door a few feet from the bed and stepped outside. Attached to the house was a wooden stall with a rain shower head. A smile played on her lips. Cassius could've bought the entire mountain, but he chose a modest cabin.

"I wanted a simple place where I can get away. No one knows about this cabin, not even my family. You're the first person I've brought here," Cassius said, coming up behind her. His body was so close. Sera felt the heat exuding off him. She yearned to curl into his fire and let it reduce her to ashes.

She waited for him to close the distance between them. Instead, he said, "Here's my secret: when I was twenty-one—fresh out of college—I climbed Mount Everest to celebrate my graduation. I already climbed it when I was fourteen, so I was confident that I knew what I was doing. I was cocky as hell about the journey.

"Honestly, I was cocky in general. A rich asshole who thought I held the world in my palms. You would've hated me." He let out a nervous cough. "Three Sherpas guided me during the climb." He fell silent, his breath tight and hitched.

Sera didn't turn around. Somehow, she understood that he wouldn't be able to finish the story if she did. "We were at twenty-six thousand feet when I got the call. We only had three thousand feet left till we reached the peak. On the last day of trying to summit, we were halfway to the top when base camp radioed me. A bad storm was coming, and they advised me to return to camp. I didn't listen. What's worse is that I didn't tell the Sherpas about the storm. I never gave them a choice. I played God with their lives." His voice cracked. "You should've seen the fear in their eyes when the avalanche swallowed their bodies. I suffered a few broken bones, but I survived. Sometimes I wish I hadn't.

"They died because of me," he said through clenched teeth. "My selfishness killed them. They had wives and children. I robbed the women of their husbands and the kids of their fathers." Cassius's sorrow crystalized the air. "My family made the whole thing disappear. That's what happens when you have billions of dollars at your disposal." Sera didn't have to see his face to know what he felt. Self-loathing radiated off him in waves.

"There was an incident with Christian years before the Everest situation. It caused a lot of scandal. We didn't want our family to be publicly humiliated again." He barked a dry laugh. "My parents had someone wipe out my plane tickets, my name in any logs...*everything*. You'd never know I went to Everest twice. Only my parents, Jacey, and our company lawyer know...and now you. Christian had already been disinherited at that point. So you see, I'm doing great. I'm wealthier than I was nine years ago and still privileged to the teeth. But what about the lives I've ruined? They can't bounce back the way I did."

It all made sense now: Cassius's generous contributions to three families in Nepal. How that money came out of his personal account. Not the Charitable Giving

Account. Sera recalled her research. She remembered reading about Cassius's Everest adventure when he was in his teens. There was nothing about Everest after that. *They really did get rid of all the evidence.* Was it guilt that led him to pursue a philanthropic path? The man donated to charities and started foundations as often as others went grocery shopping.

It dawned on Sera that Cassius might not have always been the knight in shining armor he was today. He claimed he was cocky and arrogant back then. Did the incident at Everest force him to become a better human? All her life, Sera believed that people couldn't change, but this scenario proved her wrong. *And what about Raine?* She was about to open bars in the Dominican Republic.

"You were right when you said money can't make personal demons disappear." Cassius's voice cracked once more. "But you were wrong when you assumed that I'm a good person. I'm not the golden boy everyone makes me out to be. I'm a fraud."

Sera whipped around to face him. "No, you're not. What happened was awful. I won't sugarcoat it—your actions were selfish. But you're not a fraud. I know about your humanitarian efforts. Your brother told me." That was a little lie. Christian would never shine a positive light on Cassius. "You can't beat yourself up forever. Forgive yourself. Your charitable work has changed lives for the better." Without thinking about the consequences of her next statement, she said, "You've changed my life."

"You've changed my life, too, Sera." Their eyes were fixed on each other. Feverish intensity burned in Cassius's gaze. "Enough about that topic." He swiped a dismissive hand in the air. "I didn't bring you to the cabin so you can watch me wallow in my own self-pity." He smiled, and the anguish was ironed out of his features. "Thanks for coming to Gillette. It means a lot to me."

She leaned against the shower stall. "So this is what it feels like."

Cassius furrowed his brows. "What?"

"This is what it feels like to live a normal life. To have a wonderful man with a wonderful family. To—"

"Who's your man?" he asked, the corners of his lips twitching.

Embarrassment boiled under her skin, bringing a heated flush to her cheeks. How could *that* escape from her mouth? "I didn't mean to say that you're *my* man. I know you're not. I was just—"

Sera didn't register his approach. All of a sudden, his arm was around her waist, his body pressed against hers. Bowing his head, Cassius kissed her neck. His mouth moved to her jaw next, then the lobe of her ear. "Call me whatever you like. I'm yours."

Sera put her palm on his chest. She had to push him away. The situation was out of hand. Years of grooming herself to be unbreakable, and this...*this*...was where she ended up. "Cassius..."

"Do you want me to stop?" He lifted his head and looked at her, concern darkening his eyes. "We don't have to do this."

She should definitely tell him to keep his distance. But because she no longer knew how to command her emotions, Sera wrapped her arms around his neck and pressed her lips into his. Her self-imposed shackles clattered to the ground.

Cassius growled as Sera ground her hips against his hard length. Their movements went from gentle to rabid, like animals that had been starved for weeks.

"Wait, your injuries," Cassius panted.

"I doubled the anesthetic shots. My shoulder and thigh are numb." Sera unzipped his pants and stroked him.

Cassius released a sharp breath. "You might tear your stitches."

"I know how to sew myself back up."

"What about—"

"Cassius." Sera placed a finger on his lips. "Shut up."

He abided.

Sera didn't know how they ended up inside the cabin with their clothes scattered everywhere. In their frenzy, they knocked over the lamp on the nightstand. It crashed to the ground, shards of glass shattering on the floor.

"Your lamp," Sera said breathlessly.

"Fuck the lamp," Cassius replied with equal breathlessness.

When they reached the bed, Sera's terror returned. *This is wrong...all wrong.* Sera didn't want to *just* have sex with him, and it terrified her. Sure, she craved his body, but she also yearned for his heart. Sex was supposed to be sex. A primal need that shouldn't involve the heart.

"Cassius, wait."

"What's wrong? Are you hurt?" He placed his hands next to her shoulders, holding himself up with his arms. He leashed his movements, but his eyes were savage. Barely restrained.

"I don't think I can do this. It's too much." That's all Sera managed to express. Talking about feelings wasn't her strong suit.

"All right," Cassius said slowly as if it pained him to talk. He moved off her and lay by her side.

Agonizing silence blanketed the cabin. Gathering her strength, Sera turned to face him. A muscle feathered in his jaw, the cords in his neck flexing when he swallowed. "Are you mad?"

Cassius gazed at the ceiling. "No, I'd never get mad about sex." He closed his eyes. Opening them again, he said, "Can you give me a minute or two to get myself together? I'm so hard right now. I need to think about something that'll turn me off, like my brother."

Sera laughed. "That'll do it." She brushed her hand over his cheek. "You almost broke the deal."

Cassius scrunched his face. "What deal?"

"You claimed you wouldn't sleep with me until I was in love with you." Sera slanted her eyes at him. "And you claimed you'd get me to fall in love within two weeks. You should be happy I stopped us. You would've lost your own bet."

Cassius turned to his side, propping himself up on his elbow. "Sweetheart, I won that bet." He brushed his thumb over her bottom lip. "You *are* in love with me."

Sera's breath almost stopped. He was right. She was in love with him. She realized it during the time with his family. She was barely able to admit it to herself, so she certainly wasn't going to say it aloud. "That is not tr—"

"I love you too," he said, with gentle quiet.

This time her breath did stop until she remembered

inhaling and exhaling was mandatory. Only two people had ever expressed their love for her: Lorenzo and Raine. Lorenzo's love was conditional, though. He'd take it and return it as he saw fit.

This is a disaster. She hadn't been careful with Cassius. He should've been the one she was most careful with. "Don't do this, Cassius."

His hand moved to her waist and drew circles on her skin. "Let me in, Sera."

"We've known each other less than two weeks. How do you know you love me?" Sera's eyes burned, tears threatening to escape.

Cassius placed his hand on her back and pulled her closer. "I might take extreme risks, but I'm not a man who acts on emotions alone." His heartbeat thudded against her breast, the sensation soothing her. "Why do you think at thirty, I've never been in a serious relationship? I'm not even interested in dating, as I've already told you. When I tell you I love you, I mean it. I don't use that term lightly. You love me, too, Sera." His voice lowered to a growl. "Tell me you don't."

Sera opened her mouth, prepared to refute his accusation, but her lips wouldn't form the argument. A minute passed before she spoke. "Do you recall our dinner at Kusina? I asked how enamored you'd be if I wasn't this exciting person that you think I am. Maybe you believe you're in love with me because I arouse that sensation seeker part of you.

"When we met, you thought I was mysterious and erotic. A woman who couldn't be tamed. Everyone sees me in that light. I *want* them to see me that way. I practiced to *be* that person." She might as well be honest. The conversation was too deep to be anything but. "What if we're in a relationship and you find out my idea of fun is watching history documentaries? What if I'm boring?"

"I love history documentaries." Cassius kissed the corner of her jaw. "I doubt someone who can drive two hundred seventy miles in sixteen seconds will ever bore me. You enjoy thrilling adventures as much as I do. You can have those experiences without being a criminal. That's what you are right...a criminal?"

"You know I am." Sera huffed. "I've been shot five times. So no, I don't find the lifestyle fulfilling. I also have no interest in joining a stamp collecting club either. I guess you're right about me." Sera didn't add that Cassius was always correct when it came to his theories about her. "I don't know where to go from here, though."

"We can go wherever you want, do whatever you want."

Sera was hyperaware of his hard length resting on her stomach. Fire curled inside of her, a living thing awaiting release. "How about we start over again. I won't stop you this time."

"You sure?" he asked, his lips a hair's breadth from her own.

"Yes." Sera craved him for far too long to hold back. It would be messy. Their feelings for each other complicated matters. At that moment, she didn't care.

Cassius reached to the side of the bed where his jeans were strewn. He dug a condom out of the pocket and placed it beside them. Slipping his hand between her thighs, Cassius caressed her core with his deft fingers.

"Spread your legs." The command in his tone made her quiver.

Sera draped her good leg over his hip. "Is this better?"

"You tell me." He slid a finger inside of her, followed by a second one. His thumb made lazy circles on her clit. "You're so wet. I want to taste how wet you are."

Her breath came out ragged, goose bumps flaring over her flesh. She was close. Cassius had been caressing her for less than a minute, but she was already about to burst. The pressure built, impatient in its need to climax. Yes... yes...yes...

No! Sera grabbed Cassius's wrist. "Wait."

Cassius's eyes gleamed with predatory intent. He instantly reined it in. "You've never come before? Is it a control thing?" He knew. *Of course he knows. He hasn't been wrong about me yet.*

"It's not that I don't want to." Sera's skin crawled. Trepidation pushed its way to the surface. Tidal waves of feelings rushed her, growing in magnitude and complexity. Her muscles went rigid as she tried to stay afloat—tried to tackle thoughts she didn't fully understand. They packed into her chest, drowning her. It wasn't just her body that was naked in front of him. It was her soul as well. "I...ummm...I can come if I do it by myself, not with someone else. It...ummm...it scares me."

"Let me be the first." Cassius's gaze dropped to her lips. "You're safe with me."

Sera hesitated, her mind spinning. She only felt safe around Raine. *No, that's not true.* She felt safe with Cassius's family. And with him. He was the one she ran to when the DEA chased her down. For some odd reason, he knew her more than anyone else did. "Okay, I'll try."

He gave her a reassuring smile before guiding her onto her back. Crawling on top of her, Cassius kissed her forehead, her eyes, her mouth. He traveled to her breast, rolling her nipple between his lips. Sera arched her back and moaned. Her fears remained, but she kept them at bay and focused on the sensation of his tongue.

"You're perfect, Sera," Cassius whispered. His lips trailed down her body, lingering on each of her scars. He poured love into them, his devotion a healing ointment on her wounds.

Cassius dipped his face between her legs. Sera gasped as his lips glided over her slit. He stroked her clit, his tongue slipping inside of her. Sera bucked her hips, bringing him deeper.

"I'm close…" she said, a ripple of electricity shot through her. Sera's stomach clenched as her release approached.

Could she do this? If she gave herself to Cassius—if she allowed him to take over her body, then what? *My shell of comfort will explode. I won't know how to put it back together.* She built the shell for a reason: so she couldn't get hurt. It also blocked her from finding true happiness. Vulnerability was the price she'd have to pay in order to experience joy. Was that something she was willing to do?

She was right on the edge. Her oncoming climax clouded her decision.

She wanted to …

Or maybe she didn't …

"Wait...I..." Sera pressed her hands against his shoulders.

"Trust me." Cassius looked up at her, pure adoration in his eyes. "I love you."

His words unfurled her. Untied her knots.

Gradually...then rapidly...everything felt right. The monochromatic world she lived in burst into an array of colors. Lost pieces of herself emerged. Internal wounds softened. And her lungs exhaled without effort. The alienated life she'd built didn't make sense any longer.

I love you too. It was a statement she made in her head. To Cassius, she said, "I trust you." Sera released her grip on his shoulders and allowed herself to feel all of him. The softness of his tongue. The strokes of his fingers. She spread her legs wider, opening up for him. Sheer bliss unfolded in her lower belly. "I'm about to..."

"Come for me," Cassius said.

That was an order she could easily obey. He curled his finger inside of her. Sera shook as she cried out her release.

A hurricane of emotions spiraled through her, morphing from chaotic to serene—a storm turned into a drizzle. The revulsion and self-hate Sera expected didn't appear. There was no disgust that followed her loss of control. Instead, she found infinite freedom.

"Where the hell did you learn to do that?" Sera's legs couldn't stop shaking, tremors still running through her.

Cassius's tongue continued to sweep over her, bringing her down from her climax. When her body stilled, he sat up. "I'm guessing you enjoyed yourself." His chin glistened with her wetness. It made her ache for him again.

"I *thoroughly* enjoyed myself." Sera gazed at him beneath hooded eyes. "I want you inside of me, Cassius."

"I'm here to please." Cassius moved up her body. He kissed her, light and gentle. It was a sharp contrast to the unsatisfied desire between his thighs.

She reached down and wrapped her fingers around him, her hand pumping his shaft. "You're killing me." He groaned.

Sera grabbed the condom beside her and ripped the packet open. She rolled it on his length and guided him inside of her. "Is this better?" Her hips undulated, bringing him deeper. "Or is this better?"

He groaned again. "You feel so fucking good, Sera." His arms quivered as he held himself up. "You have no idea how difficult it is not to come right away."

Sera understood. She was close to exploding herself. How was it even possible? He just entered her. "Let me get on top. I'll do the work this time."

"Your thigh..."

"If you bring up my injuries one more time, I'm going to strangle you. This is not my first time getting hurt. I can handle it."

"If you insist." Cassius smiled—savage and vicious. Without breaking their connection, he rolled onto his back, Sera straddled above him. "I've pleasured myself plenty of times to visions of you bouncing on my cock."

"That makes two of us." Sera pushed up on her legs and slid down on his length. "Let's see if reality is as good as our fantasies."

"It'll be better." He growled.

Splaying her hands on his chest, Sera rode him fast

and hard, taking his length to the hilt. Cassius's black eyes darkened even more. Grabbing Sera's ass, he worked her back and forth. "Kiss me," he said, his voice barely discernible.

She leaned down until her breasts were pressed against his chest. They kissed with fervor, grasping for something more. Hot pressure crept to her core. She was almost there. The quickness of Cassius's breath revealed he was close too.

Cassius broke the kiss. "You're the one I've waited for my whole life. I love you." He repeated the last words over and over again.

Sera's tethers came apart. She was sick of shutting him out. She lived a dangerous existence, but when it came to relationships, Sera played it safe. Not anymore. "I love you too," she whispered.

Cassius smiled. "Say it again."

Sera's legs tensed, and her body spasmed. "I love you." She barely got the words out before her fierce climax took over. Cassius's thrusts quickened, and a second later, Sera came again.

Gripping her hips, he pumped into her one more time and roared his release.

Once they got hold of their breaths, Sera rolled off Cassius. She ran her fingers over her stitches, then her shoulder. Everything seemed to be intact. There were a few tingles of pain, nothing another shot couldn't take care of.

Resting her head on Cassius's chest, she said, "I don't know what to do."

"Move to Gillette and be with me." As if Cassius hadn't

already shocked her enough, he decided to add *that* to the conversation? Maybe he was joking.

Sera knew he wasn't. "I can't do that."

"Why not?" He posed the question so calmly. It was as if he were suggesting they go to the movies instead of asking her to pick up her life and start a new one.

Sera lifted her head to look at him. "I have my father to think about. What about my businesses and my penthouse?"

"From what I can see, you barely go into the establishments you own. Have your managers continue to run them. You can take care of the rest from here. People do it all the time. I'll pay off the remainder of your mortgage. You can rent out your penthouse or leave it empty." He hesitated. "I can do the same for Lorenzo. He can move here too. I'll make sure he still gets a cut out of Christian's business." His lips set into a line as if it pained him to offer her father anything. It probably did. No one liked Lorenzo except her.

Sera tossed the idea around in her mind. "I can't just up and leave."

"What do you have to lose?" Cassius played with a piece of her hair. "You can go back to New York if you don't like it here. You'll still have your companies and your penthouse."

"Cassius, you don't *really* know who I am. You don't know the things I've done." This was Sera's opportunity to reveal her true self to him. *Well, the partial truth.* She wasn't ready to admit she had planned to assassinate him. *He'll hate me even without that information.* It was only fair that she opened up to him. Cassius confided in her. The

Mount Everest fiasco could ruin him and his family. He disclosed the incident anyway. "There are things about my past that would disgust you. Aren't you wondering what happened the night you picked me up in Jersey?"

"So tell me," Cassius said.

Sera inhaled. On her exhale, she spilled her secrets. She told him about Lorenzo's cruelness—the brutal hands and vicious tongue that left scars on both her skin and heart. She told him how she laundered money through her businesses—money she made from her job as an assassin. She told him about the three Yakuza gangsters she slayed during their dinner at Kusina. She told him what happened the evening at the drug lab. Lastly, she told him about the entire Devil's Breath operation, leaving out Christian's plot to rob and kill him. A plot Sera would put an end to when she returned to New York.

The words tumbled out of her mouth in one long sentence. She feared if she stopped talking, she wouldn't have the courage to continue. Cassius allowed her to speak without interruption.

When she was done, Cassius remained quiet. His finger rubbed his bottom lip, deep in thought. Then... "Will you continue your killing spree when you move here?"

That was his response to the rap sheet she listed? "No, Cassius. I won't continue my killing spree *if* I move here. You make me want to be a better person." Sera stared at his chest, suddenly shy.

Cassius cupped her chin, tilting her head to look at him. "I'm sorry about what your father did to you. No one should have to endure those things."

"No, no." Sera shook her head. "I painted him in a bad light. He did a lot of wonderful things as well. He tried the best he could. I owe him everything."

Cassius furrowed his brows. Sera thought he'd argue with her, but when he spoke, he said, "What's between you and Lorenzo is your business. If you come here, I'll help you legitimize your companies. You won't have to worry about getting shot or going to prison anymore. Your dad won't be at risk either."

Could it work? What did she have going for her in New York? *Nothing.* Her one true friend planned to move to the Dominican Republic and start a new life. New York brought her nothing but bad memories and pain.

"What would I do here? Be a housewife." She wanted to take back the words as soon as they left her mouth. "I didn't mean I was going to be your...what I'm..."

Cassius cocked a perfect brow. "Is that what'll get you to move here?" Amusement danced in his eyes. "I'll marry you today."

Sera punched him playfully in the shoulder. "Baby steps."

Cassius pinned her good leg with his own. "You can do whatever you want here." He planted a kiss on her forehead. "You still have businesses to run. I have plenty of work at my company if you're interested. My family will keep you busy, I'm sure. Plus, I have a bunch of toys you can play with." He dipped his head to the crook of her neck, his lips hot against her skin. "Move here, Sera. I swear I'll make you happy."

Maybe this was her chance at a normal life. *What would Tay say?* Knowing Lorenzo, he'd choose to stay in New

York. She'd continue paying his bills and giving him an allowance. For once, being separated from him didn't bother her. She just needed to take care of one issue—canceling the hit on Cassius. She'd resort to blackmailing Christian if she had to. Sera didn't give a damn about him. She never wanted her father to be part of the drug business anyway. *For what?* So he could end up in prison. She should've put a stop to the operation a long time ago.

"A month trial period. I'll leave most of my stuff in New York and keep paying my mortgage like I still live there. We can consider this a long vacation. If things work out, then we can discuss the possibility of me staying." She blew out a long breath. "This is absolutely crazy."

"Whatever you're comfortable with, Sera." His eyes lit up. Sera saw the passion in them. Lust, joy, relief. *Love.* "We're both a little crazy. That's why this works."

Sera crashed her lips against his. Cassius's presence comforted her in ways nothing else ever did. She clung to him as if he were the air filling her lungs. Rolling Sera onto her back, Cassius worshiped every part of her. He'd given her a gift she didn't earn—a chance to be normal. An opportunity to be a person that meant something to someone. Cassius shattered the walls she'd built and broke the cage that held her heart. As they explored each other, Sera held on to Cassius, afraid to let him go—frightened it was all a dream. Even when they were done, she clung to him.

"It's okay, Sera. I'm not going anywhere." He read her thoughts as usual. "I'm yours as long as you'll have me."

CHAPTER 20

The continuous buzzing of Cassius's phone woke him the next day. Carefully, he unraveled himself from Sera and slid his pants on. He gazed at her face. She looked innocent, curled onto her side, her hair splayed over the pillow, and her lips set in a pout. He loved her. Cassius had never been so sure of anything in his life. The woman was risky, dangerous, and volatile. *She was hired to kill me.* In return, he asked her to move in with him.

She won't go through with the hit. Sera faked a lot of things, but last night was real. Her steady hand when she told him she wouldn't harm him was real. The woman loved him. Cassius was almost certain she'd move to Gillette after the trial period. There was only one thing that could stop her.

Lorenzo. The man had the power to manipulate Sera into doing whatever he desired. If he convinced Sera to execute the hit, then Cassius wasn't safe. *That piece of shit.* His hatred for the man could set the world on fire. If

249

Lorenzo wasn't Sera's father, Cassius would've had him assassinated. Since that wasn't an option, he toyed with the thought of offering Lorenzo a substantial amount of money to stay away from Sera.

Cassius's phone buzzed again. *Ava.* Stepping through the sliding glass door, he walked barefoot to the middle of the meadow.

"I've been calling all morning," Ava said when he answered. Cassius pictured Ava on her third cup of coffee, triggering her own panic attack. She was a second mother to him. The woman was probably worried sick when he didn't pick up his phone.

"I'm sorry, I slept in." Cassius slipped his free hand into his pocket. "But I have good news: I'm alive."

"That's not funny," Ava snapped. "Are you with *her*?"

Not only was he with Sera, but he asked her to relocate...*into my house.*

He'd talk about that later. Ava was already on edge. "Yeah, I'm with her," he admitted. "Did Henry find out anything else? I don't have much time to talk." He glanced at the glass door, checking if Sera was still asleep.

Ava huffed. It was obvious she was biting her tongue. There was plenty she wanted to say—she *could* say—about Sera, but Cassius left no room for discussion.

"She kills in all kinds of ways," Ava said. "Her go-to is an uncut dose of Devil's Breath. She created some sort of device that goes in her mouth. It's similar to a dart blow-gun, small enough to fit under her tongue. She seduces her targets. When they go in for a kiss, she blows the drug in their face."

A fist wrapped around Cassius's lungs. "That could've been my fate."

"What's our next steps? Should we—" Ava coughed as if she'd swallowed a drink that went down wrong. "What do you mean that *could've* been your fate?"

There goes the plan on waiting to break the news. She wasn't going to like what Cassius had to say. "I asked her to move in with me."

Silence.

It stretched so long that Cassius thought Ava hung up. "Are you there?"

"You're a damn fool, Cassius." Her voice was low, her tone defeated. "You're not gambling with the stock market or making high-stakes business ventures. This is not one of your thrilling adventures or sports. This is your life we're talking about. What is your obsession with this woman? Is she that good in bed?"

Cassius laughed. "First of all, my high-stakes ventures and stock market investments are backed with tons of research. In case you've forgotten, I *always* come out on top. Have a little faith in me."

"You didn't answer the question about how good she is in bed." There was a touch of dry humor in her comment.

Cassius's mind sprinted back to a few hours ago. The softness of Sera's skin, the way she moaned when he touched her, how her back arched when she came. Cassius was stiff just reminiscing about their night. "She's amazing in bed. That's not all she is. I love her, Ava. I can't imagine being without her. Sera loves me too. You're going to say she's only pretending..." Cassius rubbed the back of his neck. "She's not. I can't explain it, but I know her emotions are genuine. She won't kill me."

Ava groaned. "Spare me the mushy stuff. I had a two-hundred-dollar brunch. I don't feel like throwing it up." She sighed. "Look, I don't like what's happening here. You're a grown man, so I'll let you make your own decisions *for now*. Like you said, you always come out on top. Just make sure this isn't like—"

"It's not like Everest," Cassius said harshly. "No one will get hurt, I promise." At least no one who was innocent. "This isn't about my savior complex either. I'm not trying to atone for Everest by protecting Sera from herself. She's not one of my charitable organizations."

"Fine, but I want you to check in with me five times a day until this is sorted out," Ava responded with equal harshness. "You better pick up when I call. If I don't hear from you for more than a few hours, I'm getting involved. Henry will follow you around as well. Don't worry, you won't know he's there. Got it?"

"Yes, ma'am," Cassius replied. "Stop worrying so much. You're going to give yourself an aneurysm."

He practically saw Ava rolling her eyes. "Whatever you say. I hope you two end up happily married with a bunch of snot-nosed kids."

Cassius smirked. He couldn't imagine Sera running after an army of children. "We'll see about that. First, I have to make sure she won't be the end of me."

"That would put a damper on things," Ava said flatly. "I'm here for you whenever you need me."

"I know you are. That's why I pay you so much."

"I'd like to keep those paychecks coming, so please

don't die." A beeping noise sounded in the background, and the roar of an engine came to life. "I'm leaving my garage, so I'll catch you later. I have a spa appointment."

"Your show of affection overwhelms me," Cassius mocked. "Are you putting your spa day on the company tab?"

"Where else would I put it? I'm certainly not spending my own money on frivolous activities." She yelled an expletive to someone who apparently almost hit her Range Rover. "Don't forget our deal. Otherwise, your little girlfriend will be buried six feet under."

Cassius ran his hand through his short curls. "Go relax. God knows you need it." The sliding door opened behind him, and Sera stepped outside. "I'll talk to you soon."

Cassius hung up the phone. Slipping it into his pocket, he turned toward the cabin. The vision of Sera liquified his insides. Her hair hung down her back in unkempt waves. Her eyes were still puffy from sleep, and her lips were swollen from kissing him all night. She wore his T-shirt, which hung down to her knees. She looked small—exposed. The woman wasn't used to baring her soul. The night made people brave. Mornings were full of remorse. Sera was panicking. Cassius saw it in her eyes. Like a prey whose hiding place had been exposed. But Cassius wasn't a predator, not to Sera anyway. He had to remind her of that.

Cassius went to Sera and wrapped her in his arms. She softened without effort. "Are you all right?"

Sera buried her face in his chest. "It's going to take me a while to get used to everything. This is all new to me."

"I understand." Cassius kissed the top of her head. "It's new to me too." She snuggled closer to him, and he stiffened immediately. *Great.* The woman's anxiety was at an all-time high, and he was aroused. "We don't have to have sex," he said quickly.

Sera snickered. "Oh, we can have sex. I'm ready for you."

"Let me at least feed you first," he said with reluctance.

"I am starving." Sera stepped away from him and rubbed her belly. "I thought you were out here foraging for food. Instead, I found you whispering to your girlfriend on the phone." Sera winked before turning to go back into the house.

Cassius caught her. Swiveling an arm around her waist, he pressed her back to his chest. Sera squealed, pretending to fight him off.

"I didn't take you for the jealous type," he growled. "You know you're the only one for me." He nibbled her earlobe. A sigh escaped her lips, and her body went limp. "Couldn't you tell last night? Don't you remember how bad I wanted you?" His teeth grazed the crook of her neck, and she shivered. "When I was inside of you..." His hand slid under her shirt, squeezing her nipple. "I never came so hard in my life."

Sera moaned and pushed herself into him, grinding her firm ass against his cock. "We can eat later," she said, her voice a command. "I want you to fuck me right now."

Cassius smiled against her skin. "Bend over."

Sera placed her palms flat on the sliding glass door and bent at the waist. She wasn't wearing any underwear. Cassius's cock throbbed at the sight. She arched her back, giving him full access to her. He ran his fingers over her wet slit, the sensation almost making him spill in his pants. The woman seriously reverted him back to a teenage virgin having sex for the first time.

Looking over her good shoulder, Sera shot him a sensual smile. It was the same smile she gave him the night they met. The same smile she gave him at the bar in the Mandarin. The fuck-off-unless-you're-going-to-fuck-me smile. "Show me how hard you get for me. Let me feel it." There was that confidence again. Gone was the vulnerable girl who stood before him just minutes ago.

Cassius licked his lips and ran his hands over her ass. He slid his fingers down, inserting two of them inside her slit. Stroking it softly, he said, "Spread your legs wider." Sera obeyed, opening for him. "Didn't I already show you how hard I get for you? Do you need a reminder?" He leaned forward and whispered in her ear, "I'm going to make you scream my name when you come."

"We'll see." Her eyes glossed over with hunger. "I think you'll be screaming mine." It was a challenge.

Cassius took his fingers out of her. He brought them to his mouth and sucked her juices off. "I could taste you forever."

Sera's lips parted as she watched. "Cassius, now."

He pulled a condom out of his pocket. Dropping his pants, he rolled it on his length. "How do you want it?"

"Fast and hard." Her voice was raspy, filled with need. "Don't make love this morning. Fuck me."

"I thought you'd never ask," he said with a smirk.

Gripping her hips, he glided into her. Slow at first, then harder. He slid his hand up the nape of her neck and grabbed her hair, pulling her head back to give him access to her throat. Sera moaned as he placed his mouth on her neck. His teeth dug into her skin, then he licked the sting away. His free hand moved under her shirt, his callused palms caressing her nipple.

The pressure built inside of him, his thrusts growing faster. His legs shook as he tried to keep his climax at bay. There was no way he'd come before her. Sera had other plans, though. She met his thrusts by pushing back into him. Grinding her ass into his waist, Sera took him deeper and deeper.

Cassius grit his teeth, unsure how much longer he could hold off. Thankfully...*thankfully*...a few seconds later, Sera's entire body shuddered. She called out his name as she came.

Cassius slowed his motions, allowing her to ride out her orgasm. "I told you that you'd scream my name."

Sera turned her head, her lips grazing his. "Pull out. I want to *taste* you."

Her words were his undoing. He took the condom off and tossed it aside.

Sera spun around and flicked her tongue over her lips. She knelt on her uninjured knee in front of him. "I'm going to give you the best orgasm of your life." She took him in her soft hand.

"You already have."

"This will be even better." Sera tightened her grip, her palm caressing his shaft. Her tongue made light circles on the tip of his cock. Too light.

"Sera..." The need to come was so intense that it physically hurt.

She looked up at him, her eyes twinkling. She was teasing him, withholding his climax. "Oh, you want more?"

"You're terrible, you know that?"

"I'm *so* good at the same time." Sera's tongue swirled over his entire length, taking all of him in her mouth. With a firm grip, she pumped him up and down.

Cassius ran his hands through her hair. His body tensed up.

Her lips were so soft...

Her tongue...

Her hands...

"I'm coming." Cassius gazed down at her. Sera met his eyes, her mouth still on him. Cassius exploded, roaring her name as he found his release.

CHAPTER 21

S era loved Cassius. She never thought she'd fall in love, especially not with a man she'd known less than two weeks. But her feelings were real. Sera had been with enough people—experienced enough life— to know Cassius Batista was the one she wanted forever. And forever wasn't a term she used lightly. She was an assassin, after all. The man accepted her, even with her flaws. *Just like the character in my favorite novel.* At least that's what Cassius told her. Sera had yet to read the ending.

An additional benefit was his insatiable sexual appetite. Hopping into the shower, he took her against the wall. Twice.

"Do you finally want to eat?" he asked, toweling her off. "We could go again."

Her body heated, but her growling stomach made the decision for her. "Let's eat first, have sex next, and go sightseeing after. I do want to explore the town I'll be vacationing at for a month."

"Don't you mean the town you're moving to?" Cassius planted a chaste kiss on her cheek before making his way to the sliding door.

Sera followed behind him, pinching his back. "If you keep fucking me the way you do, I might say yes."

"I'll always fuck you that way." Cassius went to the nightstand and pulled out a fresh pair of boxer briefs, jeans, and a T-shirt. Putting his clothes on, he tossed Sera one of his clean shirts. "I don't have underwear for you. I guess you'll have to go without. Sorry." The man didn't sound sorry at all. "What kind of food are you in the mood for? I can drive into town and pick it up for us."

Sera was already distracted. Her eyes roamed the curve of his prominent jaw, the muscles rolling in his shoulders, the flex of his arms. He was so tall and chiseled. He could've passed for a god. How'd she get so lucky?

"Are you paying attention?" Cassius asked with a crooked smile.

Sera cleared her throat. "Ummm...yes, I'll let you choose." She sat on the bed and crossed her legs. Playing with a piece of thread on the duvet, she said, "Thanks for sharing this cabin with me."

Cassius sat beside her and caressed her thigh. "You're my person. I want to share everything with you."

"Me too." Sera's eyes watered, a tear sliding down her face. She wiped it away before Cassius saw it. "You don't have to go to town alone. I'll come. Let me check my calls first."

"Of course," he said. "I have to go through some work emails too." Cassius grabbed his phone. Hopping off the bed, his fingers tapped the screen.

Sera's heart dropped when she retrieved her phone from her purse. She had twenty-eight missed calls and fourteen texts from her father. All the messages were the same: *Call me. Important.*

"It's my dad. I have to talk to him." Sera's voice shook. *Why didn't I check on him earlier?* He could be in trouble, but she was up in the mountains lounging around.

"I'll give you some privacy," Cassius said. "I need to get some things out of my car anyway."

Sera watched him through the window, waiting until he was too far to hear her conversation. Rummaging through her purse, she retrieved her burner phone and dialed Lorenzo's number. He picked up on the first ring. Sera cringed, waiting for his infamous temper to erupt. He'd definitely be livid that he hadn't been able to get ahold of her.

"Tay, I'm sorry. I didn't mean to miss your calls." Her body trembled as she spoke. The man could make her regress back to a little girl in seconds.

To her surprise, Lorenzo's voice was calm. "Are you all right, iha? I've been so worried."

"I...I..." *What?* "You're not mad you couldn't reach me?" she blurted out.

"No, of course not. I know you're with *him*, but you have to come home today. Catch a plane as soon as you can." He paused. Then... "Is Cassius all right?"

You mean, is he dead? That's what her dad really cared to know. "He's fine." Sera wasn't about to discuss her change of heart over the phone. "Why do you need me home? What's going on?"

"I can't explain over the phone." Blowing out a breath,

he said, "I'm fucking stressed and need my baby girl by my side."

Sera sat on the floor, afraid her knees would give out. Something was terribly wrong. *Is it the DEA?* Did it have to do with the secret house Christian and Damion visited? "Cassius has a private jet. I'll ask him to get me on it right away. Are you going to be okay until I get there?"

"Just hurry. I'm in a jam," Lorenzo said. "You're the only one that can help me."

"I'll do whatever it takes to fix it." Sera hung up and gazed out the window, watching Cassius dig in his car. She had a sinking feeling her relationship with him was over.

Raine would leave the city and start her new life on a beautiful island. It gave Sera hope that she could do the same. But Raine didn't have a father to look after. She had allowed her delusions to take over. *There's no starting over for me.* Sera ignored the grief thrumming in her chest, the agony bubbling in her throat. Those feelings were meant for normal people. Not killers.

Cassius rummaged in his car, searching for absolutely nothing. His mind was focused on Sera's reaction when she saw her father's missed call. *Paralyzed with fear.* As if she were standing in the middle of a frozen lake, waiting for it to crack. The man was poison—a cancer that took over Sera's mind. Cassius had a feeling the call had to do with the hit placed on him. *Why else would Sera look like that?*

Cassius sighed. He *really* wished it didn't have to come to this. He grabbed a baseball cap and a shirt out of his car. It was a ploy. He didn't need any of those items. *I do need one thing.* Opening his trunk, Cassius lifted the cover board. Inside was a small black case that held eighteen sugar glass vials of brown fluid. He shoved three in his pocket, closed the trunk, and headed back to the cabin.

As he predicted, Sera was dressed and pacing by the door. "Is everything all right?" he asked.

"I have to go home right now. Don't worry about my suitcase. You can mail it to me or throw it out. Whatever you prefer." Her eyes were wild, her gestures erratic.

Cassius grabbed her by the waist and hugged her. "Calm down and breathe."

Sera stiffened. "Cassius, I can't—"

Rubbing her back, he said, "Panicking isn't going to do you any good. Let's get in the car and head straight to my jet. I'll call Mason. He'll have everything set up when we arrive." Sera leaned into him. He was well aware by now that his touch gave her the solace she desired. "Your suitcase isn't going anywhere. It'll be here when you get back."

Sera abruptly pulled away. Frost crept over her face— the ice queen had returned. But the disguise was flawed. The ice wasn't thick enough to hide the pain underneath. "I can't come back, Cassius. I'm sorry...I got caught up in the moment. We...us...it can't work."

Cassius wasn't surprised. He figured she'd say something like that. "Let's not discuss it now. We'll talk about it after we deal with your father." He cupped her chin and kissed her. "I love you." He kissed her again. "I have to take care of a few things here, but I'll fly to the city in three days. We'll sort everything out then."

Sera ran a hand over her face. "I don't think that's a good idea. Cassius—"

"Don't say it." He stepped away from her. Leaning against the wall, he slid his hands into his pockets. "Please wait until I get to New York before you make any decisions."

"Okay," she said, staring at the ground.

Cassius was losing her. She had retreated into her shell. But he was a man who fought against the odds, and he beat them time and again. Cassius wasn't willing to let her go that easily. He ran his fingers over the vials in his pocket. Hopefully, he didn't end up dead.

CHAPTER 22

Sera sat on the lawn at Theodore Roosevelt Park. Leaning against a tree, she stared at the brick building in front of her. She was hardly aware it was there. Her heart broke at the thought of ending things with Cassius. When he came to New York, she'd make him understand it was over. She should've done it before she left Gillette, but there was no time to spare.

She was foolish to believe she could start fresh. In the end, her father came first. It was how things had always been and how they'd continue to be. Cassius would be hurt, but he'd move on. Maybe he'd even thank her for cutting ties with him. She was doing Cassius a favor by not involving him in her disastrous life. Sera had been selfish about many things, but he wouldn't be one of them. Cassius deserved better than her. She'd force him to realize it.

"My iha." Lorenzo strolled up to her. He looked around as if he thought someone had followed him before he sat down across from her. "Thanks for coming so quickly. I wanted to meet here because I'm not sure if my house or car is bugged."

It was six in the evening. Once the jet landed, Sera took a taxi straight to the park. She was exhausted and wanted their discussion to be over as soon as possible. "What's going on, Tay? You don't look too good." Lorenzo had bags under his eyes. He looked like he hadn't slept in days.

"You need to take care of something for me. It's urgent." He pulled a pack of cigarettes out of his pocket. With shaky hands, he lit one up.

Sera gritted her teeth. He *always* needed her help. Swallowing her retort, she said, "You know I have your back."

"I got into some shit a while ago." Lorenzo leaned back, supporting himself with one hand. "I got busted importing…" He cleared his throat. "That's not important. The point is, I have to leave the country as soon as possible. Like, within the next few days."

Sera frowned. "Who busted you?" She didn't ask what he imported. It was clearly something other than Devil's Breath. With Lorenzo, it was best not to pry.

He took a long drag of his cigarette. "I had to do it. I can go to prison for life, maybe even get the death penalty. They offered me a deal."

Sera's pulse roared in her ears. Her mind went back to the day the authorities showed up at the jewelry store. Someone *had* given them up. "Who did you make a deal with?"

"There was no other choice. I can't get locked up

again." Lorenzo ran his hand through his jet-black hair. "You understand, right, iha?"

"Who did you make a deal with?" Sera repeated, her voice dangerously calm.

Lorenzo gazed at her, his gray eyes shadowed. "The DEA."

Sera's stomach tightened, and bile rose up her throat. "You gave me up?"

"No, I'd never do that." Lorenzo reached his hand out as if he were going to touch her. Then, he pulled back. "I told them where Carlo's drug lab was located. I gave up *his people*, not you."

"*I was in there.*" Sera's teeth were clenched so tight she thought they might break.

Lorenzo put his cigarette out on the grass and grabbed another from the pack. "I know you and Raine wouldn't get caught. You two are gangsters. I wouldn't have told the DEA anything if I didn't have faith that you'd be able to get away." He reached out again. This time, he placed his hand on her thigh. "I never gave them your names. You're my spawn—I mean—my little girl. I love you like cooked food, iha. I wouldn't be able to live with myself if I betrayed you."

The blood in Sera's veins thinned. Lorenzo hadn't handed her to the authorities, but he put her and Raine in harm's way. They were talented in their field, but they still could've gotten arrested. *I got shot, for God's sake.* She wanted to smack Lorenzo until he understood what he'd done.

"Does the DEA know about Christian and Damion?" she asked, steeling her emotions.

Lorenzo tucked his unlit cigarette behind his ear. "Yeah, but they're holding off on taking them in. They've been tracking Christian and Damion in order to get to their real target: the cartel. The ones we bought the"—he waved a dismissive hand—"never mind. Anyway, I give the DEA any information I can. They make me wear a wire around Christian and Damion. Don't worry, I'm not wearing one now." He patted his chest and unbuttoned the top three buttons of his satin shirt. "Christian and Damion will be taken into custody soon. The DEA is close to bagging the cartel heads. I'll be put in the witness protection program." Lorenzo's face fell. "I can't do that. Witness protection isn't my style. I gotta jet outta here."

Not his style? Lorenzo was bringing down Christian, Damion, and the cartel. Not to mention, he smuggled some mysterious item into the country. A product serious enough to land a death sentence. *But witness protection isn't his style?* This whole operation had turned upside down. Sera was grateful Cassius never gave Christian any money. Otherwise, he would've been implicated for being part of the circus show.

"What were you importing?" she asked.

Lorenzo lit his second cigarette and took a long drag from it. She thought he wasn't going to respond. Then he said, "It's Christian and Damion's fault. I should've never linked up with those two wannabe thugs. Why should I take the fall for their stupidity? I told them not to work with people they barely know." He snarled. "They talked me into dealing khat. It's a plant that grows in Yemen. That shit makes you feel like you snorted meth."

"I know what it is," Sera responded, a little too harshly.

268

Unbelievable. Her father could never admit his faults. He was the rat that almost got her and Raine arrested. She highly doubted the offer to deal khat took much convincing.

"I was the one who got caught. They busted me loading the drugs into a truck at the port. Now I'm an informant." There wasn't a tinge of remorse on his features.

Sera rubbed her temples, trying to alleviate her creeping headache. Lorenzo could never settle. He had to have it all. She knew his greed would be the end of him. *Look now.* He was bringing everyone along with him.

Khat must've been what was stored in the abandoned house. Why hide it from her and Raine? They were already involved in the drug scheme. *How did they get the funds for the khat?* Sera had a sick feeling Lorenzo had used part of the money she'd given him for the Devil's Breath operation. Still, the story didn't make sense. People weren't usually given death sentences for drug charges. There was something Lorenzo wasn't telling her.

Sera released a sigh. "What do you want me to do, Tay?" Her father was a snake, but she was still going to take care of him. It would break her to see him in prison or witness protection. *What if he gets killed by the cartel?*

"I can always count on you," he said, patting her leg. "Once we're out of this jam, we'll live wherever you want. Remember when you were little, we used to talk about moving to some island?" He smiled, his bright-white teeth nearly blinding. "We can do that. We'll sit by the beach all day. We'll learn to scuba dive like we've always planned to." He leaned over and kissed her cheek.

"You'd like that, right? You'd never leave your tay, would you?"

No, she wouldn't. *Goodbye, Cassius.* Sera's eyes blurred with unshed tears. "It's you and me forever."

"Good girl." He scratched the back of his neck. "I know you have feelings for Cassius."

"I—" Sera started.

Lorenzo raised his hand. "It happens, but you gotta be done with him." His features remained soft, but his eyes thundered. "Christian found another hacker who got into Cassius's accounts four days ago. He hasn't given the go-ahead yet, because it has to be timed with Cassius's death. I told the boys I'd talk to you...to see when you can do it. Iha, I need Cassius's money this week so we can jet. You gotta get rid of him as soon as possible."

He ran his fingers through the grass. "I would've told you to take care of Cassius in Gillette, but it was too dangerous to discuss over the phone. There are eyes on me. God forbid, the DEA finds out that I'm involved in a hit. The witness protection offer will be off the table. I'll get locked up before we can skip town." Lorenzo's gaze passed over Sera with the tenderness of a dagger. "If killing him is too hard for you, Butch can do it."

Sera understood her father's message. *You manipulative bastard.* It was Lorenzo's way of telling her that Cassius was going to die no matter what. Butch would flay Cassius alive. His death would be slow and excruciating. It would either be gentle with her or unbearable with Butch.

Sera bit her tongue until she drew blood. Why did she think she could've talked her father into letting Cassius live? *I let myself get close to my mark.* Sera allowed herself to harden once again, blocks of ice stacking inside her body until it numbed every part of her. "I'll handle it. He's coming here in three days. I'll do it then. You and I can leave right after."

"Good." Lorenzo pulled out a mint container from his pocket. It held small capsules. *Devil's Breath.* What she would kill Cassius with. He handed it to Sera. "I'll get our fake passports ready and book our tickets. Where do you want to go?"

Sera shrugged. "You choose." It would've been his choice anyway. It was always Lorenzo's choice, regardless of what he said.

He patted her on the head. "What would you do for me?"

That dreaded question he'd asked her hundreds of times, knowing her answer would never change. Her devotion was to Lorenzo. Forever.

"Anything, Tay."

"Just anything?" he asked with a quirk of a brow.

"Everything."

Even kill the man she loved.

CHAPTER 23

Cassius lied. Contrary to what he told Sera, Cassius wasn't leaving Gillette in three days. He departed right after her. He wasn't completely deceitful, though. Cassius was honest about the fact that he had a few things to take care of, except the "few things" were in New York. At an abandoned house in Long Island to be exact. One Christian and his partners owned.

Cassius had been there for an hour, going through the repulsive inventory. There were thousands of glass dropper bottles labeled "Adrenochrome." He recalled the documentary he tried to watch about the drug. He picked up enough knowledge to understand that the product was evil to the core, so were the people who dealt it.

Adrenochrome was a potent drug found in the pineal gland of humans, specifically infants, when their blood was stirred with fear. Once the drug was harvested, the children were killed. It was quickly becoming a multibillion-dollar criminal industry. And his brother had taken part in it. Damion had fronted a couple thousand dollars, and Lorenzo used his daughter's money to fund the rest. Cassius was relieved to find out that Sera had no knowledge of this venture.

Christian has completely lost it. Any reservation Cassius had regarding his brother's assassination was gone. Glancing at his watch, he saw it was nearing midnight. Raine would be arriving soon. According to Henry, the woman came to the house nightly, searching for something she couldn't find. *Because the drugs are in the walls.* The one-story house had nothing inside—no furniture, no kitchen, no bathroom. It consisted of wood floors and lots of walls.

When Cassius was in Gillette, Ava had told him about Christian's involvement in the Adrenochrome business. Since the attorney was excellent at her job, she had Henry install cameras in both the interior and exterior of the home. Raine had the same idea, but Cassius scrambled her cameras. Henry found a hacker to take care of it. Cassius's money ran long, which meant anyone was at his beck and call. He didn't tap into that privilege often, but he wasn't opposed to using it either.

Footsteps neared the house. Grabbing his Remington 700 rifle—complete with a suppressor—Cassius jogged toward the side of the door and pressed his back against the wall. He waited for Raine to enter. His heart whipped against his chest, chilled blood rushed his veins. *This* was the high he lived for. He usually achieved the same satisfaction base jumping, but he was always willing to try something new. *I don't know who is worse, you or your brother.* Those were Ava's sentiments. Was he turning into

Christian? *No, this is different.* Christian was inherently evil. Cassius was…*what?* Before he came to New York, he thought the world was black and white. That's how he was raised—people were either good or bad. He'd come to realize humans were complicated. The gray areas were what made them unique and interesting. *Dangerous.*

The door flew open, and Raine walked in. Stepping out of the shadows, Cassius pointed his gun at her. Raine's two Beretta M9s were pointed back at him. He figured that would happen. If she was anything like Sera, she'd be cautious and prepared. Raine didn't seem like the type of woman who'd saunter into an abandoned house twiddling her thumbs.

"I've been waiting for you," Cassius said. He examined the way Raine held her guns as if they were extensions of her hands. It was obvious she was a skilled shooter. *So am I.* He had dozens of hunting trophies to prove it.

"Cassius." Raine let out a lethal laugh, similar to a hyena's, when they dined on a freshly killed carcass. "Fancy seeing you here. Shopping for houses?"

They circled each other like two gladiators looking for an opening.

"Not particularly," he replied.

Raine pursed her lips into a pout. "I thought we formed a truce the night I slept in your suite. I'm hurt," she said, not sounding hurt at all.

"That was before I found out you were planning to hack my bank accounts." Cassius couldn't keep the growl from his voice. His anger was alive and well. He wouldn't reveal his knowledge of his own assassination. He had other plans for that.

A glimmer of uncertainty crossed Raine's eyes. She blinked, and it was gone. "Were you the one who kept messing with my cameras? I was wondering who did that. Christian and Damion are too dumb, and Lorenzo is worthless. If you ever go broke, a life of crime suits you."

"I'll never go broke because there's no way you'll be able to hack my accounts." Cassius inched closer to her.

Raine cocked her head. "Why is that?"

"I'm always one step ahead."

Henry walked through the door, a Glock in his hand. It was directed at Raine. At the same time, Mason stepped out of a hole in the drywall, his SIG P226 handgun raised and ready.

"Ahhh," Raine said, unruffled. "Next you guys will start pulling out your cocks, trying to impress me with their sizes. Why is your gun the largest, Cassius? Are you over-compensating for something?" She briefly glanced at his crotch.

Cassius huffed a laugh. "Hardly." His eyes narrowed on her. "I have a proposition for you."

"This should be interesting." Raine cocked the hammer on both of her guns. "I can kill all of you with three bullets and walk away unscathed." An edged silence encompassed the house. Then, Raine grinned. "All right, I'll play this out. Sera has a thing for you, and I kind of like you too. You're not here to kill me. I've been in the business long enough to know when someone wants me dead. So, what *do* you want?"

"Lower your guns," Cassius said. Henry and Mason hesitated for a moment before doing what they were told. Raine *did not* lower hers. *Fine.* He assumed she wouldn't.

Holding the Remington by his side, Cassius continued. "You come here every night. I'm assuming it's not for an evening rendezvous with a hot lover." He jutted his chin toward a gaping hole in the wall. "My brother, Damion, and Lorenzo are smuggling Adrenochrome. There are thousands of bottles hidden behind the walls."

Raine's jaw dropped, her cool demeanor slipping. "Those bastards." The woman looked like she was going to be ill. Cassius heard of the expression "her face turned green." He'd always thought it was a myth. Until now.

This was the reaction he hoped for—utter revulsion. *Perfect.* He was certain she'd help him. Since he was an expert on people, Cassius picked up on a few things. The contempt in Raine's voice when she spoke on the phone to Lorenzo the night of the DEA bust. *She hates him and hopes he dies a violent death.* The way Raine thanked Cassius profusely when he helped Sera. *She approves of me.* The fact she hadn't killed him already. *She trusts me.* Raine wasn't bluffing. Cassius had no doubt she could slay all three of them in less than ten seconds.

"Before I lay out my proposal, I want to let you know I'm willing to offer you fifty million dollars. Do with it as you wish." At the family dinner, Sera revealed that her best friend planned to leave New York. *She's sick of the business and wants to start a new life.*

"What about Sera?" Raine moved closer to him. "I won't do anything with you unless it benefits her as well."

"Sera loves me." He expected Raine to balk. She didn't. *Even better.* "I asked her to move to Gillette. She was willing to give it a trial run, but I think she's going to back out."

"Because of Lorenzo?"

Cassius gave a slow nod.

Raine's eyes brewed with venom. "How about this: *if* I agree to your mysterious proposition, you don't have to give me a penny. As long as you can convince Sera to move to Gillette."

"What makes you think I can do that?"

"Because she loves you," Raine replied as if it was the simplest explanation in the world.

Sera leaving with him was the goal. He hoped it was still achievable. *Because it's a matter of life or death.* Literally. "I'll do my best," Cassius said.

"You better do more than your best, or else you'll owe me eighty million." Raine's lips curled into a half-smile.

Cassius leveled her gaze. "I said fifty million."

"I charge interest." Raine finally lowered her guns, tucking them in her holsters.

Cassius rubbed his chin in contemplation. "Fine, as long as you don't tell Sera I'm here. She thinks I'm coming in a couple of days. I'll explain everything to her after we're done."

"After *we're* done? I haven't agreed to anything yet." Raine tucked her thumbs into the loops of her black jeans. "Back to my original question. What do you want, Cassius?"

"I want to shut down the drug operation." Self-hatred coursed through him as he stated his next objective. "And, I want to kill my brother."

Raine inclined her head. The dim light illuminated her prominent cheekbones and slender neck. She looked more catlike than ever. The posture was both magnificent and intimidating. A minute passed before she said, "Okay, I'll help you." She held her hand out. "Partners."

"Partners." Cassius took her hand, shaking away any drops of reluctance.

Mason and Henry—who'd been deathly silent—each breathed a sigh of relief, loud enough that it carried through the room.

"I'm sorry about this whole thing." Cassius jerked his chin toward the men. "The guns were a precaution."

Rocking back on her heels, Raine said, "Meh, no worries. You would've been a fool if you didn't bring backup or weapons. I don't have respect for fools." Her lips twisted into a feral smile. "Now, tell me about this plan of yours."

They arrived at the warehouse lot the following evening, both dressed in black. Neither brought cars, opting for the subway instead. That made it harder to track their whereabouts. At Cassius's request, they wore disguises during their separate commutes. He didn't want to get caught on any surveillance tapes, even the ones in the subway stations. He might've been exceedingly paranoid, but he'd rather be safe than sorry. He wasn't used to committing crimes, unlike his newfound partner.

Everything was going well. The bomb was set to blow up the abandoned house, destroying the Adrenochrome inside it. *Thank goodness.* But they hadn't gotten to the hard part yet. That was coming next.

"You brought it, right?" Cassius asked. He removed his

ridiculous man-bun wig, followed by the equally ridiculous pornstache, and dumped them in a duffel bag.

"Of course. Do you think I'm an amateur?" Raine wheezed. She laughed so hard at Cassius's disguise that her breaths came out in short pants. "Here we go." Her lips twitched as she tried not to laugh again. Cassius glared while Raine pulled two audio-and-security jammers out of her backpack. "One for you, and one for me," she said in a singsong voice as if she were handing out Halloween candy. "This should muddle the security system and bugs. You know...like the bugs you installed."

After their standoff the previous night, Cassius explained how he'd gotten all his information. Raine took it remarkably well. She did hit him once, but considering it was a slap as opposed to a punch...well... "You know, Raine, you're pretty cool when you're not giving off your murdery vibe."

Raine adjusted the knife around her ankle. "You're pretty cool, too, when you're not giving off the dashing romance-novel-billionaire vibe." She placed a hand on her chest, her eyes widening with feigned shock. "I can't believe you actually have a sinister side."

Cassius slipped the jammer into his pocket. Zipping up the duffel bag, he slung it over his shoulder. "Killing my brother is definitely a character flaw." Cassius felt sick inside. Ava tried to persuade him to have a professional take care of Christian. That was the spineless thing to do. Cassius had to carry out the deed himself.

Raine placed a hand on his shoulder. "Are you sure you're okay with this?"

Absolutely not. But his choices were limited. Christian

was a menace to their family and to society as a whole. "Is what I'm doing wrong?"

Raine tilted her head to the side. "Christian is destroying lives with his drug enterprise. In a way, you'll be saving lots of people. But murder is murder. So yes, it's wrong, no matter how you look at it."

She patted herself down, then tightened her bulletproof vest. Cassius did the same. What did he expect from Raine? Did he think she'd placate him? Did he want her to? No, he wanted honesty. "How do you do it and feel good about yourself after?" He wasn't only asking about her; he was indirectly asking about Sera.

Raine gave him a strange look, biting cold sprinkled with burning guilt. "I could give you a sob story about my childhood, but I won't make excuses. It boils down to the fact that I have a complete disregard for the law and social norms." She slid her black gloves on. "Let's do this before I start thinking about the bad decisions I've made in my life. I might end up backing out. Did you call your brother and tell him to meet you here in an hour?"

Raine was right. There was no use in analyzing the situation. *It is what it is.* Cassius fiddled with the gun in his holster. Hopefully, he wouldn't have to use it. "What do you think I am, an amateur?" He repeated Raine's own words.

Raine nodded to his holster. "Actually, yes."

Cassius flushed. His knife was sheathed the wrong way. The pointed end was facing him. Just what he needed...to stab himself while trying to commit a murder. He swiftly sheathed the knife the proper way. "That was an accident."

"Nervous?" Raine picked the lock on the warehouse door and strolled in, Cassius following behind her. "I was nervous the first time I assassinated someone. Till this day, Sera throws up before each kill."

Did Raine give him that information freely, or did she not realize her slip of the tongue? Either way, Cassius was relieved to know the woman he loved wasn't a total sociopath. "How old were you?" he asked.

"Fifteen." The placid indifference in Raine's voice sent shivers through Cassius. She gave no further explanation, which was fine with him.

When Cassius was fifteen, he was attending school dances and riding horses with his friends. Raine was out gutting people. *So was Sera*, he assumed. Anger and sorrow for the women intermingled in his bones. Fortunately, he didn't have to dwell on his feelings for too long. Raine had the contents of her backpack out on the ground. Placed in front of her were the tools needed to dismantle locks.

Cassius whistled. "You are an expert."

Raine flashed him a smile. "I told you."

There were two doors in the warehouse—the front and the back, which meant two sets of locks. Raine started taking apart the locks on the back door first. The plan was to change the manual latches into automatic ones that they'd be able to control with a remote.

Cassius watched the woman work. Raine was impressive. Her fingers were graceful as a pianist who knew each chord by heart. "You made all that?" he asked, staring at the pieces of metal on the floor.

"Yup," she replied, brows furrowed in deep in concentration.

Cassius pulled out his own contraption. He couldn't let Raine have all the fun. *Great, now killing my brother is fun? How quickly we spiral.*

"Nice job, Wyoming." It was Raine's turn to whistle. "I didn't know Ivy League boys made bombs in their spare time."

Cassius turned the device around in his hand. "I learned to make one as a kid. My family is in the coal industry. We break through surfaces of mining areas using explosives. This is a less high-tech version of it." He looked it over to make sure everything was intact. "We have forty-five minutes till it blows."

Raine set the commands on her remote. "Good, they'll be here by then."

By the time Christian and Damion arrived, Raine and Cassius would be gone. The two men thought they were having a business meeting with Cassius. But it was a trap. Raine and Cassius planned to stand across the street when the men entered the building. A few pushes on the remote and they'd be locked in. A couple of minutes later, the bomb would explode. *And they'll be dead.*

Cassius pushed his disgust aside as he scanned the warehouse. His eyes landed on the left wall. Lining it were empty crates with open lids. Had Cassius given Christian the money, the containers would've been filled with Devil's Breath disguised as gems. "I'm going to put the bomb in one of the crates," Cassius said.

At least that's what he would've done if his brother and Damion hadn't walked in the front door, guns drawn.

Why the hell are they early? Cassius's adrenaline surged, a gale raging in his chest.

"What a surprise," Christian said, a not-too-sane smile on his face. "You decided to come early, too, brother. I see you brought this bitch with you." He jerked his chin toward Raine, who was now standing next to Cassius. "We stopped by our house down the street a few minutes ago. We were shocked to find it in ruins. Millions of dollars in inventory destroyed."

Shit! The bomb went off early. The timer must've malfunctioned. Cassius shot Raine an apologetic look. She wasn't looking back at him. She was watching Christian and Damion. The two men were simultaneously moving closer to them.

Fury pulsed in Cassius's brain, hot like lava. "What's wrong with you, Christian? Adrenochrome? I knew you were fucked up, but I didn't think you'd stoop this low."

Christian clucked his tongue. "Cassius, Cassius...our parents' golden boy." The gun shook in his hand. Whether it was out of fear or fury, Cassius couldn't tell. "Do you know how sickening it was to grow up in your shadow? Every time *I* took a risk, it was considered reckless. When the *golden boy* took a risk, it was a brave move."

"That's what this is about? You're destroying lives because you're jealous?" Cassius itched for his gun. He didn't try to draw it. Christian would've fired before he had the chance to retrieve it. "You do realize your self-destructive behavior is what caused the family to cut you off."

The contempt in his brother's eyes was a vicious thing. "They disowned me because I wasn't good enough to be part of the perfect Batista family. I reminded Pa that there's a stain in the family genes. It didn't help that you always had to show me up. I'd get an A, but you'd get an A+. I'd run a mile in seven minutes, but you'd run it in six. We both got into Harvard. When I chose to go to UPenn, Pa harped about it. When you chose to go to Brown, he thought it was the best decision ever."

"You went to college?" Raine sneered.

"He had two semesters left before he got kicked out for selling Ecstasy pills on campus," Cassius said flatly.

"Shut up. *Shut up*." Christian waved his gun in the air. The erratic action made even Damion duck.

"Chill out, man," Damion snapped. "Let's do this and get the fuck out of here. We're wasting time."

"How are you going to hack my accounts if you kill Raine?" Cassius challenged.

Christian and Damion blinked at the same time. "What?" his brother asked, appearing less confident.

"I know about your plan." Cassius carefully set the bomb on the ground. Christian's gun followed his movements. "That's the problem with you, brother. You never think things through." He gave Raine a sidelong glance, glimpsing her hand creeping to her belt. He had to keep the two men engaged. "You know why Pa doesn't want anything to do with you? It isn't because he likes me better. He's cried over you more times than I can count."

Cassius's gaze discreetly remained on Raine. He caught her fingers circling the hilt of her knife. "They disowned you because of this." Cassius extended his arms, encompassing the room. "Your memories are off. You got A's because you cheated on tests. You ran a mile in seven minutes because you pumped steroids into your veins.

285

You wanted to go to UPenn because you had drug connections there, which got you busted. That was the final straw. Pa disowned you because he was sick of giving you chances. Our family was all over the news, for God's sake." Cassius rolled his shoulders back. "I never gloated when Mãe and Pa yelled at you. I always tried to help you. Why do you think I came to New York? I want you to do well, but you repay me by trying to rob me?"

"I'm devastated." Christian clutched his chest in a mock gesture. "Thanks for the stroll down memory lane. I think I'll kill both of you now. We don't need either of you. I have a hacker waiting in my car. He got into your accounts five days ago. Once you're dead, I'll give him the 'okay.' And your money will be in my hands."

Again, Cassius was a step ahead. The bank locked down Cassius's accounts two days ago. At this point, it was hacker-proof. "Has your hacker tried to get into my accounts since then? Your minion can't—"

Raine's knife flew in the air, slamming into Christian's shoulder. Christian stumbled as his gun went off. Wrapping his arms around Raine, Cassius ducked and brought them both to the ground. The bullet hit the wall behind them. Two more bullets came toward them. One from Damion, another from Christian. Raine and Cassius tucked and rolled, avoiding the shot.

"Twenty minutes till the bomb explodes," Cassius said, briefly looking at his watch.

"We'll kill them in ten." Raine pulled her Beretta out and cocked it.

Cassius did the same with his 9mm. "Leave Christian

to me." The feud was between him and his brother. Cassius had to be the one to end it.

"Good luck," Raine said, running to the crates. Ducking behind them, she shot over the top, making her way to Damion.

Cassius bolted to the steel table in the middle of the warehouse. He tossed the table onto its side and hid behind it. His brother released a round of shots, the bullets denting the frame. Cassius waited, his pulse thrumming. Christian was bound to run out of bullets. When he heard the click of an empty gun, he jumped over the table.

Cassius made it to Christian before he finished loading his magazine. He slammed his fist into Christian's mouth. His brother's head snapped back, blood spraying from between his lips. Elbowing Christian's arm, Cassius knocked his gun to the floor. Then, he pressed his 9mm against his brother's sternum.

Christian burst into manic laughter. He spat out a wad of crimson. "See, Cassius, you always win."

"I don't want it to be this way." Cassius held his gun steady even as his stomach lurched. He couldn't bring himself to pull the trigger.

He looked into Christian's eyes—unnaturally black like his, their features nearly identical. Was there another way? Maybe he didn't have to kill his own brother. Cassius hesitated too long. Even with a knife embedded in his shoulder, Christian was fast. Christian whacked the gun out of his hand and dove for it, catching it before it hit the floor. Bringing the gun to Cassius's chest, he pulled the trigger. The force slammed Cassius onto his back. His skin burned as if it had been lit on fire.

"Of course you have a bulletproof vest on." Christian roared. Crouching next to Cassius, he pressed the cold barrel against his brother's temple. His eyes ignited with savage joy. "I have a secret to tell you." He lowered his voice to a whisper. "Your *lovely* girlfriend, Sera...I hired her to kill you. I understand you more than you think. I knew you'd fall for her. She studied you for months. She learned what gets you off. What makes you hard. What makes you want to wife her up. It was all an act. She played you, brother."

The revelation hit like an arrow through his heart. *Yet...*Christian was wrong. Sera's feelings might've been part of a plot in the beginning. *It isn't anymore.* With equal quiet, Cassius said, "I don't care." That wasn't true, but he wasn't about to hash out his emotions with Christian.

"You don't care?" The gun dug deeper into Cassius's temple. "You're fine with killing me, but you're giving that whore a free ride?"

Cassius steadied his breath. "Sera was hired to assassinate a stranger. You're *my* brother, and you put out a hit out on me. Who's next? Our parents? Jacey?"

"I don't want to hear it anymore," Christian screamed. "I want you out of my life." He pulled the trigger.

With gazelle-like speed, Cassius rolled away from Christian, the bullet barely missing his head. The deafening sound of the gunshot rang in his eardrum, muffling any noise around him. He didn't wait for Christian to pull the trigger again. Cassius grabbed the knife out of his belt.

Turning toward his brother, he rooted the blade in Christian's neck.

"What the—" Christian dropped the gun and grabbed his throat. "Cassius, help..." He scooted backward, gasping for air.

Cassius sat up and watched his brother struggle to stay alive. A part of him died right there. His heart had been plucked from his chest, and his soul withered in his body. "I worshiped you when we were young, Christian. I wish things could've been different for you—for us. I never stopped loving you. None of us did."

The blazing fury didn't leave Christian's eyes even as he battled for air. His mouth opened and closed like a fish. Until his breath ceased altogether.

Cassius sat frozen in horror. His limbs were numb, his lungs unable to take in oxygen. He couldn't move, the significance of his actions crushing him. He was lost in the hellish vortex of sorrow. Cassius knew he'd never be the same again. *I murdered my own flesh and blood.* This wasn't like Everest. He couldn't pay away his guilt. The memory of his brother's death would forever torment him. *I'm sorry, Christian. I'm so sorry.*

When he finally found the strength to stand, he went to his brother. Cassius stooped and cradled Christian's head in his arms. Tears splashed his cheeks, and sobs racked his body. His surroundings melted away.

Nothing else mattered...

Until it did.

A familiar voice snapped Cassius out of his trance. *Raine.*

A couple of feet away, Damion had the woman pinned against the wall, his gun against her jaw.

Cassius hopped up, awareness seeping back into him. "Damion, wait...hear me out." He placed his hands above his head. "Look, I have no weapon. I just want to talk." He blinked his tears for his brother away. "My accounts are locked down. I put in the order when I found out about Christian's plot. There's no way your hacker can access it." He took a small step forward. "Let her go, and I'll pay you. Name your price."

"How do I know you won't call the cops?" Damion asked, his eyes unhinged.

Another small step forward. "That's a risk you'll have to take. You'll have a chance to change your identity and leave the country before the cops find you." A third step. "We'll stay with you until you get your money. What's your other choice? Christian is dead, the Adrenochrome is gone, and you're broke."

The gun in Damion's hand faltered. He was contemplating it. A decision had to be made soon. Cassius guessed they had ten minutes left before they all turned into charred bones. "What do you say?" He glanced at the bomb on the other side of the room.

"Two hundred million."

"Done."

"All right...let's move." Damion shoved Raine toward Cassius.

He caught her in his arms. "We have nine minutes left," he whispered, peeking at his watch.

"You're not paying this asshole shit." Raine snarled through her teeth.

Cassius was about to agree when Raine pulled a knife out of her sleeve and tossed it. The blade slammed into Damion's stomach. She grabbed another knife from her ankle. That one landed in his sternum. The entire act was performed within seconds.

"You caught my blind spot earlier." Raine seethed at Damion. "If I had more time, I'd flay the skin off your face. But you'll be dead any minute now, and I have a bomb to worry about."

Damion's free hand clutched the hilt of the knife lodged in his stomach, the arm holding the gun dropping to his side. "You bitch. You whore. You piece of shit." He lifted the gun again and pulled the trigger. The bullet went toward Raine's forehead.

Cassius leaped in front of her, the bullet hitting his side. Doubling over, he clutched his ribs. "Fuck...that *hurts.*"

"Damn it." Raine placed a hand on his back. "Why did you do that? Did it break skin? *Please* tell me it did not break skin." There was genuine worry in her tone.

"Don't know." Cassius wheezed, pain searing down his body. "Damion..."

Cassius didn't need to finish the sentence. Damion dropped in front of them. Raine's stab wounds proved to be deadly, after all.

"There's your answer," Raine said dryly. "Lift your shirt. Let me see how bad it is." Cassius did as he was told, allowing Raine to examine him. "You're good. It didn't go through the vest." She released a sigh of relief. "Thanks for saving my life."

Cassius waggled his eyebrows. "That's what dashing billionaires from romance novels do."

"Don't *ever* do that thing with your eyebrows again. It's highly disturbing." Raine rolled her eyes, but her lips twitched as she tried to hide a smile. Then her expression morphed. She was suddenly somber. "Cassius, I'm getting out of this life. Sera should too. All that shit I said about giving me money if you can't persuade her to move to Gillette…I don't care about that. I *need* you to convince her. She'll die if she keeps going down this path. Lorenzo pushes her and pushes her and pushes her. Please tell me you'll try your hardest." The raw sadness exuding off Raine didn't match the lethal demeanor of a woman who ran two knives into someone minutes before.

"I'll do everything in my power to get Sera to leave with me." Cassius rubbed the spot on his chest where Christian's bullet hit him. It hurt more than the one on his ribs. Like a permanent hole in his heart. "Neither of us are going to be able to do anything if we don't get out of here, though."

"What about the hacker in Christian's car?" Rained picked up her gun from the ground. "We have to get rid of him."

He looked at the time. "We only have three minutes left."

"Perfect," Raine said, sprinting toward the door.

Cassius grabbed his gun as well. "Are you sure you want to get out of the game?" He ran alongside her. "You seem to be enjoying yourself."

"Don't spoil my final celebration," Raine teased.

Together, they stepped out of the warehouse. Christian's Benz was parked ten feet from the door. The hacker was snoozing in the back seat. It was an easy kill for Raine. One shot to the sleeping man's head.

"Well, that wasn't any fun. How boring," she said with a yawn. "Anyway, I'll take care of the car and the body. Go to Sera."

Cassius glimpsed the key dangling from the ignition. "No, I've got this."

"What are you doing?" Raine frowned.

"I'm going to drive the car into the building." He hopped in the driver's seat. "The bomb will destroy it."

"There's less than two minutes left." Raine ran her fingers through her hair. "You won't make it."

"That's plenty of time." Cassius turned the key, and the engine roared to life. Putting the pedal to the metal, he took off.

"You're insane," Raine yelled.

"Sera wouldn't love me if I was boring," he yelled back.

The car crashed into the warehouse. Cassius bolted out of it and sprinted to the door. His feet barely touched the pavement before the building exploded behind him.

"I'm going to repeat what I said..." Raine placed her fists on her hips. "You're *insane*. What the *hell* made you think you could survive that?"

Cassius buzzed with adrenaline. "Are you kidding? I live for this kind of shit."

CHAPTER 24

Who the hell is ringing my doorbell at two in the morning? Not that it mattered. Sera was wide awake. She hadn't slept well since her meeting with Lorenzo. Grabbing the gun from her nightstand, Sera padded down the stairs to her door. She glanced through the peephole and nearly fainted. Standing on the other side was the man she was supposed to murder. *Shit!* She wasn't ready to see him.

"I thought you weren't arriving until tomorrow," she said, opening the door. Cassius glanced at the gun by her side. With a sigh, Sera placed it on top of the entry table. "Come in. Do you want a drink?"

Cassius shook his head and wordlessly followed her to the living room. Sera sat on the couch and patted the empty space beside her, signaling for him to sit. That's when she noticed his bloodshot eyes. *He's been crying.* "Cassius, what's going on? And how did you get past my security?" She wasn't mentally prepared to kill him right then and there. She'd never be ready, but a surprise visit in the middle of the night *really* threw her off her game.

"I came here earlier than expected. I needed closure on a family issue." He turned his body to face her. "Raine got me past your security. Apparently, she knows the doorman well." He gave her *that* smile—the one meant only for her. Sera's chest twisted. It would be the last time she'd see it. "I've been calling and texting you since your plane landed." Cassius placed his hand over hers. "Why weren't you responding?"

Sera stiffened and pulled away. His touch was the sun, torching the glacier she'd encapsulated herself in. "I didn't want to talk to you." *What am I doing?* She needed to woo him in order to kill him. But she couldn't do it. She'd rather shoot him from afar. To take him to bed—like she did with Carlo and countless others—was too personal an act.

Cassius winced, hurt dulling his features. "I just wanted to know what happened with your father. You left Gillette so abruptly. I was worried about you."

"My dad is none of your bus—" Something he said wormed into her brain. "What do you mean Raine got you past security?"

He watched her, his eyes dark pools of endless abyss. "I asked Raine to meet me. She gave me her number the night you were shot. Christian—"

Sera raised her hand, her palm facing him. "I don't care about him." Cassius's family issues were of no concern to her anymore. Christian was going to be arrested soon. And in less than forty-eight hours, she'd be on a plane with her father.

She shouldn't have asked about Cassius's meeting with Raine. All it did was extend their conversation. She'd get the information from her friend later. At the moment, Sera had to get away from Cassius before she lost the courage to kill him.

"You should go," Sera said, scooting away from him.

She made up her mind. She'd follow him to his car and snipe him from a distance. *Easy and painless.*

Sera started to stand, but he was too fast. Before she could stop him, Cassius closed the distance between them. Cupping her chin, he asked, "Why do you want me to leave?"

Think about Tay. Sera fastened her mask of indifference. "The plans we made in Gillette can't happen. We had a great time, but it's over. I don't want to build a life with you. I got swept up in the moment."

"You're lying." Cassius's gaze sliced Sera open, exposing her lie. "Tell me what made you change your mind?"

She removed his hand from her chin. "Nothing happened. I get bored easily. You were a passing phase." Sera got up and walked to the staircase, her own presence making her sick. "I'm going to sleep. You can show yourself out."

Do not cry. Do not cry. Sera pictured Cassius's body on the ground, a bullet fixed in his head. In a few minutes, his life would be over.

"What's it like, Sera?"

She looked over her shoulder. Cassius stood a few feet away from her. The grief on his face made her want to slit her own throat. He resembled a man whose heart had been carved out of his chest. She yearned to tell him she'd go anywhere with him—do anything to be with him. *But Tay...*

"What do you mean?" she asked, stunned at how well she maintained her detached tone.

Cassius's jaw flexed. "What's it like to not feel anything?"

Sera leaned on the stair railing and faced him. She could give him a few grains of truth. He at least deserved that. "What if you've been taught your whole life the only way to survive is to put yourself in a cage? One day, someone comes along and wants to unlock it. But the cage shielded you from harm for twenty-nine years. How can you ask them to leave the place they feel safe?"

Cassius slowly moved toward Sera. "Your scenario talks about surviving, not living. Don't you want to know what it feels like be free?"

A tear slid down Sera's face. She cursed herself for it. "I am who I am, Cassius. I can't change that."

He moved even closer. Sera didn't know what to do. She should stick to her plan. But she couldn't bear the thought of never seeing him again. Her indecision kept her frozen. Before she knew it, he was in front of her.

Cassius placed his hands on the railing, bracketing her shoulders between his arms. "Tell me you don't love me, and I'll go."

Sera tried to form the words. They wouldn't take shape.

"Tell me," he growled.

Say it. He's your mark. He has to die.

"Tell me," he repeated, his lips brushing over hers.

"I...I don't...I can't," she said. *I'm worthless.*

"I know you can't." Cassius kissed her.

With gentle ease, he removed her clothes and made love to her. The tenderness of his touch unraveled Sera. Something inside of her blossomed despite her own frost. Like a jasmine flower flourishing in the winter, unperturbed by the snow. Their limbs linked together, and her heart melted. Cassius's touch seared Sera's skin, burning away the facade—molding her into something new. His breath filled her lungs, giving her life. And his voice was a song composed only for her ears. Sera's climax splintered her to pieces. Yet...she never felt so whole.

Moving to Sera's room, they explored each other as if it were their first time. Cassius reminded her of his love every time he was inside of her. When they were done, his name was written on her bones.

They lay facing each other, their bodies entangled. Sera watched Cassius sleep, his breath soft and easy. *How am I going to live without him?* Regardless of what occurred, she had to go through with the plan. Lorenzo's future depended on it. Despising herself, Sera slid out of the bed, put her clothes on, and entered the walk-in closet. She sobbed in silence as she removed a burner phone from one of the drawers.

Do it at 7 a.m. Sera sent a text to Raine.

Her friend was to drain Cassius's accounts in two hours. Christian might've had a new hacker, but Sera had the upper hand. Christian couldn't give his man the order until Cassius was dead. Right now, she was the only one who knew when that would be.

Sera had changed her mind...*again.* She wouldn't snipe

Cassius from afar. She'd kill him in her penthouse. She wouldn't be a coward.

He should know how truly terrible I am.

Sera sat in her closet for thirty minutes, waiting for Raine to respond. It was early, but her friend was usually awake by now. When Raine didn't reply, Sera put her phone away. She wasn't worried. The woman always pulled through.

Opening her sock drawer, Sera removed the mint container that held the Devil's Breath capsules. She shoved one in her pocket and put the tin away. Stepping out of the closet, she found that Cassius was awake.

"What were you doing?" He sat up and rested his head against the headboard. The sheets bunched around his waist, exposing his solid frame. All Sera wanted to do was curl into him. The universe—or rather Lorenzo—had other plans for her.

"I needed to think," Sera said.

"About if you're leaving with me?"

"Yes." Sera lingered at the foot of the bed. She had to do it now. Her determination faded the longer she waited.

"You're not going to Gillette, are you?"

Sera shook her head. The words wouldn't roll off her tongue. Admitting it made it too real.

"Can you come here so I can hold you one last time?" There was no denying the grief in Cassius's voice or the unshed tears in his eyes—evidence of an already broken heart.

This is the part where I kill him. Soon, the nightmare would be over...*for Tay.* It would be the beginning for her. A vicious surge of anxiety rushed Sera's veins. "I'm going to use the bathroom first. I'll be right back."

"Sure, take your time," Cassius said, his eyes following her. There was something alien in his gaze. A cruelness she had never seen before.

Sera entered the bathroom and stared at herself in the mirror. She wanted to scream, to punch through the glass. Her reflection offended her. Turning the sink on, Sera vomited. Then, she gargled, splashed cold water on her face, and wiped off on a towel. *Get it together. You've got this.* Pulling a capsule out of her pocket, Sera stuck it under her tongue. All she had to do was blow the powder in Cassius's face. *Easy.* His death would be pain-free. Merciful.

I've always wanted to live on a beautiful island.

Tay and I will have more money than we'll know what to do with.

Sera ran down a list of reasons why Cassius's death would be a blessing to her and Lorenzo.

Looking in the mirror one last time, Sera took a deep breath. She forced her mind to remain calm. The emptiness gutting her was temporary. *In a few months, I won't even remember his name.* She repeated the thoughts in her head until she believed them. She had to believe them. That was the only way she'd go through with this heinous act.

Plastering a smile on her face, Sera strolled back into the room. Cassius was still on the bed. Except he was dressed. *Interesting.* Was he heading out? She did tell him she wasn't going to Gillette. Something was off. There was a warning in his eyes, or was it a challenge? It almost seemed like he knew what Sera was about to do. *I'm being paranoid.* There was no way Cassius was aware of his impending assassination.

Sera crawled on the bed and straddled his waist. "I'm sorry I can't go with you." She meant it. She'd give up almost everything to be with him. But not Lorenzo. Never Lorenzo.

"I'm going to miss you, Sera." Cassius's fingers caressed her hairline. "I'll always love you. I honestly can't imagine loving anyone else."

Each sentence was a hot knife against her flesh. Sera's soul cracked like glass, the shards severing her veins. "You don't know the real me, Cassius."

"You've said that many times before." He rubbed the pad of his thumb over her lips. "What I know is that you're the one I want by my side...until my dying day."

Sickness roiled in her stomach. Little did he know she was about to make his wish come true. "Please sto—"

"Thanks for giving me what you could of your heart." He pressed his palm on her chest. "You did warn me you'd break *my* heart." A soft smile. "It was worth it."

Sera almost lost it. Cassius was still alive, but he was already gone in her eyes. Losing him stung like a stab wound. Sera would have a chance to stitch it up, but she'd let it bleed out. She wouldn't throw the memory of him away that easily.

As her face inched closer to his, Sera thought she saw something shimmer in his mouth. *Great, I've become delu-*

sional. She closed her eyes, unable to watch Cassius take his last breath. "I love you," she said. "I'll love you forever."

Her lips hovered over his face.

Sera's heart thudded as she pushed the cellulose capsule between her teeth. Her mouth puckered as she prepared to blow out the powder.

One second passed...

Two seconds...

Three...

Four...

And...

Sera swallowed it.

She couldn't go through with it. She loved Cassius too much. No matter how hard she tried to lock up her feelings, he'd smash the bolt open with a hammer.

Shoving Cassius aside, Sera stumbled out of bed. "I'll be back," she said on a gasp, holding on to the walls and staggering to the bathroom.

The sensation was instant. Flashes of light obscured her vision. Everything around her moved too fast and too slow all at once. Sera only had a few minutes to get the drugs out of her system. Probably not even that long.

Cassius called after her. Sera ignored him.

She had one thing on her mind: not dying.

By the time she reached the toilet, her body was drenched in sweat. Sticking her fingers down her throat, Sera vomited. She repeated the process three times. *It's not working.* No amount of purging would remove the Devil's Breath from her system. Human survival instinct was the only reason she tried to save herself. Her arms and head collapsed on top of the toilet seat. Her heart stuttered like an old car attempting to start up. Keeping her eyes open took effort. It would be over soon.

At least Cassius is alive.

I'm sorry, Tay.

A strong pair of hands pulled her off the toilet. She couldn't make out who it was. "Sera, hold on." The hazy figure cradled her head, placing it against the edge of the tub. "Open your mouth."

It was a man. It was…it was…

"Cassius?" Why was talking such a struggle?

"Yeah, it's me. I need you to open your mouth." *What's he saying?* His words entered her ears and got scrambled in her brain. "Do you understand me?"

"Mmm…." Sera murmured.

"Shit, Sera. Why the fuck did you swallow it?"

Sera felt pressure on her cheeks as if they were wedged in a vise. A gush of fluid slid into her mouth and glided down her throat. Each swallow brought her back to consciousness.

Sera's heartbeat regulated.

Her vision cleared.

The sweating stopped.

Finally, her voice returned. "What…what did you give me?"

Cassius cupped her face in his hands. "Are you all right?" His chest rose and fell at an unnatural speed.

"I feel high as a kite, but I think I'm okay." How was she going to explain what just happened? She'd have to come up with a hell of a lie. *I'll say…* Realization slammed into her. "Wait, how did you *know* what to give me?"

Cassius released his hold on her and picked a vial up off the floor. "A friend gave me this. It's made of sugar glass, so it's edible. It contained the medicine needed to stop overdoses." He shoved the vial in his pocket. "Devil's Breath overdoses."

The air thinned. Sera found it hard to breathe. It had nothing to do with the powder still floating in her system. "You *knew* the whole time?"

Cassius leaned against the sink cabinets, opposite the tub Sera rested on. He extended his legs and crossed them at his ankles. "Not the *whole* time. But yes, I learned about my brother's plot to steal my money and kill me." A muscle feathered in his jaw. "I discovered that you use Devil's Breath for most of your targets. I had an antidote made. I carry the vials wherever I go. When we were in Gillette, I thought you might back out of the plan, then your father called. That man is your weakness."

Sera pulled her knees up to her chest and wrapped her arms around her legs. She wanted to disappear. Her shame was life-ending on its own. Sera tried to kill him, and he saved her. It all made sense now. Cassius got dressed when she went to the bathroom so he could quickly leave. She wasn't delusional when she spotted the glimmer in his mouth. He'd stuck a vial underneath his tongue. "Where did you get all your information?"

Every inch of him appeared at ease, but Sera saw the shackled rage beneath his poised exterior. "Here's a lesson for you to carry throughout your life, Sera. Don't fuck with people as powerful as me. My kind of money goes a long way."

Sera blinked. How did she not see it before? The man

was kind, but there was a dangerous edge to him. Cassius had two major advantages. First, he was disgustingly wealthy; many people were at his disposal. Second, there wasn't much that frightened him.

"When did you find out?" Sera asked meekly.

"I found out about the assassination plan after I arrived in New York." He rubbed the back of his neck. "I didn't know the identity of my assassin until we were in Gillette."

"Oh, I see..." Sera rested her chin on her knees. He baited her the entire time. Everything he told her had been fake. Sera's heart sank. She felt betrayed, which was ridiculous. The only person that had a right to be upset was Cassius. "Why did you come here tonight?"

"I had to know." Cassius inclined his head, gazing at her through hooded eyes. "I didn't think you'd go through with it. I was right."

"This was all a game to you?" Bitterness coated her tongue. It was selfish of her to be upset. But she couldn't help it. "That sensation seeker brain of yours must be really happy. I'm guessing this is the biggest risk you've ever taken. How are you going to top this?"

Cassius folded his arms over his chest. "Sure, it gave me a thrill. But it wasn't a game, Sera. I meant everything I said. I love you."

Sera threw her hands in the air. "Why? I tried to...tried to..." She couldn't say it. The words sat like cement in her stomach.

"You didn't go through with it. In fact, you almost killed yourself so you wouldn't have to kill me. That's how much you love me." Cassius looked down at his watch and stood abruptly. "I have to go." He started walking out of the bathroom.

"That's it?" Sera blurted out without thinking. *Of course that's it.* What the hell did she expect? That he'd ask for her hand in marriage? "Sorry, I have no right to question you. Before you leave, I have something to tell you." She owed him the truth. "Christian has another hacker. You're not safe, Cassius. My dad—"

"Christian has been taken care of." He stopped at the bathroom door and faced her, his eyes wet and wounded. "I don't have to worry about him anymore." He ran his fingers through his hair. "I don't want it to be over between us, Sera. The offer to come with me is still open. You can stay in Gillette for a month or for however long you'd like."

Sera didn't respond. She didn't care about the trial period anymore. She wanted to be with Cassius forever. But she still had Lorenzo to think about. She screwed up. *Badly.* How was she going to tell her father what she'd done?

"I love you so much, but it's more complicated than that."

"No, it's not." Cassius slid his hands in his pockets. "You need to make a decision: your happiness or your dad's. My jet is at JFK Airport. I have a few things to tie up, but I plan to board at eleven a.m., which is in three hours.

"If you don't show up, then I promise I'll leave you alone. You'll never have to hear from me again." Cassius sighed. "There are things you should know. It's not my place to tell you. Talk to Raine before you decide anything. I love you, Sera."

Without waiting for a response, Cassius left.

CHAPTER 25

Sera waited until she heard Cassius's footsteps descend the stairs before she pulled herself up off the floor. Her legs shook when she walked, like a baby calf taking its first steps. When she reached her bed, she grabbed her phone from the nightstand. Slumping to the ground, she dialed Raine's number.

"Hey," Raine said, picking up on the third ring.

"Did you get my text earlier about the bank?" She wasn't on the burner, so she chose her words carefully.

A slight hesitation. Then… "Yeah, I'm not doing it. You'll have to find someone else."

"I don't want you to do it anymore." Sera was both relieved and taken aback. "Can you please come over? It's important."

"I'll be there in ten minutes," Raine replied.

She arrived at Sera's penthouse in eight minutes. Together, they sat on the living room couch. Sera was grateful her high was mostly gone. She needed a clear head for their discussion.

"Thank you for coming." Sera picked at a string on her shirt. "I couldn't kill Cassius because I love him." Why did she start the conversation with *that*? Maybe she was still high.

"I know you do." Raine placed her hand on Sera's leg. "That's why I didn't respond when you texted me." A sheepish grin crossed her face. "I ignored it."

Sera raised her brows until they disappeared into her hairline. "You chose a man over me?"

Raine fluttered her lashes. "He is a hell of a catch."

Sera laughed. It felt good, like fresh air in her lungs. "I agree. I've never met anyone that puts up with as much shit as he does." Resting the side of her head against the back pillow, Sera told Raine everything that transpired since she went to Gillette—from Cassius confessing his love, to her meeting with Lorenzo, to what occurred that evening. When Sera was done, she said, "Cassius still wants me to move. He asked me to meet him in three hours at JFK."

Raine lay down, placing her head on the arm of the couch. "I'm not surprised. The man is crazy about you. You should go with him, Sera."

"I can't. I have to find a different way to get Tay out of the country. He can't do this alone." Sera scrubbed her hand over her face. "He's going to hate me for ruining this job." She was not looking forward to Lorenzo's wrath.

Raine tousled her hair in frustration. "Sera, you're intelligent and levelheaded, but your father manages to get beneath all of it. It's to a point where you deprive yourself of healthy things. Every move you make is based on his happiness. Can't you see how absurd that is?"

Of course Sera saw it. She chose to tuck her resentment into forgotten corners in her mind. That was until Cassius came along and stripped her down, exposing her vulnerabilities. The thought of him reminded Sera of the reason she asked Raine to come over. "Cassius said you had things to tell me."

"I do." Raine sat up and crossed her legs. "I'm not sure if you're ready for this…"

Raine's stories were a whip against Sera's skin. A dark pulse in her belly. The aftershock of an earthquake. Raine recounted her meeting with Cassius—how he had offered her fifty million dollars to help bring down Christian and Damion. She spoke of Cassius's plan to blow up both the warehouse and the abandoned home. She told Sera how Cassius had killed his own brother and saved Raine by taking a bullet for her.

The most shocking revelation was the Adrenochrome. *That's* what Lorenzo left out when Sera spoke to him at the park. *That's* what he got caught smuggling into the country. *That's* what would've gotten him the death penalty. It wasn't khat he imported, after all.

Lorenzo had done a lot of horrible things in his life, but this was the worst. Innocent kids were trafficked and killed in order to obtain the drug. Sera was no saint, but there were lines no one should cross.

Sera clutched her stomach. "I think I'm going to be sick." She bent forward and vomited on her pristine living room floor. Raine patted her back as she heaved.

"Cassius is a different breed," Raine said when Sera was done. "There aren't many people like him. I mean that in a good way." She placed her palm on Sera's forehead as if she were checking for a fever. "I helped Cassius because I wanted what's best for *you*."

Raine grabbed both of Sera's hands. "I found a house in the Dominican Republic. The closing date is in a month. I'm leaving, Sera. You should leave too. You deserve a chance at happiness." Raine looked at her Rolex. "You have two hours left. I hope you make the flight." She kissed Sera's cheek. "Be happy." Standing up, she draped her purse over her shoulder. "Do you need help cleaning your vomit?"

Sera shook her head. "No, I'll do it. You've done enough as it is."

Raine adjusted the strap of her bag. "If you need my help with anything, let me know. I'm out of the business starting today, but I'll always make an exception for you. Lylas, chica."

Be happy. Sera couldn't do that unless she settled things with her father.

Taking a deep breath, Sera entered the apartment she grew up in. It was located on the first floor of a worn-down brownstone. The building consisted of dark hallways and dingy carpets. The inside of the apartment wasn't much of an improvement. There were chips in the white paint—now turned yellow—and the wood floors needed refinishing.

Unbeknownst to Lorenzo, Sera purchased the apartment from the slumlord who owned the building. It wasn't up for sale...*but everyone has a price.* Sera paid her the cost of the building just to possess the one-bedroom rathole she spent seventeen years of her life in. She never had it furnished and only visited the place once in the five years she owned it. Sera didn't know why she kept it in the first place. Maybe it was to help her remember where she came from and the person she used to be. *The person I still am.* The only thing that changed was that she had more money. Sure, she was educated and rich, but in the end, she was still an alley cat disguised as a lion.

The door creaked open, and Lorenzo walked in. "Hi, Tay," Sera said.

The man looked terrible. His face was puffy, his eyes inflamed. *He's been drinking all night.* "What are we doing here, Sera?" Lorenzo scanned the living room they stood in.

"I told you on the burner phone I wanted to talk somewhere private, where the authorities can't find us." She looked him up and down. "You weren't followed, right?"

"No, I made sure of it." Lorenzo fidgeted as if he were uncomfortable being in his old home.

Sera knit her brows. "Nervous?"

Lorenzo responded with a shrug.

"I bought this place five years ago." Sera walked up to her father and gave him a hug and a kiss on the cheek. "I put it under your name. It's your apartment."

Lorenzo scowled. "Why the hell did you do that? I don't want any ties to this shithole." He tapped his feet and pushed Sera off him. "We need to leave. I have the plane tickets and passports. Everything on my end is done." He patted the pocket of his leather jacket. "What about you? Is he gone? Are the finances in order?"

Ignoring her father, Sera strolled to the kitchen. Her fingers traced the rusted stovetop. The hairs on her arms stood as she recalled all the times he burned pieces of her flesh on it. The reasons were plenty—she spoke too loudly, she bought him the wrong brand of cigarettes, she botched a robbery.

"Sera, what's going on?" Lorenzo asked, following behind her.

She whipped around to face him. "I was almost caught by the DEA. You gave me up." She should've brought up the Adrenochrome, but she didn't want to discuss that atrocity with her father. She'd overlook it just like she overlooked his other faults.

"No, I didn't." Lorenzo blinked. "We already talked about this."

Sera tapped her fingers on the counter. "What if I got caught?"

"Iha, why are you bringing this up again?" His voice was syrup-sweet. The kind that hurt your teeth and gave you a bellyache. "Have faith in me. Come on, give me some credit. I mean, look how awesome you turned out. All because of me."

Sera gazed at the wall behind him. When she was fifteen, he slammed her head against it. She had a concussion that lasted a month. To add insult to injury, he made Sera plaster the hole in the drywall. Why didn't she see how abusive he was? What a user he was? "You raised me to be a stickup kid. I'm *still* a stickup kid. I just graduated to a professional level."

Lorenzo's eyes watered, and a tear fell down his cheek. Sera had seen him cry only a handful of times. The display of sadness took her aback. "I wasn't perfect. You deserved better." Another tear. "But I am what I am, iha. I taught you what I knew. You can't blame me for that." He held both her hands, entwining them with his own. "This is our chance to start fresh. I'll be a better father. I'll make you proud to be my daughter."

Sera's throat tightened. These were the words she'd wanted him to say for years. *Why now?* She could never win. Lorenzo always sucked her back in.

"Where are we going?" she asked, her resolve disintegrating.

"That's my iha." Lorenzo let go of her hands and wiped his face with the back of his arm. "Indonesia, baby girl."

"That's where we've always wanted to go," Sera whispered. When she was young, Lorenzo made up stories of their life in Indonesia. They were mere fantasies then. Now it was about to become a reality. "Things will be different there?"

"Absolutely." Lorenzo cupped her chin. "We'll have more money than we'll know what to do with. We'll buy a house near Pink Beach."

"We'll visit the grandest spas in Bali?" Sera was a little girl again, craving her father's affection.

"Yup, and we'll go surfing in Kuta," Lorenzo added.

"We'll visit the Borobudur Temple?"

"Visit?" Lorenzo ruffled her hair. "We'll buy the fucking temple." He gazed at Sera, his eyes a storm-ridden sky. "We'll explore the jungles. We'll do it all. Together. You and me. It's always been you and me, right, iha?"

"Yes, Tay." They'd have a perfect life. Sera could see it already.

315

Except for one thing…

How am I going to tell him about Cassius? Would he still accept her after she confessed that she let Cassius live? That she didn't rob him?

"Let's go." Lorenzo put his arm around her shoulder.

"Okay, I have to use the bathroom first." She patted his arm before walking through the living room and into the bathroom.

Closing the door, Sera placed her forehead against it. Life was unfair. She had her mind made up before she arrived at the apartment. Now, the circumstances had changed. She should text Cassius and tell him she wasn't coming. But Sera left her phone at home. She couldn't risk the authorities tracing her whereabouts. Cassius would figure out Sera bailed on him when she didn't show up.

It's always been you and me, right, iha? She belonged with her father. Slipping the Devil's Breath capsule out of her mouth, Sera flushed it down the toilet. Shame coursed through her. To think she was going to blow the deadly powder in Lorenzo's face when she kissed his cheek. She almost killed the man who raised her.

"Sera, are you almost done?" Lorenzo called to her.

"Yes, just a second." Sera washed her hands and wiped her palms on her pants.

"I almost forgot. Butch has some documents to give me. I gotta finish up a few things at the house. Can you grab them? We can meet at the airport at noon." Sera heard his footsteps stop in front of the bathroom door. "Before we leave here, why don't you give me the info to the offshore accounts you put Cassius's money in, so we both have it. What do you say?"

Sera froze with her hand on the doorknob. She had to meet up with Butch? Her father's psychopathic-killer friend. Triggers exploded in her head. *If I ever leave you alone with Butch, you know your time is up.* In Sera's twenty-nine years of life, Lorenzo had never asked her to do a single thing with Butch. And why did he need access to the offshore accounts now? Accounts that didn't exist since Cassius was still alive. "I thought everything was taken care of?"

A long pause. Then… "It's been such a stressful day. I forgot about other paperwork we need."

Sera pressed her forehead against the door again. Her chest rose with sluggish, forced breaths. "What does Butch have to give me?"

Another long pause. "Social Security cards and birth certificates."

That's when Sera knew for sure. *Tay, you bastard.* Butch was a brawler, a murderer, and a drug dealer. He lacked the brain capacity to forge important records, nor did he have connections with anyone who did.

"Okay, Tay. I'll get them," Sera said, one fist clenched by her side.

Lorenzo was sending Sera to her death. *He could at least do it himself.* The man was a coward. Was it greed that made him want to kill her? Perhaps he thought she was a loose cannon. Sera clutched her stomach and turned on the sink to hide the sound of her retching. Once done, she wiped her mouth with her hand.

Breathe in.

Breathe out.

Breathe in.

Breathe out.

Sera stepped out of the bathroom with a smile on her face. "Let me get my purse." She went to the kitchen counter, grabbed her bag, and slung it over her shoulder. "Tay, wait," she said when they reached the door.

Lorenzo's lips pressed into a thin line. "What now, Sera? We don't have time for this bullshit."

She stood on her tiptoes and planted another kiss on her father's cheek. "I love you, Tay." The taste of goodbye coated her tongue.

Lorenzo sighed as he wrapped his arms around her. "I love you, too, iha. When we're living it up in Indo—"

He didn't get to finish. Sera slid a Glock out of her purse and put the barrel against his ribs. Pulling the trigger, she shot him three times. Lorenzo slumped into her arms. She held him until the light left his eyes.

"I'm sorry," she said, crying, while she placed him on the ground. "I'm so sorry." Tears streamed down her face as she pulled her father's burner phone out of his pocket. She choked back sobs as she dialed Raine's burner number.

"Hello," Raine said.

"Can you—*hic*—do me—*hic*—a final favor?" Sera hiccupped between her words.

"Of course. What's up?" Raine's voice was a gentle embrace through the phone.

Sera placed her hands over her father's eyes and closed them. "Can you help me clean one last time?"

"Tell me where, and I'll be there."

CHAPTER 26

Cassius sat at the terminal, checking his watch every five minutes. It was noon. Sera was an hour late. *Or she isn't showing up.* As time ticked on, it became obvious she wasn't coming.

"What do you want to do?" The pilot strolled up to him with a giant pretzel in his hand. "Should we keep waiting, sir?"

Cassius looked at his watch again. Three minutes had passed since the last time he checked. It felt like forever. His mind warred with his heart. Leaving meant accepting that they were over. Perhaps it was for the best. She *did* try to kill him. *She also saved me.* That internal argument was moot. Cassius loved her regardless.

He had to let her go. "All right, let's get out of here."

In silence, they walked out of the terminal and headed to the jet. Sitting down on the plush leather seat, Cassius stretched his legs in front of him and closed his eyes. Everything hurt. How was he going to forget about Sera when she was ingrained in his mind? Her scent was embedded in his lungs, her touch sticky on his skin. His memories of her were vivid. It was as though she were there now, watching him with stormy eyes. Ones he fell into and couldn't crawl out of.

"Dreaming about me?" a husky voice filled his ears.

Cassius's eyes fluttered open. Standing in front of him was Sera. Her face was flushed, and her usually pristine ponytail was a tangled mess. *Is that blood on her shirt?*

"I'm sorry I'm late. I had to tie up some loose ends with my dad." She pointed to the crimson stain on her top.

Oh. *Oh.* "Are you all right?" Cassius asked.

"No. Maybe I will be…" She seemed oddly shy. "Do you still want me to come with you?"

In one swift move, Cassius pulled her onto his lap. "Why do you think I'm still here?"

Sera curled into him, resting the side of her head on his chest. "I didn't mean to be late." Sera played with the buttons on his shirt. "Things got complicated."

"You're here now. That's what matters." He tugged her ponytail lightly. "You could've sent a text."

"I left my phones at home. Your number is saved on my regular cell and my burner. I didn't have either with me. And I don't have your number memorized. I was going to ask Raine to contact you, but she dumped her main phone where your information was saved. She's leaving for the Dominican Republic in a month and doesn't want to deal with people. Except me, of course. There was no way to get ahold of you. I tried to rush, but what I had to do took longer than I expected." Sera wrapped her arms tightly around him. "Cassius, I'm terrible at this. I want to be better. I promise I'll try my hardest." Her arms wrapped even tighter. "You waited for me. After everything…you didn't give up on me."

Cassius's heart hurt for her. He had grown up in a home filled with love and affection. Excluding Christian, Cassius's family did everything to make sure he flourished. Sera spent her entire existence fending for herself. Lorenzo had used her as a tool and abused her mentally and physically. All she knew was pain and suffering.

"I'll never give up on you," Cassius said, burying his face in her hair.

Sera lifted her head to meet his eyes. She scanned them, looking for a lie she wouldn't find. "There are many things I need to work through. My past might haunt us. And I'm broken…really broken."

Cassius hushed her with a kiss. "We'll work through anything that comes our way, together, as a team."

Sera traced her fingers over his jawline. "I don't understand why you love me."

"'There are some who can live without wild things, and some who cannot.'" Cassius repeated the Aldo Leopold quote he recited to her during their first date. "You're the wildest person I know." He grabbed her hand and kissed her palm. "I'll always love you, Sera."

"Just *always*?" she asked, biting his lower lip.

He caressed her cheek with the back of his knuckles. "Until the devil takes his last breath."

ABOUT THE AUTHOR

Lang Johnson worked in IT for ten years, where she spent her lunch breaks crafting stories on scraps of paper and stuffing them in her desk drawer. When her secret stash was close to overflowing, Lang took a leap of faith and quit her job to pursue a career in writing. As a lover of true crime and romance books, Lang embarked on a journey to write her first romantic suspense novel, *Devil's Breath*. When Lang isn't typing away, she enjoys globe-trotting with her husband, cuddling her three fur-babies, diving, snowboarding, back-country camping, and dreaming up characters to fill the pages of her next novel.

STAY CONNECTED

You can follow Lang Johnson on the following platforms to stay up-to-date with her latest projects.

Website: authorlangjohnson.com
Instagram: @writer_langjohnson
Facebook: @authorlangjohnson
TikTok: @authorlangjohnson

Printed in Great Britain
by Amazon

25111313R00189